LOST

For a complete list of books, visit

JamesPatterson.com.

LOST

JAMES PATTERSON

AND JAMES O. BORN

GRAND
CENTRAL
PUBLISHING

New York Boston

Copyright © 2020 by James Patterson
Preview of *Fear No Evil* copyright © 2021 by James Patterson

Hachette Book Group supports the right to free expression and the value of copyright. The purpose of copyright is to encourage writers and artists to produce the creative works that enrich our culture.

The scanning, uploading, and distribution of this book without permission is a theft of the author's intellectual property. If you would like permission to use material from the book (other than for review purposes), please contact permissions@hbgusa.com. Thank you for your support of the author's rights.

Grand Central Publishing
Hachette Book Group
1290 Avenue of the Americas, New York, NY 10104
grandcentralpublishing.com
twitter.com/grandcentralpub

Originally published in hardcover and ebook by Little, Brown & Company in January 2020
First oversize mass market edition: November 2021

Grand Central Publishing is a division of Hachette Book Group, Inc. The Grand Central Publishing name and logo is a trademark of Hachette Book Group, Inc.

The publisher is not responsible for websites (or their content) that are not owned by the publisher.

The Hachette Speakers Bureau provides a wide range of authors for speaking events. To find out more, go to hachettespeakersbureau.com or call (866) 376-6591.

ISBNs: 9781538750070 (oversize mass market), 9780316493987 (ebook)

Printed in the United States of America

OPM

10 9 8 7 6 5 4 3 2 1

LOST

CHAPTER 1

MIAMI INTERNATIONAL AIRPORT isn't exactly a tranquil space on a normal day—if there's such a thing as a normal day at MIA. Now, as I watched a human trafficker strolling toward the immigration portal with six kids in tow, it felt like a hurricane was about to hit indoors. An ill-tempered Customs supervisor from the Department of Homeland Security fidgeted next to me.

The supervisor's pudgy fingers beat on the tan veneer counter, thumping out a rhythm I almost recognized. The only thing Customs supervisors hated worse than a Miami cop asking for help was a Miami cop on an FBI task force asking for help.

The man stopped tapping out "Jingle Bells"—hey, I got it—and shifted to rubbing his gut, which was hanging over his belt despite the extra holes he'd punched in it. He looked up at me and said, "So what kind of task force is this?"

"International crime."

"Who from Customs is on it? There's no way you can have an international crimes task force without Customs."

He was right, but I ignored the question to concentrate on the operation.

We were acting on a serious tip we'd gotten from the Dutch national police. They were looking at a smuggling group associated with the Rostoff crime organization, and I was now looking right at the suspect, Hans Nobler.

The Dutch national was about fifty years old and dressed like he was trying to impress twenty-year-olds. In his skinny jeans and leather bracelets, the dude was more creepy than stylish. He wore a blue and orange Dutch World Cup jacket with the swagger of someone who'd played, but the colors were too close to the University of Florida's for it to seem genuine. I had at least eighty pounds on him; he didn't worry me.

I turned my attention to the children Nobler was herding, four girls and two boys. The two teenage girls looked scared. The two younger girls, a blonde and a brunette with olive skin, were striking; they couldn't have been more than ten or eleven years old. When the creepy Dutchman caressed the face of the blond girl, I almost snapped.

But part of police work is patience. Besides, I was in charge of this operation, and it looks bad for the boss to break the law during an arrest. I didn't want other members of the task force telling the FBI that I was some sort of lunatic.

The Dutchman steered all the kids to the same line for entry.

Why that line? There were seven lines open, and others were shorter or moving faster. Had to be significance to that choice.

The inspector was alert and moving people along reasonably quickly. I checked the roster and saw his name was Vacile. Vacile waved the four older kids through with barely a glance; next up was Nobler with the two younger children. Nobler casually draped his hand over the little blond girl's shoulders and played with her hair.

My stomach knotted. This wasn't my usual assignment, some shitty dope deal in the city between lowlifes I didn't really care about. I desperately wanted to get these kids out of here safely—and, to an extent that surprised me, I wanted this task force to succeed.

I phoned Stephanie Hall. As she answered, I felt a tap on my shoulder.

I flinched and turned quickly to see Stephanie herself. She said, "Are you jumpy, Tom Moon? Let's grab this shithead and call it a day. What else do you need to know about this guy? Remember, curiosity killed the cat. And will make me late."

I said, "I want to see how he accounts for the kids." My mind ran through scenarios of what could happen once we made our move. Crowds of tourists, kids in danger—the complications made me shudder.

The other two members of our task force— Anthony Chilleo, who worked for the Bureau of Alcohol, Tobacco, Firearms, and Explosives (ATF), and Lorena Perez, a Florida Department of Law Enforcement (FDLE) agent—were also lurking in the area. I used my police radio to urge everyone to be alert and gave a detailed description of the suspect.

Stephanie said in a singsong voice, "Sounds like you're trying to impress someone."

"You're the only one I ever try to impress." That made her smile, which seemed to brighten the whole room.

CHAPTER 2

AFTER I MADE detective, I realized that different law enforcement agencies always talk shit about one another. Here's the first joke I heard an FBI agent tell: "What's blue and white and sleeps four? A Miami police patrol cruiser." (Made me laugh, if I'm being honest.)

But sometimes the suspicion among agencies came from genuine issues, like the one I was having now with Customs. These agents at the airport had their own little fiefdom; they didn't care about how we gathered evidence for different crimes. They liked things quick and simple: *You're smuggling contraband; we seize it; you plead guilty; case closed.*

I tried to keep things pleasant. I turned to the Customs man and said, "Someone from the task force needs to lay hands on him before you guys."

"Ah, politics. I guess I shouldn't be shocked the FBI wants to get some publicity from this." The supervisor gave me a dirty look, yanked a radio from his belt, and said, "Raoul, pull the guy with the two kids out of line three. The guy who looks like a reject from some half-assed *American Bandstand,* the one wearing the wannabe Gators jacket."

I guess he showed me.

I looked out over the crowd. At least I had a good view of the room. There were only a few people as tall as me, and we all stuck out like giraffes. There were Europeans eager to get out in the sun, Americans returning from vacations in Europe. And rising heat in a room where too many people had been pushed in too quickly.

I watched as a lanky Customs officer in a rumpled blue uniform — Raoul — stepped away from a back wall.

I followed him. A guy my size can usually cut through a crowd, but these were people escaping U.S. Customs. Before I could even squeeze past the first heavyset tourist coming to visit America's most exotic city, the Customs agent was already making contact with the suspect, waving him over. It looked casual, at best. Raoul clearly didn't know the circumstances of the crime.

The Dutch suspect had the children behind him when he stepped up to the Customs agent. Without telegraphing his intentions, Nobler headbutted Raoul. Soccer moves to match the jacket! Then he punched the stunned Customs man in the throat and drove his whole body into Raoul's long, lanky frame. As I stood helplessly watching, Nobler somehow managed to get a hand on Raoul's pistol. He had it out of his holster before the Customs agent flopped onto the cracked tile floor, gasping for air.

I turned to the supervisor and said, "I think your man just made my point for me. Now this asshole is armed. Cover the exits, quick."

Nobler frantically searched for a way out of the crowded room, then pointed the semiautomatic pistol into the air and fired twice. The rounds sounded like bombs in the enclosed space. The smell of gunpowder quickly reached my nose.

When my hearing returned to normal after the gunshots, I heard the higher pitch of screams as the shocked crowd realized what was happening. Soon the whole place sounded like a police siren wailing.

People scurried in every direction without regard for where the danger was coming from. I'd seen it a hundred times; panic caused more panic, and few people used common sense.

I broke free of the lines entering passport control, Steph Hall right behind me. We both sprinted, trying to catch the suspect, who knocked down about four people as he fled. The sight of the armed man made everyone panic even more, and the crowd parted in a wave to get away from the guy holding the gun.

I caught a glimpse of Nobler just in time to see him find an open access door and disappear through it.

CHAPTER 3

THERE'S AN OLD police saying: Only rookies jump into a foot chase. My own philosophy was that only an idiot chased an armed suspect on foot. But sometimes, you have no other choice. I ran like a sprinter—albeit a sprinter who weighed 240 pounds—gripping my pistol in my right hand. I had an equal match in Stephanie Hall, who stayed neck and neck with me as we kept the suspect in sight. Steph ran gracefully; I was just plain determined. There was no way this jerk-off was going to get away, even if he was considerably faster than I'd anticipated. The skinny jeans alone should've slowed him down.

The last guy we'd chased together was a murder suspect who had shoved our colleague Lorena Perez. It was embarrassing to check a prisoner with black eyes into the jail, but I had never even touched the man. No one noticed Steph Hall's bruised knuckles. I'd hate to be this guy if she caught him first.

Nobler didn't look back as he sprinted across the rough concrete floor, his longish hair streaming behind him.

Ahead of us, a black Delta baggage handler who

looked like he could wrestle professionally took in the sight of the man running in his direction with the police right behind him. He moved into position to block the suspect. I appreciated it. Cops didn't see that kind of help much anymore.

Then the Dutchman raised his pistol and fired once on the run. The sound of the shot echoing through the cavernous area made the well-built baggage handler dive behind a stack of luggage.

Unexpectedly, the Dutchman spun, raised the semiautomatic pistol, and fired two rounds at me. One of the bullets pinged off the floor a foot to my right. Jesus Christ!

I dived to one side and Steph to the other. We both took cover behind concrete pillars. My heart raced and I had to take a gulp of air. Then I leaned around the solid barrier to squeeze off a shot at the suspect.

When I peeked around the pillar again, he was back to running as hard as he could. It had been a good use of a couple of his bullets; it pinned us down and gave him time to put some distance between us. I hate smart criminals.

We sprang back into the chase. The suspect was still keeping up the pace, and I was starting to get frustrated. He looked over his shoulder and saw that Steph and I were not about to give up. He changed course slightly, zigging and zagging through stacks of luggage like a striker weaving through defenders, then dived headfirst down a steel baggage chute. As he did, he dropped the pistol, and it clattered onto the concrete floor.

I scooped it up on the fly as I hit the same chute, hoping to catch up to this moron before he reached the bottom. Steph took the stairs to cut Nobler off.

He did a pretty good roll at the end of the chute, landed on his feet, and went back into an all-out sprint. That pissed me off even more. When I hit the bottom of the chute, I was gasping for air.

I stood up and started running again. Now Steph was in front of me and I could just barely see the Dutch suspect. He was making for a far door on this lower level of maintenance and storage.

A large black woman with an MIA Services jacket was the only thing between the suspect and his freedom. At least he didn't have a gun anymore.

Nobler skidded to a stop in front of the airport worker as she leaned against a souped-up golf cart that looked like it could climb a mountain. He tried to slip past her to get into the cart. When she resisted, the man took a swing at her.

She dodged the punch and lifted her knee hard into his groin. He was stunned. Then she drove an elbow right into his face.

I could hear the cartilage in his nose crunch from twenty feet away. It made *me* wince.

He tumbled onto the concrete floor, wheezing and gurgling.

As Steph and I pounced on the fallen man, I heard the woman say, "I finally got to use my Krav Maga classes."

I put cuffs on the idiot Dutchman quickly, looked at Stephanie, and said, "I love Miami."

CHAPTER 4

STEPH HALL AND I walked back through the terminal with our prisoner in tow. He didn't want to talk, but the scam was easy to figure out. He held the passports for the kids. He'd brought the kids to the U.S. after someone had paid for their transport. Paid a lot. The kids were expected to work off the cost of their transport—usually in the sex trade. It pissed me off just thinking about it.

The other two task-force members, Lorena Perez and Anthony "Chill" Chilleo, fell in next to us. The whole team marched past the corpulent Customs supervisor. Not to show off, of course, but I hoped he'd take notice; these were the cops who'd passed the FBI requirements to join the task force on international crime.

A uniformed Miami-Dade cop took our Dutch prisoner to the tiny holding cell at the airport until we were ready to transport him to Miami MCC. The federal detention center never seemed to fill up the way it should.

Anthony Chilleo had a tough aura about him, forged by fifteen years in the ATF and five before that as a Tampa cop.

Lorena, as usual, looked like she'd just stepped out of a fashion magazine. Even after running through the terminal after us, she wasn't flustered and her clothes weren't disheveled.

She said, "You okay?"

"Yeah. Do I look that bad?"

"Your hand is wrapped in a paper towel and dripping blood, your shirt's ripped, and you're sweating like you're in detox. Didn't you play football in college?"

I was about to make a snappy comeback when a man wearing a nice polo shirt and madras shorts stepped in front of me. He was only an inch or two shorter than me and had a little muscle as well.

He didn't waste any time on pleasantries. "My name is Randall Stone, and I'm an attorney here in Miami. Let me tell you something—that was some of the most careless, stupid police work I've ever seen. You put people at risk to stop someone who's just trying to get into the country. Let me guess—he insulted the TSA? Or maybe it's just another arrest to pad your statistics."

The lawyer made sure he said this loud enough for everyone in the immediate vicinity to hear. Then a woman trying to comfort her little boy stood up and walked over to me. She didn't say anything as everybody stared at us. Then, without warning, she slapped me. Kinda hard.

The slap brought Steph Hall over. Moving fast, she grabbed the woman by the shoulders. Steph was mad and I didn't want this to get any more out of control. As the boss, I had to set the tone. I'd been slapped before. Punched, bitten, and stabbed as well. This was Miami, not Disney World.

The woman said, in a strong Brooklyn accent,

"My son was almost crushed by the panic you caused. You should be ashamed of yourself."

I stood there silently, staring at the woman. I wanted to point out that it was the suspect who'd fired a pistol and run, but years of experience had taught me to let this go. In fact, from an early age, I'd learned to let most things go—my lack of achievement on the University of Miami football field, my failed love life, and even parts of my family life.

Lorena said to the lawyer and the woman who'd slapped me, "How can you people be so stupid?" Then she glared at the attorney and said, "I understand an ambulance chaser like you trying to stir up a crowd, but this lady is way out of line. You have no idea what was going on."

I cut her off and waved at the team to start walking again, away from the crowd. "It's okay, Lorena. 'The only true wisdom is in knowing you know nothing.'"

Lorena said, "Socrates."

I turned and smiled at her. "Very good. That's impressive."

She laughed and said, "You rotate between Plato, Socrates, and politicians. I took a shot. You're right—no matter how much we explain, assholes like that lawyer hate whatever the police do."

I even avoided bumping into the attorney as we took our walk of triumph.

Everything in police work depended on experience. I wanted to lead everyone away from these loudmouths before someone said or did something stupid. Lorena had a temper, something she'd have to learn to control. Maybe my example could serve as a lesson; I figured it was easier than some of the teaching methods I'd seen at local police departments.

When I was a rookie, I'd arrested a local crack dealer. The narcotics detectives set up to interrogate him and made a big deal out of allowing me, a new patrol officer, to watch it over a closed-circuit TV in the next office. I had to lock up my service weapon and promise that I wouldn't make any noise or tell anyone I was allowed to watch the interrogation.

I sat there quietly with an older narcotics detective and watched as two of the better-known narcotics detectives sat across a small table from the thin, antsy crack dealer. One of the detectives wore a shoulder holster.

Less than a minute into the interview, the crack dealer started to shout, and then, without warning, he reached across the small table and grabbed the pistol in the shoulder holster.

It happened so fast I didn't react until he was standing behind the table with the gun raised at the two detectives. Then he pulled the trigger. I still remember seeing the flashes on the fuzzy TV. *Bang, bang,* and both detectives were on the floor.

Holy shit.

I sprang out of my seat, burst through the door into the hallway, and yanked open the door to the interrogation room. That's when I got one of the biggest surprises of my life: the two detectives were sitting on the table laughing, and the crack dealer was laughing right next to them.

The crack dealer was one of their regular informants and they'd put blanks in the gun. The idea was to have a laugh at the expense of a rookie and teach him two important lessons, both of which I have never forgotten: don't wear a shoulder holster, because it's tactically unsound, and don't take a gun into an interrogation with a prisoner in the first place.

I also learned that a person could literally have the piss scared out of him from a prank like that.

Today, I'd learned never to underestimate the speed of a skinny guy. And Lorena had learned that it never paid to argue with an idiot.

CHAPTER 5

ABOUT AN HOUR after the airport worker had used her martial arts skills to disable our Dutch suspect, I found myself sitting at a long table in a Department of Homeland Security conference room with all six of the children Nobler had brought over. We looked like the weirdest corporate board meeting in history.

I said, "My name is Tom Moon. You can call me Tom."

The kids and I started chatting. At eighteen, Joseph from Poland was the oldest. His accent was thick, but he spoke decent English. We talked sports. He said, "Real football players are the best athletes, both in skill and endurance."

"I still prefer American football."

Joseph gave me a sly grin and said, "I would too if I were as big as you."

The two youngest kids didn't speak much English, but I doubt they would have said a lot even if they'd understood what was going on. They were shy and quiet. Considering what had just happened to them, I got it.

Michele, a little blond girl, was only nine years

old. She was not ready to talk about how she'd ended up in this situation. She spoke only French. Our office was trying to find her parents or guardians, who were somewhere outside of Paris.

The other little girl, Olivia, was eleven years old. She was from Madrid and thought she was on some kind of field trip. I still wasn't clear on the details of how the traffickers had tricked her into coming, and I didn't know if she had family back in Spain, but we had no problem finding a translator for her. More than 70 percent of the population of Miami–Dade County was fluent in Spanish. Even *my* Spanish was good enough to just chat.

I asked her, in Spanish, "What do you like to do when you're not in school?"

"I have Rollerblades and roller skates. I'm faster than anyone in my apartment building." Her eyes positively shone as she boasted of her skill.

"I bet you are." I couldn't hide my smile.

Monnie, the teenage girl from Kenya, turned to fifteen-year-old Jacques from Belgium and whispered in his ear. They both giggled. I smiled to let them know it was okay to speak, but they were happy in their private joke.

I looked over at the Finnish girl, fourteen-year-old Annika, and said, *"Hei, kuinka voit."*

Her blue eyes opened wide and she hit me with a slew of Finnish.

I held up my hands. "Whoa, sorry. 'Hello, how are you,' is all I know in Finnish."

She smiled and switched to English. "Where did you learn to say that?"

I said, "'If you talk to a man in a language he understands, that goes to his head. If you talk to him in his language, that goes to his heart.'" The quote covered the fact that I didn't remember where I'd learned the Finnish phrase.

"What's that mean?"

"It's a famous quote."

"Who said it?"

"Nelson Mandela."

"Who's he?"

"A smart man who changed the world."

Joseph said, "Aren't you a policeman? How do you know things like that?"

"A policeman can read and go to college," I told him. I turned back to Annika and said, "What kind of music do you listen to?"

She fixed her blue eyes on me and said, "Mostly I like Top Forty pop. But sometimes I listen to classical music like Brahms or Mozart." She looked at Joseph and said, "Joseph played me a Mozart sonata on the piano before we left Amsterdam. He's really good."

I said, "My mom plays piano."

Annika asked, "Did she teach you to play?"

I let out a laugh. "She tried, but in South Florida, there are an awful lot of things for a boy to do that are more interesting than playing piano."

"Is she a piano teacher?"

"She …" I decided to let that one go.

A short while later, a dark-skinned man wearing a jacket that said DEPARTMENT OF HOMELAND SECURITY INVESTIGATIONS stepped into the room and announced, "Time to get your stuff together, kids. It's a little bit of a drive to the place where you'll be housed."

I looked at the man and said, "Where is that?"

"Krome Detention Center."

"These kids are *victims* of a crime, not suspects.

You dumb-asses let the damn suspect run. *We* caught him. Can't you find a better place than Krome for them?"

The man gave me a hard stare for a moment, then said, "Look, pal, there are certain procedures we follow, and that's where I'm taking them."

As soon as the DHS agent stepped out of the room, I gathered everyone together. Joseph looked at me with big brown eyes and said, "What are we doing?"

I smiled and said, "We're making a break for it."

CHAPTER 6

IT WAS A little bit of a challenge to fit all six kids in my unmarked FBI-issued Ford Explorer, which was made less spacious by the steel box bolted to the floor in the back. It held an MP5 machine gun, a few hundred rounds of ammunition, and a ballistic vest.

In the eight months I'd been on the new task force, I hadn't needed the extra firepower. It still amazed me how much money the federal government had to spend on international crime investigations. It was the hot new flavor of the month, and the FBI wanted all of us to look and act the part.

Even the way they'd selected us was unique. There were actual tryouts for the unit that included a fitness test, reviews by the applicant's bosses, and a breakdown of his or her three biggest cases. I'd liked the whole challenge, even the fitness test, which was held in the middle of a hot afternoon, maybe to see if anyone complained.

I'd known about half the cops there. One of them was Alvin Teague, a Miami detective like me. The thirty-year-old Florida A and M graduate who never seemed to have a hair out of place and whose wardrobe looked like it would have bankrupted a Wall Street broker had been talking shit to everyone, trying to get in the other candidates' heads. It looked like it was working on some of them. He called me by my street name, "Anti." The name the Miami residents had given me was a source of pride.

I said, "Hello, Smooth Jazz." He was a good enough cop to have earned a street name. His was a nod to how he spoke—like an announcer on a late-night jazz station.

Steph Hall, whom I didn't know at the time, asked, "How'd you end up with a street name like 'Anti'? What are you opposed to?"

Before I could answer, Teague looked at the group and said, "Only one other brother and he's on the stout side. I'll smoke you all like cheap cigars."

The heavyset Fort Lauderdale cop looked offended as he glanced down at his stomach. Then he looked up, smiled, and shrugged.

Steph Hall stepped up and said, "I'm black. Did you overlook me because I'm a woman?"

Teague didn't miss a beat. "I couldn't overlook someone as beautiful as you. But I ran track in high school. I was the all-county champion in the four hundred meters. There's no way someone here beats me."

That's when Lorena Perez said, "Sounds like you're worried about the other parts of the tryout. Didn't you have any good cases to go over? You run your mouth so much, I don't see how you would ever hear anyone offer you a decent case."

"I recognize you. You're that financial-crimes genius from FDLE." He didn't hide the fact that he admired Lorena's curves.

"And you're the Miami cop that I'm going to bet ten bucks can't beat my girl Steph here."

It was a great afternoon and gave me some insight into my new partners. It also gave me a good laugh. I may not have been the fastest one on the track, but I finished the one-and-a-half-mile run within the twelve-minute time limit and I had a great view as Steph Hall's long, graceful strides wore down Alvin Teague. She crossed the finish line a full ten seconds before he did.

Alvin didn't have to be reminded that he owed Lorena ten bucks. Being a resourceful detective, he used it to his advantage. He started to hand the ten-dollar bill to Lorena, then snatched it back and said, "Any chance I could pay off the bet with a nice dinner?"

"You can eat all the nice dinners you want. As long as I have your ten dollars to get a pizza later."

Everyone roared with laughter, even Alvin Teague. He was a loudmouth and a braggart, but he wasn't a bad guy, and everyone recognized he was one hell of a cop.

But he didn't get chosen for the task force.

Now, as I ushered the kids through the halls of the Miami Police Department headquarters, I was hoping to avoid Teague and any other cop I knew. I stashed the kids in an interview room with a dispatcher who I knew could handle them.

As I slipped out of the room, the dispatcher said, "Anti, you know you owe me a big favor after this."

"Anything you want, Tosha."

I raced up the stairs, wondering if witness services could help me find a place for the kids for the night, and ran into the one person I'd most wanted to avoid.

Alvin Teague, wearing a starched shirt and a

blue Vineyard Vines tie with a sailboat design, stood in the middle of the staircase. He gave me a smug smile and said, "Hey, Anti, you still holding my spot on the task force?"

I just stared at him. I didn't have time to trade burns.

"I'm not joking," he said. "I'll be there one day. I hear that if you don't keep making arrests, you're rotated off."

"That's what they say."

"That's what *I* say too. I wish every unit was so strict. Maybe we'd get rid of some of the dead-weight."

"You can have my spot when the Dolphins win a Super Bowl."

Teague let out a laugh. "Look at the philosopher making jokes. I thought your only joke was your football career."

It was pretty much the same shit I heard every-where in Miami. It didn't faze me.

"By the way, is that fine Agent Perez still on the task force?"

I said, "She's still on the task force, but I doubt she'd give you the time of day."

"Lesbian?"

"Good taste."

Teague laughed again and waved as he brushed past me on the stairs. He called over his shoulder, "Stay safe, Anti."

"You too, Smooth Jazz."

That interaction went better than my conversa-tion with the witness advocates. They told me the only place they could house that many kids together was Krome. I had already decided that wouldn't happen. Now I had to make another decision.

CHAPTER 7

I DROVE OUT of Miami slowly so the kids could get a decent look around. They marveled at the speeding, swerving cars, and I explained that in South Florida, hitting your brakes is considered a display of fear. It's best to avoid it.

I mentioned a few historical facts so the trip would be educational. For instance, I told them the city's name had come from the native word *mayaimi,* which meant "big lake." (No one cared.) And that Al Capone had lived here in the 1930s. (No one knew who Al Capone was.) I grew a little desperate and dredged up the legends of Blackbeard and Jean Lafitte, pirates who, it was said, used to visit the area and hide treasure on the coastal islands and the mainland.

Joseph said, "Can we look for treasure?"

"Maybe. It's not common to find it anymore, but we can go to the beach and try." That seemed to satisfy everyone.

We stopped to pick up three gigantic pizzas from Pizza Brew, and by the time we reached our destination, everyone was hungry and tired. Each kid carried a small suitcase or backpack; I balanced the three pizzas like a Ringling Brothers act and opened the front door.

When the kids stepped into the cool, wide room, they all asked some version of the same question: Where are we?

I still had some explaining to do. I'd been avoiding phone calls from my FBI supervisor that I was sure were related to me taking the kids. He was a stickler for rules, and I was fairly certain the FBI had a rule about not kidnapping minors. I wasn't worried. I intended to return them once I was certain they'd be treated right.

Jacques, the Belgian boy, stared through a sliding glass door at the patio with the pool wedged into the backyard. He turned to me and smiled. "I am a good swimmer."

I patted him on the head and said, "We'll put that boast to the test after dinner."

All of the children turned and looked at the hall-way on the far side of the room. I let them stare in silence for a moment at the two women standing there like ghosts. They didn't move and both happened to be dressed in light clothes. The effect was perfect. I wasn't sure how this would play out, but the time had come to see how good my decision-making abilities were.

I cleared my throat, raised my voice slightly, and said, "Hey, guys, let me introduce you to some people." I waited as the children all gathered around me. "This is my mother and my sister. You can call them Mrs. Moon and Lila." I turned to my mom and sister. "Mom, Lila, this is Michele from France, Olivia from Spain, Joseph from Poland, Annika from Finland, Monnie from Kenya, and Jacques from Belgium. They're going to be our guests tonight."

My whole body tensed as I waited to hear what would come out of my mom's mouth. The longer the silence stretched, the worse I felt. Then a smile spread across my mother's face and she said, "It'll be so nice to have kids around the house for a change." I glanced at my sister, who just winked.

The relief I felt was incredible. I knew I should've called first, but I'd been afraid that if my mom was having a bad day, I would've lost my nerve and changed my mind about breaking the kids out of the Department of Homeland Security.

My mom looked at me and said, "Thomas August Moon, this is the best surprise you could've brought me."

My mom was the only one who ever used my middle name, August, and she did it only for emphasis. My little sister's middle name is June. We called her Junie for a while when she was a baby, but my dad put a stop to it. He wasn't on board with my mom's semi-flower-child love of odd names.

My mom walked across the room to greet the kids. To little Michele from France, she said in perfect French, *"Bonjour, Michele. N'est-ce pas jolie?"*

The little girl grinned like a Texan holding a gun.

My sister, Lila, leaned in to me and said, "You got lucky. How'd you know she was having a good day?"

"I didn't. It was a calculated risk. Immigration wanted to hold these poor kids at the Krome Detention Center. I just couldn't let that happen." I didn't comment on the alcohol I'd just smelled on Lila's breath.

Lila was a vivacious twenty-four-year-old who partied a little on the hard side, but she never missed a day of work and took good care of our mom. I sometimes felt like my mother and I were stealing part of her youth.

"That's my big brother." She slapped me on the back. "Have you started throwing all those quotes at them? You know that's annoying, right?"

"Maybe a couple of quotes. It's one of the few skills I can show off."

"I can tell the kids already trust you. Sounds like tonight will be lots of fun. Sorry I'm gonna miss it."

"Why? Can't you cancel whatever you're doing?"

"Nope—I've got a date. You're on your own tonight with both Mom and the kids. Are you okay with that?"

"It depends on who you're going out with. If it's Blake, the idiot PE teacher from your school, then no, I'm not okay with it. He has a man-bun. If it's Melvin the accountant, I'm reasonably okay with it."

My sister cocked her head and gave me the same look she'd been giving me since she was a kid. "Funny. But if it were either of those two, I wouldn't have told you I was going on a date. I don't want to hear shit about dating Blake just because you think he's a slacker. And I don't want to be encouraged to date Melvin just because he's got a good job. Besides, last time Melvin was here, all you guys did was talk about the University of Miami and Florida State."

"Our alma maters. At least we have college degrees."

"And Melvin even uses his degree in his job."

"Ouch. That hurt."

Lila smiled and said, "I think having the kids around will be good for Mom. At least for one night. Where'd they come from?"

"I already told you. From all over the world."

"You're an ass."

"That's the word on the street. Hey, what did the doctor say this afternoon?"

Lila shrugged and brushed her light brown hair away from her pretty face. "Nothing new. He gave me a little notebook to keep track of when Mom loses her grip on reality. He told me to cherish the days that she's lucid. Big help, huh?"

"He obviously didn't go to the University of Miami's med school. He probably went to Florida's." I looked over at my mother, who I loved so much and missed at the same time. She was talking with the kids, who'd gathered around her like she was giving away candy.

I saw my mother smile, and suddenly all the problems I'd had today just faded away.

CHAPTER 8

Amsterdam

HANNA GREETE LOOKED out the wide bay window of the apartment she'd converted into an office. She and her twelve-year-old daughter, Josie, lived in the apartment next door. She'd spent a small fortune to purchase both apartments and have a door installed between them so that she could go from one to the other easily.

She stared down at the tourists rushing around on the street below. Hanna liked living in the De Wallen District of Amsterdam, the old town quarter, because of the nice apartment buildings and safe streets. Tourists loved to tell people back home that they'd wandered through the red-light district and looked at the canal from Oudezijds Voorburgwal, just below her window. There were even organized tours of the red-light district, with guides and everything. The guides always said how great the young girls in the brothels had it. How they chose their own hours. Took only the customers they wanted. Didn't mind showing off their bodies in the windows. The charade made Hanna sick. She knew what these girls really went through. There was no glamour in prostitution.

Not unless you controlled a whole stable of prostitutes.

But the tourists ate it up. They'd take photographs around the sex shops and tell their friends back home about how they'd seen real-life prostitutes. Big deal. Amsterdam was a city that had historic sites in every form, but all the tourists wanted to talk about was legalized marijuana and prostitution.

Hanna had just finished speaking to someone in the United States. She made a quick calculation in her head and realized the six kids she'd been trying to smuggle into the U.S. had cost her about eleven thousand euros so far, and that wasn't even factoring in Hans's expenses and salary. She didn't like letting him sit in jail in Miami, but she wasn't in a position to bail him out. She hoped he'd understand.

There were other issues with the failed operation, the load. She'd borrowed money to cover expenses and then had essentially gone into business with Emile Rostoff, a local Russian gangster who had more than fifty thugs working for him in and around Amsterdam. But Hanna had heard that was a fraction of the men Emile's older brother, Roman, employed in Miami. The two were known as the Blood Brothers for reasons Hanna preferred not to think about. She had seen what happened to people who disagreed with the Rostoffs—missing ears, severed fingers, and scars from beatings. The local criminal population was a walking advertisement for why you shouldn't cross the Russian gang.

One of the worst punishments Hanna had seen was meted out to a young woman who hadn't paid her "tribute" to the Rostoffs to sell heroin to tourists and who'd mocked a Rostoff lieutenant. Now she had Emile Rostoff's initials carved in her cheeks, one letter on each side, and the end of her nose was missing. The girl was a tourist attraction all by herself.

Now Hanna had to explain to these same people why she couldn't make a payment on her loan.

Hanna turned and saw the three young women she employed as administrative assistants staring at her. She understood the fear in their eyes. The loss of the kids was a major blunder. Someone on her staff was responsible. Someone had talked too much.

She knew it wasn't Janine, who had been with her the longest. And it wasn't Janine's sister, Tasi, who was an airhead and therefore not given much responsibility. That left Lisbeth.

Hanna could tell by the way Lisbeth's eyes darted around that she knew she was the focus of Hanna's rage. Lisbeth had made all the flight arrangements, so this was her fault. Now she was going to learn a lesson about owning up to one's mistakes. Hanna had rescued Lisbeth from prostitution, taught her some basic clerical skills, and given her a life without strange men accosting her every night. But Lisbeth had screwed up somehow, and Hanna couldn't have that.

At thirty-five, Hanna was a lot older than these girls. Sometimes, she felt almost like their mother, and occasionally, parents had to punish their kids. She started slowly. She held Lisbeth's gaze as she started walking across the hardwood floor of the enormous room to where the twenty-one-year-old sat.

Hanna said, "Lisbeth, did you hear about the cockup in Miami?"

The young woman shivered and nodded. The expression on her pixie face showed her fight against tears. "I know Hans was arrested. I don't really know anything else." Lisbeth brushed her blue-streaked brown hair out of her eyes.

"Don't I pay you to know what's going on?" Hanna kept advancing.

"I made the flight arrangements and ensured the kids had all the right paperwork."

"And spent plenty of my money doing it. Now that's all gone. We have nothing to show for it. This is a business. We need cash flow. Especially now. How do you think I should handle this?"

"I...I...I mean, I'm not sure what you're talking about."

Hanna reached down, snatched the girl's long multicolored hair, and jerked her out of the seat. The rolling office chair spun from the force of it. Hanna dragged her across the floor to the balcony.

Lisbeth said over and over, "Please, I didn't do anything wrong."

Hanna released her when they were both on the balcony. She said, "Who did you tell about the trip?"

"No one, I swear."

Hanna repeated the question slowly. "Who did you tell?"

The girl started to cry.

The tears made Hanna snap. She grabbed Lisbeth by the shoulders and shoved her so that she was dangling over the brass railing of the balcony. Hanna held on to her belt, leaving the girl suspended upside down six stories above the cobblestone sidewalk.

Hanna said again, "Who did you tell about the trip? Was it the Russians? Did you speak to the police? You'd better start talking or the last sound out of you will be a scream on your short trip to the ground." She relaxed her grip so the girl slipped a little bit more.

Lisbeth was crying and screaming now. "I swear I didn't tell anyone!" She begged for mercy, then mumbled several Hail Marys and another short prayer some priest had probably told her would protect her. He was wrong.

CHAPTER 9

HANNA LOOKED DOWN at the terrified girl dangling off her balcony. She wasn't sure what to do with Lisbeth, but at least she was getting her message across. Her other two assistants would be much more careful in the future.

Hanna heard the chime that told her the inside door between the apartments was open. That meant her daughter, Josie, was home from school. With some effort, she pulled Lisbeth back onto the balcony. She straightened the girl up and brushed her hair out of her face. Lisbeth kept sobbing.

Hanna said, "Shut up, you stupid cow. Don't let my daughter see you upset."

Lisbeth nodded nervously and wiped her nose with her bare hand.

Hanna pulled the girl close and said, "I was going to drop you, but I changed my mind. Maybe you aren't completely useless." She kissed Lisbeth on the forehead. "You know I love you girls. Now go get cleaned up."

Lisbeth scurried off to the powder room as Josie and Hanna's brother, Albert, who often walked Josie home from school, came in.

Josie trotted out to the balcony. Hanna gave her a quick hug and told her to do her homework before they went out to dinner. She watched as the twelve-year-old scampered back to their apartment, high-fiving her uncle on the way.

Hanna had needed to see a little gesture like that to calm her down. Thank God her brother was such a help.

He joined her on the balcony, where she explained the disaster in Miami.

Albert shrugged his broad shoulders and said, "Just the cost of doing business."

"I know you're not involved in the finances of the business, but the money I was going to make from those six kids would have covered a lot of our debt to the Russians."

"I told you not to borrow money from the Russian mob. Emile Rostoff doesn't fool around. He and his brother are big on messages. He sent one to the guys in Aalsmeer who were making their own meth instead of buying from him. Two of them were skinned and then dumped on the sidewalk in front of the apartment where they were cooking the meth. They were still alive and screamed for five minutes until paramedics arrived. It was a mercy they died on the way to the hospital. There's still a bloody outline of their bodies on the sidewalk. *That's* a serious message."

Hanna had heard the story but insisted that she'd had to borrow the money. "If we hadn't gotten that money last year, we'd be living on an abandoned farm somewhere down in the south. Josie's idea of culture would be American TV. Besides, what's done is done. We have to pay them back soon."

Albert ran a hand over his neatly trimmed

goatee. "You always seem to have something in the works. Are you telling me you don't have any plans now?"

Hanna gave him a faint smile. "I've been trying to put together a big load for a month. At least twenty people. Right now, I'm still waiting for two more to come from Germany. I have them stashed all over the city."

"And the diamonds? How long do you intend to hold them?"

"Not much longer. I need you to buy an electronic tracker, one we can put in a backpack. I'm going to hide the diamonds in the pack, then give it to one of the people in the next load bound for Miami."

Albert looked at his sister and said, "You're not worried about Customs finding it when they go through the airport?"

"They won't be going through the airport. Twenty is too many people to fly. This time we'll send them by ship. And when it's all over, we'll be debt-free with cash in hand. That's all any business owner could ask for."

CHAPTER 10

HANNA AND HER brother, Albert, spent much of the rest of the afternoon visiting various contacts around Amsterdam. They hoped someone could tell them something about what had happened in Miami. There was no way Hanna was going to lose that much money without getting some kind of explanation.

But so far, they hadn't gotten much information. The longer this went on, the more frustrated Hanna became. And if Hanna was frustrated, Albert was on the verge of fury.

They crossed into the Noord District by way of the Coentunnel and walked until they were a couple of blocks from the city office on Buiksloter-meerplein. Their contact would meet them near the bronze statue of children playing.

At the edge of the park, Albert nudged his sister and pointed to a young woman and a man huddled in conversation.

Hanna said, "What about them?" Then the woman looked up and Hanna saw her clearly. It was the girl who'd had Emile Rostoff's initials carved in her face, an *E* on her right cheek and an *R* on her left. Each scar covered almost the entire cheek.

The missing end of her nose was also jarring, but in a different way. It took a moment to recognize the blunted tip of an otherwise normal nose.

The man next to her was missing the fingers on his right hand.

The image of the two sent a shudder through Hanna, just as it was intended to. That was one of the reasons Emile Rostoff could live in a waterfront penthouse without anyone ever touching him: everyone was terrified of him.

Hanna and Albert had spent most of their lives in Amsterdam. They hadn't heard of this kind of violence until the Russians arrived en masse and took control of much of the city's criminal enterprises.

Hanna looked away from the Rostoff victims and spotted Heinrich, her contact from the city office, a corpulent little bald man who'd been bleeding her dry for years by claiming to have connections in law enforcement worldwide.

She saw a smile spread across the man's face as he watched her approach the bench he sat on. She'd never really liked the way Heinrich looked at her. Hanna knew his preference was for young girls because she'd provided him with some over the years, but the grubby, forty-five-year-old civil servant didn't impress her as being particularly discriminating when it came to women.

Hanna did like the way Heinrich's smile faded instantly when he noticed Albert walking a few feet behind her. Her big brother had looked out for her ever since they were kids.

A light breeze blew the man's thinning hair into odd angles. Even though temperatures were mild now in the late summer, he had sweat stains blossoming under his arms.

She wasted no time on small talk. "I'm quite bothered about losing an entire load in Miami."

Heinrich hesitated, then said, "Is that why your brother is with you?"

Hanna said, "Don't worry about Albert. I just need a few answers."

"I would prefer to speak with you alone."

Albert stepped closer; he towered above the seated man. "What's wrong, Heinrich? You got something to hide?" He didn't wait for an answer. Albert plopped down on the bench right next to him. He pulled a long survival knife from under his light jacket. Then he made a show out of using it to clean his fingernails.

Hanna stayed on her feet. She looked down at Heinrich with her hands on her hips like a schoolmarm. "No games. Do you know anything about it or not?"

"The American FBI got the tip from the Dutch national police about your man with the kids," Heinrich told her.

"You know who gave the tip?"

He shook his head, but Hanna couldn't tell if it was a nervous gesture or if he was saying no.

Albert slammed the point of the knife into the bench's wooden seat less than an inch from Heinrich's leg. That made him jump. Albert said, "C'mon, Heinrich, it's not like someone from the Dutch police will cut off a body part if you tell us who called the tip in to the Americans."

Heinrich said, "I think you both know who it was."

Albert said, "Tell us."

"I thought we were business associates. I don't appreciate being threatened," Heinrich said.

Albert jerked the knife out of the bench and swung it like a tennis racket toward the civil servant's face. He froze it just as the edge of the blade touched Heinrich's throat.

Both men sat perfectly still, like statues. A thin trickle of blood dripped from the tiny cut Albert's knife had made.

Even Hanna flinched at the suddenness of the action and the sight of blood. But she held steady as Heinrich whimpered.

Albert acted as if nothing had happened and smiled as he said, "A name?" He lowered the knife.

Heinrich hyperventilated as he lifted his left hand to feel his neck. He mumbled, "Detective Marie Meijer."

Albert said, "That wasn't so hard, was it?"

CHAPTER 11

HANNA CALLED FOR a cab, then turned to her brother and said, "Was that really necessary?"

Albert put on an innocent look. "What? You mean the shave I gave to fat boy? People are beginning to take advantage of us. They no longer fear us. Something's got to change."

"You have a point. But threatening a public official, no matter how petty or corrupt, could come back to haunt us."

"If you weren't with me, I would've sliced off one of his fingers or an ear. Just to show that we mean business."

"That doesn't change the fact that we're facing scrutiny by the national police as well as the Koninklijke Marechaussee. We have to be careful."

Albert said, "I trained with the Koninklijke Marechaussee when I was in the army. They're mostly muscle. They don't really investigate. This all has to do with that one detective, Marie Meijer. She has it in for us."

Hanna nodded. He was right.

"I have no idea what we ever did to her," Albert said. "Maybe we should offer her a cut of our profits."

"I don't think so. She's a true believer. A bribe won't work this time."

"I could deal with her. Permanently. I could even make it look like an accident, although that's more work and less fun. Drop her in the Markermeer."

"No. Bodies always wash up on the shore eventually. Besides, cops never give up chasing someone who's killed another cop."

Albert looked down the road at the approaching cab and pouted like a little boy. "You don't let me have any fun at all."

CHAPTER 12

Miami

THE TASK FORCE was officially called Operation Guardian, mostly because when it was known as International Criminal Investigations, ICI, everyone referred to it as "Icky." Now we had an okay name and office space in North Miami Beach, a few miles from the main FBI office.

No one outside of law enforcement seemed to understand that Interpol didn't make arrests. Interpol was just a global organization that shared information. For instance, if there was a jewelry heist in Paris that was somehow connected to Miami, a French detective would fly to Florida and work with either the FBI or the Miami police.

That was one of the rationales for taking the best investigators from the most active agencies— now there was a single unit that took on the biggest international crimes. And we had to make a name for ourselves. Make a big splash.

The problem with an active unit, though, was that the office was always busy. It was hard to find a space where six kids could hang out.

I'd moved my laptop into the conference room so that I could work at the end of the table and also keep an eye on my new posse. No one in the office had shown much interest in helping me babysit.

The kids were a distraction, but only because they seemed like they were having fun and I didn't want to be left out. I abandoned my report to play the Monopoly game someone had brought in to keep them occupied.

Monnie said, "I've never seen this game before."

Jacques was amazed. "It's old. I saw a TV show where they said the British POWs in World War Two played it."

Olivia said to me in Spanish, "Can I play?"

I hugged her. "Of course. We're all a team. We all play or no one plays."

And that's how one of my best days started.

Forty minutes later, while I was considering putting houses on Ventnor Avenue, Anthony Chilleo stepped into the room. Sometimes, dealing with Chill was like dealing with a wild animal; he might disappear or he might eat out of your hand. I hadn't quite figured out the quiet ATF agent yet.

Chill was about average size, but he was solid. He also had a certain intensity to him that made everything he said seem vital. I hated to generalize, but that was a characteristic I'd noticed in all the ATF agents I'd worked with—they brought this intensity to everything they did. I figured it was one of the reasons they had such a high conviction rate. And I guess if I worked for a small, under-funded agency whose main task was getting illegal guns off the street, I'd develop the same kind of determination.

He placed a black camera bag at the end of the table. All he said was "This is for you."

As he started to leave the room I called out,

"Whoa, Chill, what are you trying to give me? That doesn't look like a gift."

The wiry forty-five-year-old ATF agent said, "It's a bag of electronic-surveillance shit. As the second in charge of the unit, you're supposed to keep it in your car in case we need it in the field. A couple of recorders, a camera, and a tracker. Usual stuff."

He hesitated like he had something else to say, then motioned me out of the room so the kids wouldn't hear us. He said, "I heard something that might be related to your new case."

"What's that?"

"Roman Rostoff was part of the group trafficking the kids."

"Rostoff? I thought he was more of a drugs/extortion/pimp kind of gangster. Now he's involved in human trafficking?" Roman Rostoff tried to present himself as a legitimate businessman who had a ton of political influence from his donations, but most cops knew he was the Godfather of Miami.

"He's involved in anything that'll make money. I'm looking at him for exporting guns to Syria."

"You got any snitches into him?"

Chill shook his head. "It's tough to get someone close enough. He only has other Russians near him. They're the ones that talk to people outside the organization. He's a shifty one. I hear things through the grapevine. And I heard he's pissed. He had plans right away for the girls in your new little family."

I shuddered at that thought.

I said, "Do you think he could cause trouble?"

"He can always cause trouble. The question is if it's worth it for him. If he thinks losing these kids reflects badly on him, he might do something. I just have no idea what."

"I thought you said he only cares about what makes money."

"Yeah, but Rostoff thinks ahead. If he believes losing a load of people hurts business later, he might do something crazy. I'll keep my ears open."

"Thanks, Chill."

And just like that, he was gone. Chill didn't like wasting time in idle chitchat. He wanted to get things done right away. That's probably why he'd joined the ATF instead of the FBI.

CHAPTER 13

A FEW MINUTES after Chill left, Stephanie Hall popped her head into the conference room and greeted us; she addressed each kid by name and in his or her native language. Maybe what people said about the education you get at Ivy League schools like Brown, Steph's alma mater, was accurate. I could barely pronounce some of their surnames.

Steph pulled me out of the conference room to give me a quick heads-up. "I've heard that the bosses are annoyed you took the kids without anyone's approval. Be ready if the skipper calls you into his office."

She must've seen the concern on my face because she added, "Don't worry. You handle him really well. We're all glad you're the second in command so we don't have to talk to him."

I said, "Does he always start off with the 'I have two years before I retire' speech?"

"He does it more during stressful situations. I think it's a mantra he uses to keep calm. By telling someone else about his retirement, he's reassuring himself."

Right on cue, after my conversation with Steph,

I got a text saying the boss wanted to see me, and I didn't waste any time getting to the office of the FBI supervisory special agent in charge of our unit. He seemed like a decent guy, but I'd heard his background as an accountant made him risk-averse. He weighed every decision and tried to anticipate every possible outcome, even though any cop out of the academy knew you couldn't plan for everything. Shit turned bad at a moment's notice and you had to improvise.

One thing my mom had taught me was not to overthink things. Make a decision and go with it. I had helped my mom since my dad left, when I was fifteen and Lila was only seven. That's why I chose a college so close to home. While my friends went to far-off Florida State in Tallahassee, almost five hundred miles away, at the University of Miami, I was never more than forty minutes from home. Some of my teammates used to call me a mama's boy. If being raised by a strong, decisive woman made me a mama's boy, I was not offended at all.

I was still getting used to having a friendly, measured boss. Police department supervisors are much more straightforward than FBI bosses, and they don't have too much regard for your feelings. I always knew when a Miami PD captain was mad at me because he or she would yell and maybe even throw something. I liked that directness. No fuss, no muss. Get it out in the open, know where you stand, and move on.

The FBI didn't seem to work like that, but they liked the fact that I had done well at UM and knew how to talk to people. And this time, when I sat down, my FBI supervisor was direct and to the point.

"Next time you intend to kidnap a group of kids, give me a call first. DHS is all bent out of shape. They're being a pain in the ass about getting the kids back to Amsterdam."

"What? When did you intend to send them back?" I asked.

"I'm sorry, did you want to play board games with them a little while longer? We need to get them home as soon as possible."

"Fine, let *me* escort them home. That way I can confer with the Dutch authorities and maybe gather some more evidence on this shithead we locked up yesterday."

"You have any idea how much that would cost?"

"You sound like it's your money. Someone is gonna have to fly back with them. Why not me?"

"What if something happens here while you're gone?"

"Steph Hall can handle anything that pops up. I thought that was why we had a whole task force to work with. You can't imagine what these kids have been through. And it happens to kids every day. We've got to make a case on the entire ring smuggling people into the U.S. That might make a difference. I can't do that if I let my best witnesses disappear."

I studied the supervisor's face. He didn't look worried. He was thinking. Thinking this through to see how it might affect him over the next two years.

Finally, he sighed.

That was usually a good sign.

"Make the arrangements and be on your way in the next two days."

CHAPTER 14

AT LUNCHTIME, I took all the kids out. No one seemed sorry to see us leave the office. Maybe I was already used to how much noise my new posse made. They were kids; what were you going to do? Maybe they were a little rambunctious. After all, most of them hadn't had much parental supervision for a while. But God, I enjoyed spending time with them.

As we hustled out the door, Monnie said, "Where are we going?"

I said, "You can't visit Miami and not have a little fun. We're going to do some sightseeing and have a *lot* of fun." I didn't tell them that I also wanted to be away from the office in case my supervisor changed his mind and sent them back to Amsterdam with a DHS representative.

I drove through the city, giving the kids more fun facts, like how it was the only major city in the United States founded by a woman.

Annika asked, "Who was she and what'd she do?"

"Her name was Julia Tuttle. She did it by sending an orange to a railroad magnate named Henry Flagler. It was after a frost, and everyone thought the

Florida orange crop was destroyed. She convinced Flagler to extend his railroad all the way to where Miami sits today."

I glanced around the car and realized they needed a different form of fun.

We visited the Miami Seaquarium, where I had a contact who let us in for free. It's amazing that a couple of University of Miami football tickets twelve years ago still got me free shit around the city. This city loved its team, warts and all.

The kids thought they were at SeaWorld. I explained to them that SeaWorld was two hundred and fifty miles north and this was a local attraction everyone loved.

Once they saw the sharks, they thought the Seaquarium might be the greatest place in the world. I agreed. I remembered my dad taking me here when I was a kid. I didn't care if the other kids thought it was lame; I was with my dad. It was cool.

Monnie pointed to a flock of parrots noisily fighting in a tree. "I didn't know there were parrots in the U.S."

I smiled. "There weren't, originally. People brought them to Miami as pets and let them go. Without natural predators, they multiplied fast. Now they're everywhere."

Finally, the kids were appreciating my Miami trivia.

After a couple of hours of fun, we got back in the car and started to make our way north toward my house. Joseph and I got into a deep debate about the merits of soccer versus American football. The next thing I knew, I'd bought a football at a local Walmart and we were in a park next to the Pompano Beach airport.

I explained the basic rules, which they seemed to have a hard time understanding. We tried some simple plays with me as a quarterback and each kid taking a turn as receiver. I told Joseph, "Run a pattern along the sideline, then cut to the middle, and I'll drop a pass right over Michele into your hands."

I called out a fake signal and Jacques hiked me the ball. I watched as Joseph ran in a random manner, went past Michele, then ran back toward me. I tossed the ball a few feet and he caught it.

When he was done, I said, "Why didn't you run the pattern I suggested?"

He looked at me like a kid explaining something obvious to a parent and said, "I didn't understand anything you said after *Run*."

That made me laugh. Hard and loud.

After we were once more in the car and headed back to my house, Annika said in her elegant accent, "Did you play football in school?"

"I did. I even got a scholarship to play football at the University of Miami."

Jacques was excited. "Did you play professionally after that?"

I chuckled. "No, I never got close to the NFL. I barely played at the University of Miami. My position coach reminded me often that I had run the slowest forty-yard dash of any tight end ever at the school."

Olivia said, "What's a tight end?"

That made the older kids laugh.

I said, "It's a receiver who also blocks. Usually they're bigger than wide receivers."

Annika said, "You're really big."

I laughed. "Back then, I lifted a lot of weights, and I was thirty pounds heavier than I am now."

"Did you like playing?"

"I did. It also paid for my schooling, and then, when I went back for law school, they gave me a huge discount. I'm pretty happy with my limited football career, even if I never did go pro."

Joseph said, "Did you have a nickname? Like 'the Rocket' or 'the Greatest'?"

After I finished laughing, I thought about how happy I was that no one from my old team had heard the question. Then I told them all my current nickname, "Anti."

Annika said, "Like someone's aunt?"

"No, like you're against something or the opposite of something. Like anti-government means you're against the government."

"What are you against?"

I hesitated. "In this case, it's a name people in the neighborhood gave me. They say that Ray Lewis is the greatest defensive player who ever came out of the U, so the real nickname they gave me was 'Anti-Ray' because I was the opposite of him. They were saying I was the *worst* offensive player to come out of the U. Over time everyone shortened it to just 'Anti.'"

"Isn't that an insult?"

"Yes and no. The local residents wouldn't give me a street name unless they knew me and trusted me. I like to be called Anti by people in Liberty City. It means I made some kind of impact."

Joseph said, "Should we call you Anti?"

"Not unless you want me to make up a mean nickname for you."

CHAPTER 15

WE MADE IT back to my house in Coral Springs late in the afternoon. Lila met me at the door and said, "Tough day."

That meant my mom wasn't herself. Or, more accurately, that she was herself at a different time and place.

I followed the piano music, which was always great no matter what kind of day my mother was having. When I stepped into the small parlor, she looked up and said, "Hey, Chuck."

Ugh. Chuck was my dad. He'd divorced my mom sixteen years ago, and that was where she'd flashed back to when she'd checked out for the day. I suppose that was a time when everything seemed to be going well. I had given up trying to understand this goddamned disease a long time ago. I just wanted my mom to be happy. I didn't care what the doctors called the disorder; whether it was dementia or Alzheimer's, she was just as lost to me. I felt like one of the pillars of my life was gone.

I pulled Lila into the kitchen and told her about my pending trip to Amsterdam with the kids. My sister poured her heart into working with special-needs children every day, and she still managed to deal with my mom without complaint. I felt guilty piling more on her.

She said, "I can probably take care of Mom on my own, but it's a scary prospect. I thought the reason you went with the Miami Police Department instead of a federal agency was so that you could help me."

"You're right. If you really think I need to stay, I'll work it out."

She thought about it for a moment, then said, "I can handle it. I think it's great you want to take these kids home personally."

"I'm glad somebody thinks it's great."

Lila cocked her head and said, "I've never heard Mom play Beethoven before. She's more of a show-tune-and-pop-music kind of gal."

We walked back into the parlor and I was surprised to see Joseph sitting next to my mother on the bench playing Beethoven's Piano Sonata no. 4. It was the first time my college music-appreciation class had come in handy. It was haunting.

All of the kids stood around the piano, and my mother looked positively thrilled.

And that made me positively happy.

CHAPTER 16

I WAS GROGGY the next morning as I pulled over by the park in Hallandale Beach, right next to the county line. It was so early that the presence of police cars and a crime scene still hadn't attracted many onlookers.

Hallandale's South City Beach Park used to be referred to as "Needle Junction" and "Body Drop Park." It had been cleaned up a lot since then, but there was still room to do shit without anyone seeing you.

The phone call from Anthony Chilleo at 5:15 that morning had startled me out of a sound sleep. I'd raced over here from my house, twenty-five miles to the northwest.

I held up my badge to the young patrol officer who was maintaining security around the perimeter of the crime scene. She seemed like a kid to me even though she was probably in her midtwenties. That's what six years of police work in Miami can do to you.

I followed her directions and carefully walked along the path marked by tiny flags. Crime scene people were busy combing the area on both sides of the path, and I could see Chill talking with a Broward County Sheriff's Office homicide detective.

Chill made the introductions, and the homicide detective reminded me that we'd met once in a class on money laundering.

After the small talk, I asked, "So did you think I needed to come down to the beach so early?" I said it with a smile, even though I was confused.

Chill said, "I told you about the rumors of Roman Rostoff being involved in everything, including human trafficking."

"I remember."

"I think he's showing his displeasure with how we interrupted his shipment of kids being smuggled into Miami International." He pointed to a set of screens hiding something that a crime scene technician was photographing.

I stepped over to the screens and looked behind them. I knew there was going to be a body. There wouldn't be this much commotion over cocaine that washed up on the beach or some recovered stolen property. But the image shocked me, and I knew it would haunt me for a long time.

The young woman, a teenager, lay sprawled on the sand, naked. She had blond hair and a beautiful girl-next-door face. Her blue eyes were still open and staring straight up at the sky.

There was a neat slit in her throat with dried blood on both sides leading to the sandy ground. I squatted down to make it look like I was getting a better view, but in fact the scene disturbed me. I needed to wrap my head around this nasty business. She reminded me of some of the girls I'd rescued from the Miami airport.

Chill squatted down next to me and held up a plastic evidence bag.

I struggled to see past the spatters of blood on the inside of the bag. "What am I looking at, Chill?"

"Someone stuck her Florida driver's license as well as her ID from Serbia into the wound on her throat. We've already done some quick background on her. She was a dancer at one of Roman Rostoff's clubs. The two IDs and a talk with a coworker indicate that she was smuggled into the United States. Rostoff wants us to know that if we screw with his business, someone is going to get hurt."

I looked down at her pretty, lifeless face. Somehow I felt responsible. At the same time, I was pissed. Who did this asshole think he was?

I stood up and backed away from the body. I looked at Chill and said, "How do you feel about doing something the FBI wouldn't approve of?"

"To tell you the truth, I do that every day. Just on principle."

I smiled. The ATF agent didn't say much, but I was getting the idea that he'd be useful in an insurrection. People like that are hard to find.

CHAPTER 17

A FEW HOURS later, I found myself on Biscayne Boulevard in front of a beautiful skyscraper overlooking the bay. It housed the headquarters of AEI Enterprises, and I cringed when I realized that it also housed the law offices of Robert Gould, the man who was now married to my ex-fiancée.

Chill met me in the lobby. He'd thrown on a sports coat and looked remarkably professional. I was still wearing my 5.11 Tactical pants with my gun on my hip. We were in the city of Miami now. This was my territory.

Chill said, "I worked a case in front of here once."

"The Che Guevara shirt?"

He smiled. "Exactly. You were on it too?"

I hadn't been, but I remembered it well. A Cuban immigrant had taken deadly offense to a tourist's Che Guevara T-shirt. "I had just come on the PD and was working patrol," I said. "When I heard someone had been shot in this area, I was curious. I guess that hipster from Chicago learned his lesson the hard way; even *I* knew you didn't praise Castro or Che in Miami."

Chill nodded. "People who don't understand shit

like that shouldn't be allowed to leave home. I was surprised the jury even convicted the Cuban shooter."

"Of manslaughter, not murder. He was a hero in the city when he came home three years later. I heard he never has to pay for a meal on Calle Ocho."

I glanced around the opulent lobby and said to Chill, "What does *AEI* stand for?"

"American Entertainment and Investment. It's Rostoff's supposedly legitimate business, the one that handles his nightclubs, alcohol-distribution companies, and foreign investments. He's listed as the president, and there are half a dozen other Russians in the top corporate spots."

"Hiding in plain sight."

"Roman Rostoff doesn't even try to hide. He just donates truckloads of money to the county and city commissions. One of the state senators in the area has stepped in four different times to help him out with business licenses and real estate issues. He's an old-time gangster who brings in money from a dozen ventures and understands that he needs politicians in his pocket to keep going. They're giving him some kind of award in Miami Beach soon."

We rode the elevator up to the forty-first floor. All of the offices here were occupied by AEI Enterprises. A sharp-looking receptionist who wore superthin glasses, probably as a fashion statement, asked if she could help us.

I said, "We'd like to speak with Mr. Rostoff."

She looked us over, and we clearly didn't pass the test. "I'm sorry, Mr. Rostoff's schedule is quite filled today."

"When does he have some time?"

She glanced at her computer, hit a few keys, then

smiled and said, "Unless you have an appointment that he's agreed to, his next free time is in April of next year." She smiled again and somehow made it seem sincere.

That was my cue to walk past her. If you're not making some kind of effort, I don't have time to deal with you.

Chill let out a low chuckle as he followed me to the giant double doors that I assumed led to Rostoff's office. I opened both doors to make our entrance seem more spectacular. But our entrance couldn't compare to the incredible view of Biscayne Bay, South Beach, and the Atlantic Ocean beyond. It might have been the best view I'd ever seen in Miami.

That pissed me off a little bit more.

We walked toward a man in a blue Joseph Abboud suit sitting behind a carved oak desk. He looked to be about fifty-five years old. Before we'd gotten three steps, two other men sprang into action. The tall, muscular one turned to me; an older guy in a suit moved toward Chill.

I held up my ID quickly and said, "This is a police matter."

The man near Chill said, "I know. It's called criminal trespass. And you're going to get arrested for it."

CHAPTER 18

I APPRECIATED THE quick comeback by the jerk in the suit.

The tall man closer to me didn't say anything, which meant he was the one who was going to take action first. He was about an inch taller than me. I'm not used to men with a longer reach than I have, but he didn't try to punch me. He reached out with both hands to grab me by the shirt. It was like a drill we used to do on the practice fields—someone grabs your jersey, you knock his hands away. In this case, I put my weight into it, and after I knocked his hands away, I gave him an open-handed slap on the back of his head. That is one of the most disorienting blows you can suffer, the good old Gerber slap. It might not cause much damage, but for a couple of seconds you're knocked stupid.

He stumbled forward, fell onto an expensive Asian carpet, then slid into the decorative baseboard.

I reached for my gun, and the man near Chill started to reach into his suit jacket. This was turning ugly fast.

Just as everyone was about to pull a gun, Roman Rostoff yelled, "Enough!" We all froze. Rostoff said,

"Billy, help Tibor up." He looked at Chill and said, "What can I do for you, Agent Chilleo?"

Chill said, "I'm impressed you know who I am."

"I always learn the names of people trying to hurt me or my business. But who have you brought with you? He looks more like a professional wrestler than a cop," Rostoff said. He had almost no Russian accent. I was surprised that he was neither intimidated nor flustered. That was a disappointment. I'd been hoping to scare him a little bit, but mostly I'd just wanted him to know we were watching.

I said, "My name is Tom Moon. I'm a detective with the Miami PD working on an FBI task force."

"What kind of task force, Detective?"

"International crime. Right now we're looking into human trafficking."

Rostoff clucked his tongue and said, "Is there such a thing as human trafficking? There are so many people that wish to come to America, how could there be human trafficking here?"

I knew his smile was designed to annoy me. It worked. I took a moment to size up the other men. The one named Billy looked like he was in good shape. He had dark, thinning hair and a goatee with a blue tinge to it. I guessed he was trying to look younger, but no hipster I'd ever met wore a thousand-dollar Brooks Brothers suit or had hands that looked like they could crush granite.

The other guy was standing now and trying to look tough even though I had just smacked his ass onto the floor. He was younger than the other one and had long hair tied in a ponytail and the sides of his head shaved. A tattoo of a blossoming branch came from under his collar up his neck to the right side of his face. It looked a little like the van Gogh painting of almond branches. I was willing to bet each white blossom represented something, like a person he'd killed. None of these ass-wipes had tattoos for the hell of it.

I said, "Wasn't the girl found murdered on Hallandale Beach trafficked? Poor Serbian girl was brought to the U.S., thinking she was going to live the dream. Instead, she ends up working at one of your shitty clubs."

Rostoff kept his smile. "Who are you talking about?"

"Valentina Cerdic."

He shrugged and said, "Don't know her."

Chill said, "She worked at Club Wild." He looked at the man with the dyed goatee. "That's one of the places you run, right, Billy? You're the guy people call Billy the Blade."

Billy gave him a smile and then looked over to his boss.

Rostoff turned his attention to the ATF agent. "Did you enjoy watching this dead girl dance?"

Chill was far too cool and collected to let a comment like that get to him. Cops who bite at that kind of bait never get much done.

Rostoff said, "Now, why did you gentlemen really come up here? Was it just for the view? Perhaps to practice your martial arts on my associates?"

I said, "I wanted to get a look at what kind of shit-heel murders a girl and stuffs her ID into a hole in her neck."

"Then I suggest you start searching for the killer."

"We already are." I looked at the well-dressed, fit man who had confronted Chill. I said, "Billy, is it? What kind of Russian name is Billy?"

The man lost his smile and said, "One you should remember."

"No need to worry about that. I remember almost everything. Plus we'll be keeping a close watch on you."

Rostoff clapped his hands together. "Excellent. You can never be too safe. Tell me, Detective Moon, do you think you're safe? Being a police officer is a terribly dangerous job."

I stepped a little closer and said, "You think you're smart. Beyond our reach. Let me assure you that you're wrong. This isn't a seventies NYPD movie. No one is untouchable. Especially if the FBI is after your ass. You should have learned that from Al Capone. Another Miami resident."

"We shall see."

I turned to leave. "We'll be in touch."

As we stepped through the door, I heard Billy mumble, "So will we."

CHAPTER 19

I SPENT A long, tiring day making sure everything was in order to take the kids back to Amsterdam.

Virtually everything in the police world ran on favors. The more help you gave, the more help you got. So even though I was crazy-busy, when a homicide detective asked me to swing by the PD to help him interview a witness, I couldn't refuse.

The witness, Hazel Branch, was an elderly woman who lived off Miami Avenue and had known me since my first days on patrol. She was an eyewitness to a drive-by shooting and she said she'd only talk to me.

I had to help, but it wasn't because of the detective's request. It was because Miss Hazel had helped me out once. When I was on patrol as a rookie, she'd warned me about a gang-initiation ambush. Two beefy young men with baseball bats were planning to break my legs when I walked through the apartment complex. Thanks to Miss Hazel, I changed my route and walked up behind those two young men while they were waiting for me. I said, "Can I help you fellas?"

They both jumped and turned quickly. One of

the men inadvertently whacked the other in the arm with the bat. That started an argument between them, which led to some good swings, and each man took some lumps.

I didn't make an arrest. I couldn't risk tipping them off to Miss Hazel. Besides, it was fun watching those two punish each other more than any judge would have. And I never forgot what I owed her. I always came when she called.

I stepped into the comfortable interview room. Miss Hazel, who wore a simple, dignified dress, as she always did, looked up and said, "Hello, Thomas. Would you explain to this young man that I don't need trouble with any of the local gangs?"

I sat down in the chair across from the elderly woman. "Miss Hazel, he's just trying to figure out who killed that young man in front of your apartment. I know you said you heard the gunfire, but do you know what time? Did you happen to glance at the clock?"

"Thomas, if I looked at the clock every time I heard gunfire in my neighborhood, I'd never get any sleep."

I tried not to laugh—I didn't even know if she was trying to be funny—but I couldn't help it; the detective and I both broke up. After some casual chatting, I finally got something worthwhile from Miss Hazel. I asked, "Do you have any idea who shot him?"

She smiled slyly. "Now, that's a good question. The youngest Gratny boy shot him."

"How do you know that?"

"Because I heard him tell Bean Pole, who lives in the apartment next to me."

I glanced up at the detective to see if he knew who

Bean Pole was. He nodded, looked at Miss Hazel, and said, "Why didn't you say that at the beginning of our interview?"

She said, "I don't know you from the pope. But I know Thomas. He won't tell anyone what I told you. And he wouldn't have asked the question in front of you if he thought you'd tell anyone."

Now the homicide detective owed *me* a big favor.

CHAPTER 20

THAT EVENING, LILA slipped out again with some friends, this time to go dancing in Fort Lauderdale. Looking after both my mom and the kids that day had sapped my last bit of strength.

Which was why I was sleeping so hard when Lila called in the middle of the night.

"Hey, are you okay?" I asked.

"I am great, big brother," she slurred. "Come down to the beach and join me. That way you can give me a ride home when I'm done."

"It sounds like you're already done. How much have you had to drink?"

"Just a few vodka-and-cranberries and some champagne."

I heard someone say something behind her and caught snatches of music. I figured she was in the ladies' room or maybe outside one of the clubs.

Lila added, "Oh, and we had a few shots too."

Ever since men started realizing my little sister was a beauty, I'd told her that if she had too much to drink she should call me and I'd come pick her up, no questions asked. I didn't mind missing a little sleep if it meant my sister didn't accept a ride from a stranger.

I said, "Where are you?"

"Beach Rockets, between Sunrise Boulevard and Las Olas."

"Isn't that the new place for spring-breakers? I thought it had a young crowd."

"I'm only twenty-four! Just because I act like an old person around you and Mom doesn't mean I'm not young. It's a fun dance club and tonight was ladies' night."

"Okay, I'll be there in twenty minutes."

I slipped through the house quietly. There were kids sleeping on couches and air mattresses everywhere. At least, that's how it felt. I checked to make sure my mom was asleep.

I was a little nervous about leaving, but I had no choice. I didn't want to wake up six kids and drive them twenty minutes to wait outside a bar. Everyone had my phone number, and they all knew how to use the house phone. Kids in the U.S. might not know what a landline was, but these kids did.

When I pulled up to trendy Beach Rockets, I could feel the music pulsing through the walls even from my car. The bright colors and decorative rockets near the door covered up the fact that the place had been a dive bar six months ago. Of course Lila wasn't waiting outside for me, and she wasn't answering her phone. I could hear the beat of the bass through the thick concrete walls, so there was no way she could hear her phone inside the club.

It'd been a while since I'd had to pass a bouncer and a uniformed cop working the door to get into a dance club in Fort Lauderdale. Or anywhere else, for that matter.

The place wasn't all that big, but I didn't see Lila. I stood there for a few minutes, hoping she'd walk by. Then someone said, "Are you waiting for your sister?"

I was about to say yes, but then I turned and saw who had asked me the question: Rostoff's man Billy. Billy the Blade. His blue goatee seemed to make his teeth glow in the low light of the club. And standing at the bar right behind him, wearing a goofy smile, was Tibor, the tall Russian I'd smacked. Even in the dark, I saw the flowering tattoo running up to his face.

CHAPTER 21

I STARED AT the two Russians casually drinking Budweisers at the end of the bar. My right hand involuntarily moved toward the department-issued Glock that was stuck in my waistband with my shirt hanging over it.

It was one of the few times I was at a complete loss for words. I wanted to just pull my pistol and put a bullet in the face of each of these lowlifes.

Billy, as friendly as ever, said, "Lila was here just a minute ago. I'm sure she'll be right back."

The other Russian, Tibor, winked at me.

I don't know what he thought would happen. I don't know who they were used to dealing with. But it didn't matter. I brought my hand up to his crotch and used the strength I'd been working on since the coach had told me I needed a better grip on the football twenty years ago. I felt Tibor's testicles mash in the palm of my hand.

He gasped and his eyes rolled back in his head as I maintained my hold and pushed him against the bar. No one saw what was going on except for his friend Billy.

I turned to Billy and calmly said, "My next move

will be to rip his balls right off him. I doubt he wants that to happen. What do you think?"

Billy struggled to maintain his composure and said, "I think you just committed felony assault. I think you need to release him right now. We're part owners of this club and there's a Fort Lauderdale police officer working the front door."

"Why don't you go get him? I've got a few questions to ask him myself. And if I don't see my sister in the next thirty seconds, your buddy here isn't going to have any kids and you're going to have a pistol stuck halfway down your throat. Is that what you want to happen in your nice little club here?"

Then I heard Lila from the other end of the bar. "Hey, Tommy, I see you met my friends."

I turned to see my little sister wobbling toward me with a stunning young woman whose arm was draped around her shoulder.

I released Tibor's balls. He stumbled back and plopped onto a barstool without a word.

I turned to Billy and said, "This is not cool."

"What do you mean? Your sister making new friends? I thought it was very cool."

Lila came up to me, unaware of any potential violence, and said, "This is Nadia, Billy, and"— she looked at the man I had nearly castrated—"and their friend."

I took her by the arm and started to drag her out of the club.

Lila tried to yank her arm away from me and said, "Hey, what the hell are you doing? I thought you were okay with me calling you for a ride now and then."

We burst out of the club into the warm night air of South Florida. No one paid any attention to us.

This wasn't the time to explain things to her. As soon as we were both in my Explorer, I pulled out of the spot and rolled past the club.

Billy stood just outside the door and gave me a friendly smile and a wave.

CHAPTER 22

THE TALK WITH Lila went about like I'd expected it would. She said I was too suspicious; I told her she was too naive. In the end, she agreed not to go back to that club or any of the other ones Rostoff owned. She also promised she'd check in with Anthony Chilleo every couple of days while I was away.

Chill told me that he'd keep an eye on things. When a guy like Anthony Chilleo tells you he'll take care of something, you can be confident it will be taken care of.

Two days later, the kids and I were all on a KLM flight from Miami International to Amsterdam. The two youngest girls were next to me, and the other four kids were across the aisle spread out over two rows in front of me. The man across from me asked if we were on some sort of school field trip. Some of the passengers looked relieved I wasn't sitting beside them. No one wants to be stuck next to a big guy in economy for eleven hours.

The kids were not excited about going back to Amsterdam. Annika from Finland had told me she lived there with her mother, but her mother's drug problem had gotten so bad that she could no longer function. Once Annika's mother had gotten into the social services network of Holland, Annika had lost touch with her completely. Two months ago, she'd learned her mother had died, and she'd decided to start fresh in the United States. She met a woman who promised to get her to America and said Annika could work off the debt once she got there. She had no other choice at that point.

Joseph's story affected me deeply, maybe because I was so close to my sister. He had left Gdańsk, Poland, with his sister, Magda. While traveling through Germany, they were caught up in a protest of the European Union's refugee policy. They'd gotten separated in the crowd just as the police arrived. Joseph waited four days in Berlin, avoiding social services, hoping to find his sister. He hadn't had any success. Now she was all he thought about.

The younger girls, Olivia and Michele, had essentially been tricked into coming to the United States. I didn't even want to think what someone had had in store for them.

I noticed Jacques fidget in his seat, then lower his head. I went over and knelt down by the fifteen-year-old Belgian boy and said quietly, "You okay, Jacques?"

"It's embarrassing."

"More embarrassing than me admitting I was the worst football player on my college team?"

That made him smile. Finally, he said, "I'm a little scared. This is only my second flight. This waiting is making me nervous. I wish we'd just take off."

I glanced around, then said to Jacques, "Close your eyes and take a deep breath."

He did as I asked.

I said, "Now think about the most exciting thing you can. Feel the excitement."

A smile slipped across the boy's face.

"What are you thinking of?"

"A girl."

I laughed. "A pretty one, I assume."

"Beautiful. She's nice too."

"Oh, is this a real person? Not some fantasy?"

"She's real."

"Who is it?"

He didn't answer. Then he blushed.

"Jacques, you can tell me."

"You won't tell anyone or get mad?"

"Of course not. Who are you thinking about?"

"Your sister."

"Lila? She's ten years older than you."

"Nine."

"Are you crazy, telling me that?"

"You said you wouldn't get mad."

I smiled and snapped my fingers. "Foiled by a loophole." That made Jacques giggle.

The flight attendant announced we were about to take off.

I said to Jacques, "You okay now?"

He nodded.

"By the way, my sister can be a handful. You might've dodged a bullet by leaving town."

He liked that.

As I went back to my seat, I looked at the smiling Michele and Olivia and pulled a deck of cards out of my back pocket. "How would you guys like to learn a counting game? It's going to be hard because of our language differences, but I think you'll like it."

Olivia managed to say, "What game?"

I smiled and said, "It's called blackjack."

CHAPTER 23

Amsterdam

WE ARRIVED AT Amsterdam's Schiphol Airport about midmorning. The children had slept during most of the interminable flight, but I'd stayed awake. I felt like the kids were too vulnerable. I didn't want to risk taking my eyes off them.

This airport was either a lot less busy or a lot more organized than Miami International because walking through it seemed like taking a quiet stroll. The airport even had its own shopping mall. I held Olivia's and Michele's hands and let the boys fight over who would push the little cart with everyone's luggage.

A tall woman wearing a tailored blue dress approached us before we reached the police substation where I was supposed to contact my Dutch counterpart. She wasn't walking so much as marching. A few feet in front of me, she stopped and said, "Detective Moon?"

I gave her my best smile and said, "You must be psychic."

"I'm hardly psychic. I was told to look for an American over one hundred and ninety centimeters tall who looked like he played professional rugby and who was accompanied by six children." She held out her hand and said, "My name is Marie Meijer. I'm your liaison with the Dutch national police."

She had an elegant accent, graceful movements, and a grip that could crack a walnut. I wouldn't want to be on the wrong side of her.

Marie leaned down and spoke French to little Michele, then greeted each of the kids by name.

"Wow, you learned everyone's names before we arrived. You're quite thorough."

"I've been working on this ring of human traffickers for more than a year. I finally have someone to feed me information, so I'm hoping we make some serious arrests soon."

Olivia was either scared or bashful. She hid behind my right leg, peeking out like a puppy. The other kids had gravitated behind me too, and we now faced this woman as a single group.

Marie smiled and said, "I'm happy to see the kids trust you. That must mean you're trustworthy. Kids and dogs are rarely wrong about such things." She focused her blue eyes on me and said, "Shall we get to work?"

After being at the FBI for the last eight months, I liked that attitude.

A few minutes later, we were in front of the airport looking at a long white Mercedes passenger van. A blue VW hatchback with an official police emblem on the dashboard was parked behind it. Marie directed the kids into the van, then turned to me and said, "You can say your goodbyes. I'll drive you in my car."

I almost didn't understand. I saw the stunned expressions on the kids' faces. I said, "If you don't mind, I'd like to ride with my posse. I want to see where they're staying and what the conditions are like."

Marie didn't miss a beat. "Of course."

I watched her walk toward her car. Jacques looked up at me and said, "I wouldn't mind riding in her car."

I laughed as I playfully shoved the Belgian teenager toward the van.

About twenty minutes later we arrived at an apartment building. I'd been relieved to see that the Dutch drove on the right side of the road. And so far, aside from about three thousand bicyclists, traffic didn't look all that much different from what you'd see in a big city in the U.S.

Marie showed great patience as I checked out the rooms, questioned the two social workers, and made sure the children were all settled with their bags next to their own beds. I'd friended them all on Facebook and gotten their e-mail addresses, and they all had my e-mail address and my cell phone number.

I couldn't believe how upset I was to say goodbye to them. I promised I'd see them again before I flew back to Miami. Everyone wanted a hug.

I couldn't meet Marie's gaze as we walked out of the facility because I was trying to keep the tears out of my eyes. I hate that kind of shit.

CHAPTER 24

AFTER I'D HAD a sandwich accompanied by an eight-ounce Coca-Cola in a glass bottle that made me feel like a giant, Marie gave me a quick tour of Amsterdam. I didn't want to explain that I'd been up all night on an airplane and that my circadian rhythms were all screwed up. I just tried to take in the sights and listen to what this sharp detective had to say.

"I heard you had to chase the man bringing the kids into Miami. Do you have many foot chases?" Marie asked.

I shrugged. "Some. I guess it depends on how badly you want to make the arrest."

"Do you get angry at runners?"

"No. I learned early in my career to keep it in perspective."

"What happened?"

"I was a rookie in uniform and saw a young man selling crack on Miami Avenue, right in the center of the city. When he ran, I chased. As I ran, I kept screaming, 'Police, stop,' like that might help.

"Finally, near a highway underpass, I tackled him. I was mad and yelled, 'Why'd you run from me?'

"The crack dealer kept calm and said, 'It's my job to run. It's *your* job to catch me.' I had tackled a philosopher. He was right and I've kept it in mind for every chase I've ever been in."

I liked that Marie found the story funny. She had a beautiful smile and an engaging laugh. I noticed now that her left eyelid looked heavy, half closed over her dazzling blue eye. But her creamy skin was flawless. I was finding her more and more interesting.

Marie said, "This is the De Wallen District of Amsterdam. It's the largest of the red-light districts, although it's almost nothing more than a tourist attraction now. No one wants to risk a tourist getting hurt, so everyone makes sure the streets are safe."

"Is this where most of the human trafficking occurs?"

"The whole city is used as a hub to traffic people, mainly to the U.S. The Amsterdam police joke that we should be classified as an official rest stop for Russians in transit. The local Russian mob is constantly running people through Amsterdam."

I said, "I wondered if they were causing problems here like they do in the U.S. The northern part of Miami–Dade County has seen a huge influx of Russians over the past few years."

"Do the Russians in Miami organize in groups to commit crimes as much as they do in Europe? I know the criminal justice system is different in the States."

"No. They're like any other immigrant group— they tend to keep to themselves. The problem is the criminals prey on other Russians, and the crimes are difficult to investigate. One crime lord in particular, Roman Rostoff, is engaged in some human trafficking as well as a long list of other crimes."

"I'm familiar with Rostoff, unfortunately. His brother, Emile, has a smaller operation here in Amsterdam."

"Is he as big an asshole as Roman?"

Marie smiled and said, "I'm glad we both view the family the same way. But from what I hear, Roman is much more brutal. Emile is vicious, but he tries to keep things quiet. We don't have the same level of violence as you do in the U.S."

"But somehow every country has organized crime and people like the Rostoffs who screw things up for everyone else."

Marie pulled over on a block with a lot of pedestrians. I had to unwedge myself from her VW. We walked down the street to a series of four-story apartment buildings that looked like they'd been there a long time. I stared at a line of people that stretched around the block. "Is this a place where you find a lot of human smuggling?"

She smiled and shook her head. "No, this is the building where Anne Frank lived in hiding. I thought you might like to see some of the history of the city."

I felt like a moron. I didn't want to tell her I was too tired to see anything like this, so I just followed along.

I had no idea the day would stretch into the evening. The detective took me through the Heineken factory and on a drive along the IJmeer coastline. She also showed me several dilapidated buildings where the police suspected human traffickers kept people on a regular basis.

"For a party city, I don't see anyone walking with a beer in their hands like they do in New Orleans," I said.

"No beer allowed on the street, just in pubs. Alcohol makes people aggressive."

"Let me get this straight. You can smoke a joint in the red-light district and no one will bother you, but you can't drink a beer on the street?"

She smiled. "When was the last time you saw a person high on pot punch someone?"

She had a point.

I noticed something on the glass of a decorative street lamp. I stopped to look closer at the image of a man with a guitar. It was remarkably detailed and lifelike.

Marie chuckled and said, "This is a rare treat. Usually when he puts those up, people steal them quickly. The artist is Max Zorn. He makes these incredible images using nothing but packing tape and a razor."

I studied the figure illuminated by the lamp. It was extraordinary. I murmured, "'The purpose of art is washing the dust of daily life off our souls.'"

She said, "Excuse me?"

I turned to her. "Picasso said that."

She smiled. "You are not at all what I expected of an American police officer."

"Is that good or bad?"

"Just surprising." She started to stroll down the street and added, "I like surprises."

As we continued on, I couldn't stifle a yawn. Marie said, "Is a big, tough American police officer like you getting sleepy?"

Her mocking tone made me smile. She sounded like Stephanie Hall or my sister. That meant she was okay. It also meant she was giving me some kind of a test. She might have wanted to see if I would take offense or show me how tough she could be by outlasting me. I didn't need any convincing.

When I saw the Hilton sign in the Noord District, I knew salvation was at hand.

CHAPTER 25

IT WAS LATE in Amsterdam, but it was a good time to call home. I wanted to check on my mother and Lila, though I knew my mom didn't like that I worried so much about her; she always said I needed to get a life.

Lila picked up the home phone on the second ring. The first thing I did was get Lila to talk a bit so I could listen to her speech and make sure she was sober. Then I ran through our regular checklist of concerns: Did Mom have any doctor appointments coming up? Was she getting exercise? Was she staying occupied? That was a big one; we'd learned that her dementia was worse when she wasn't busy. When she focused on the piano or crochet, she tended to stay grounded. Even reading helped quite a bit.

One thing I'd noticed recently was that my mom tended to read the same books over and over. I thought she was just a huge Brad Meltzer fan until I realized she had read the same book of his, *The President's Shadow,* at least four times in a row.

It was tough to deal with my mom's issues, but I could never put them out of my head. It

was part of my upbringing; I'd been raised a good
Lutheran and still attended services with my mom.
I still believed. But like most humans, I had questions. That's what had attracted me to philosophy
in the first place. That whole notion of the search
for truth.

Philosophy came down to opinions. It wasn't
science. It was one man's or woman's idea of what
life should be. So far, I hadn't found any answers
that would solve all my problems.

I'd read what Plato and Schopenhauer and various other philosophers had said about adversity, but
it was former president Bill Clinton who'd said it
best: "If you live long enough, you'll make mistakes. But if you learn from them, you'll be a better
person. It's how you handle adversity, not how it
affects you. The main thing is never quit, never quit,
never quit."

It was that quote that kept me going sometimes.
In football, in police work, and especially in dealing
with my mother.

Everything at home was fine, and after the call,
I conked out almost immediately. In fact, when my
room phone started ringing at seven forty-five the
next morning, I was still lying on top of the covers
in the khakis and blue button-down oxford I had
been wearing the day before.

It wasn't a good idea for a guy my size to cram
himself into a tiny airplane seat for a transatlantic
flight and then spend the next twenty-four hours
walking around town. As I reached for the phone, I
heard creaks in my joints that reminded me of every
time I'd caught a football and then been knocked to
the ground by some defensive back.

"Good morning, Detective Moon," Marie Meijer

said cheerfully. "Are you ready for another day of excitement in Europe's most interesting city?"

I know I made a sound like a groan before I said, "Please call me Tom, and please call me again in two hours."

She laughed and said, "I'll meet half your demands. I'll be in the lobby waiting for you in about ten minutes, Tom."

Before I could object, she hung up.

CHAPTER 26

SOMEHOW, TEN MINUTES later, I was in the lobby wearing clean clothes and searching desperately for a cup of coffee.

Marie bounced into the hotel as if she'd just gotten back from vacation. She greeted the doorman by name and then we hopped in her official VW hatchback.

It seemed like every third building was some sort of museum. When they talked history in Amsterdam, the topics were events that had occurred before the U.S. was a going concern. In South Florida, *history* meant the Cuban migration or Jackie Gleason living there in the seventies.

It wasn't all sightseeing; there was a purpose behind it. Marie explained how the city was laid out and told me where different crimes were most common. She also showed me potential safe houses for the Russian mob. At one point, we stopped by a building next to a canal.

Marie said, "These apartments are often used to house people before they're smuggled to their next destination. There's going to be an operation to make some arrests tonight. I wanted to bring you so you can see what it's like. There are some legal prostitution houses in this block as well," she added.

I was genuinely curious. "Did you find that legalizing prostitution had much of an effect on crime?"

"There's never an easy answer to things like that. Even if you legalize something, there's still a black market. People think that decriminalization eliminates black markets, but those are people who don't experience life on the streets. For customers who want to avoid taxes or identification, there's always a market that the government can't control. Legalizing prostitution has made Amsterdam a destination for desperate people, and that provides an avenue for human traffickers. They convince runaways or young people with drug problems that if they can just get to somewhere else, everything will be all right. It's basically the same scam every criminal has used for the past two hundred years."

In the early evening we stopped at a café. I'd expected to throw down half a gallon of coffee to perk up, but as soon as we settled into a small table in the corner, I realized this was no ordinary café. This was one of the coffeehouses Amsterdam was famous for, the kind where they served pot along with coffee.

It was not dark or dank. The different strains of marijuana were proudly displayed in glass containers. The conversations in the small coffeehouse were muted and private. A light shone on a poster of the Rolling Stones at Altamont. Except for the odor of pot in the air, it could've been any hipster hangout in the States. Commercial cigarettes and alcohol were both strictly forbidden in the coffeehouse.

When I told Marie I knew what was up, she gave me a sly smile. "It's completely legal here. At least, inside a place like this."

I glanced around at people enjoying pot-infused pastries or smoking joints or hookahs.

Marie said, "Would you like to try marijuana legally?"

"Just because it's legal here doesn't mean I'm allowed to try it."

Marie said, "Have you ever tried pot?"

I laughed. "I went to the University of Miami. Of course I've tried it."

She ordered in Dutch. Before long, I had a cup of coffee and a lovely-looking pastry in front of me. Marie had the same. She also had a single, perfectly rolled joint.

I said, "Knocking off early today, are we?"

"No. Just breaking all kinds of rules."

I watched as she lit the joint with a plastic lighter and took a single puff. She handed it to me. I thought about it for a moment, then copied her single, light puff. If it was a test, I'd passed it. She put out the joint by crushing it under the edge of her coffee cup.

Marie said, "I was hoping you weren't one of those by-the-book cops who are so insufferable."

I let out a laugh and said, "I can be insufferable even while breaking the rules."

We chatted about differences between the U.S. and Europe. It was as nice an evening as I'd had in years. The pot seemed to hit me in waves. At first, it was just some ringing in my ears, but before I knew it, I felt the full effects.

This shit was so much stronger than anything I'd ever tried in college. Of course, I hadn't smoked a lot back then, and the few times I had, it was to fit in or impress a girl.

I guess things hadn't changed much.

Marie asked me about the task force and I felt like I was slurring my words as I told her about it. Finally, I said, "No one realizes that Interpol is basically a series of databases with no real arrest powers."

"Isn't it funny how people assume they know all about police work from movies?" Marie said. "My father always asks me if I have a CSI team with me. He watches reruns of the American show."

"I get that all the time. Especially with my size, people assume I'm duking it out with bad guys every day."

Marie laughed. "It's true that much of our view of Miami police work comes from reruns of *Miami Vice.*"

"It's a good show, but it's about as realistic as *Game of Thrones.*"

"Another favorite. I prefer a good fantasy to some of the horror we have to face in real life."

I raised my coffee cup and said, "Amen, sister."

It might have been the pot, but we both laughed for a really long time.

CHAPTER 27

HANNA GREETE LOOKED across the small table at the two men she'd been chatting with for the past half hour. The older of the two men, Alexi, worked directly for Emile Rostoff. She said, "Can't you talk to someone on my behalf?"

Her overriding feeling was relief that she had not brought Albert with her.

Alexi acted as if he was trying to help her. But she knew that, with the Russians, it was all about business. They wanted her to pay them back, and she couldn't pay them back if they killed her. That's why she'd left Albert at home with Josie. Her brother would have stirred up even more trouble. He didn't handle threats well.

Alexi said, "We're not a bank. You can't pay in tiny installments. You owe us almost five hundred thousand euros. We want at least half in the next month."

"Five hundred thousand? That's crazy. We borrowed three hundred thousand less than six months ago."

"Money is a commodity. Right now, the value of money is up."

"Not according to the European Union or any reasonable banks. Their interest rates are all hovering around one percent."

Alexi was not impressed with that reasoning. "You are most welcome to take out a loan to pay us back. One of the advantages would be that banks aren't going to break your leg or follow your daughter home from school if you miss a payment. Why don't you try for a loan?"

That comment made the younger man with Alexi snicker. He was clearly Alexi's answer to Albert—in his thirties, tall, well built, unshaven. He looked like a movie thug.

Hanna said, "No, I don't think I'll get a loan from a bank. I have some money coming in soon and I'll use it all to pay you off."

Alexi sat back and smiled. He had scars on his face that seemed to brighten when he smiled. They were like a map of his professional life. He had clearly been an enforcer when he was younger, and now he ran the operation for Rostoff out of the Noord District. Of course, Emile Rostoff ran the whole city. No one dealt directly with Emile, but if you did something to displease him, the results were almost always disastrous.

Alexi said, "Everyone knows about the diamonds you bought. We'd be willing to cancel a hundred thousand of your debt for five nice diamonds. We don't care where they came from."

Hanna had to be careful about how she played this. "If, hypothetically, I had any diamonds, they would be worth the full five hundred thousand." She knew her estimate was about right, and she would jump at the opportunity if Alexi agreed.

Instead, he shook his head and said, "I don't

deal in hypotheticals. And I don't pay retail for diamonds. I hope your next load goes better for you so we can get paid. Mr. Rostoff's man in Miami will help set everyone up with jobs. That will go a long way toward paying down your debt. But you're going to have to do more. We are starting to lose patience."

The other man, whose English was much more accented than Alexi's, said, "Tell your crazy brother not to do anything stupid."

Hanna looked hard at the younger man. "I can control my brother only so much. I can tell you're afraid of him. That means you're a little smarter than I thought."

She walked away before he could respond.

CHAPTER 28

THE NEXT DAY, Hanna and Albert went to check out the port at Rotterdam. She'd decided it was too dangerous to move the load out of Amsterdam. Between the police and the Russians, someone would cause headaches.

In the late afternoon, they arrived back in Amsterdam to the apartment that held half a dozen of the younger people going on this trip. She had two older Indian men and several women at another apartment across town.

The Indian men had paid for the trip up front. They just wanted a fast way into the U.S. Hanna used their money to pay for everyone else's expenses.

In addition, she had six girls divided among two apartments. The apartments held people going on other shipments with other groups. Hanna and her brother felt it was a way to minimize exposure and keep traffickers from turning other smugglers in to the police.

She and Albert visited an apartment near the Emperor's Canal. One of the teenage girls she'd stashed there stepped into the main room wearing tiny shorts and a T-shirt that looked like it was made for a little kid.

Hanna greeted the girl and pulled her close to sniff her hair. "Where'd you get shampoo that smells like that?"

The girl just shrugged and said, "The lady that works for you, Janine, bought it for us."

Hanna said, "Where's Gregor?"

The girl said, "He's taking a walk with Freda."

Hanna grabbed Albert and pulled him out the door. As they walked down the hallway, she said, "First thing I want to do is scream at Janine for buying luxury items for these girls. They don't need to worry about expensive shampoo until they're in the U.S. getting ready for a job. And second, I told that prick of a landlord, Gregor, not to fraternize with the girls. Now, when I need to talk to him, he's out touring the city with one of them."

They stepped outside the main entrance to the building and saw Gregor with his arm around the shoulder of the teenage girl. Albert said, "I'm guessing someone is about to be yelled at. If you need me to do anything more than that, just nod."

Hanna wasted no time walking up to the squat, middle-aged landlord. She poked him right in the chest until he took his arm away from the girl. "I told you not to have any social contact with these girls," she said.

Gregor backed away, raising his hands. Dark hair bristled on his forearms.

Hanna glared at Freda and said, "Get back to the apartment now." The girl ran into the building.

The landlord said, "I'm not making any money housing these girls. All I want is a little bit of fun. It would be easy for me to go to the police and explain what you're forcing me to do."

That was over the line. Hanna turned to her brother and nodded. Albert didn't disappoint. He pulled out his favorite survival knife and let it dangle from his hand right in front of the landlord.

Gregor stared at the knife for a moment.

Hanna said, "This is a critical time. You will not tell anyone about what we're doing. Not the police, not your friends, no one. And in case you don't understand, Albert is going to make it clear for you."

She had no idea what her brother had planned, but she watched with great interest.

Albert was very casual. He simply leaned forward slightly and flicked the knife up between the landlord's legs. The sharpened tip was enough to pierce the man's off-brand blue jeans and catch him right in the testicles.

The landlord grunted, grabbed his groin, and dropped to his knees.

Albert said, "And that was for even *thinking* about going to the police. Imagine what will happen if you really do."

As the siblings walked away, Hanna said, "I'll admit that sometimes you're more articulate than me." She waited until they were at the end of the block and said, "This will be our last dealing with Gregor. Once the girls are on their way, make sure he doesn't talk to anyone."

Albert just smiled.

CHAPTER 29

AFTER THE EFFECTS of my single puff of marijuana had worn off and Marie and I had had a decent dinner, she brought me back to the apartment complex she'd shown me earlier. We were at the edge of the Nieuwmarkt neighborhood in the Centrum-Amsterdam borough.

Marie said, "I've tried to give you a good overview of the city's criminal issues. The information I get on the group that tried to smuggle the kids into Miami comes from a couple of sources. The woman who runs the group is named Hanna Greete. She's managed to keep a relatively low profile, but she deals with Russians, and Russians always talk about their competition among themselves."

I said, "It's been my experience they don't hesitate to talk about their competition to the police too."

"I haven't been able to conduct decent surveillance on Hanna's group because of a lack of resources. All anyone seems to care about anymore is terrorism. Human trafficking has taken a back seat. That's why I work closely with our paramilitary agency, the Koninklijke Marechaussee. And that's why I brought you here tonight."

I noticed the activity at the far end of the block. "You're taking me on a police raid for our first date?"

She smiled. "No, on our first date I dragged you all around the city after you had traveled for twelve hours. This is our second date. And things will only get more exciting from here."

"Are these guys going to arrest Hanna Greete?"

"This apartment is used by several different smuggling groups. I got this specific tip from some Russians, which means they're not holding any people here themselves. We don't have a lot of information, but we know that the man who owns the apartment building tends to like younger girls. It's very common among these safe-house owners. And that's not something our friends in tactical gear down the block appreciate."

I felt a twinge of excitement. This was a big deal. It also meant that Marie trusted me. She'd gone out of her way to involve me in this. After spending time with the kids we'd rescued from Miami International, I had a genuine interest in watching human traffickers taken down. I wanted to see a whole group rounded up. I wasn't satisfied with the skinny Dutchman I'd grabbed at the airport.

It was a swiftly evolving, complicated crime, but it didn't capture the public's attention as much as terrorism or narcotics did. I'd learned in the short time I was involved with this case how dangerous these human traffickers could be.

Obviously, the Dutch police felt the same way. They were taking no chances. I watched as two different groups of men dressed in black tactical clothes with body armor and carrying MP5 machine guns hustled along the street in the shadows. They looked like a SWAT team from any major U.S. city. This was getting interesting fast.

I said a silent prayer for the poor people in the building who were trying to get to the States. They might not have realized the danger they were in from these scumbags who viewed them only as a source of income.

CHAPTER 30

I WATCHED AS the SWAT team lined up outside the wide, decorative wooden door that had probably been handcrafted three hundred years ago. They were all precise and quiet, the definition of a good SWAT team.

TV shows make SWAT teams look sexy and glamorous. In real life, it is a tough, physical job with endless training. Critics call them *militaristic* or *threatening* without ever considering the decisions SWAT members must make in a split second. And just the sight of a team has saved lives; that alone has made barricaded suspects surrender and dangerous crowds disperse. A SWAT team is the big dog you don't always have to let off the leash.

At the end of the block, the support officers were pulling into position. They would be the ones to enter the building after it was secured.

This was one of the most dangerous activities for any SWAT team. When noncombatants or victims are inside a house with the suspects, tactics change. Like most cops, I don't know how I could live with myself if I accidentally hurt an innocent, like a child, while executing a search warrant.

I felt nervous for the team about to enter the apartment building. You never know; the next entry might be your last. Marie listened on a radio. I couldn't understand any of the Dutch being spoken, but I recognized the tone. They were getting ready to breach the main door. I'd bet there was another team that would make entry from some other point.

An older apartment building like this would have several doors. Most would crumple under a strike from a battering ram.

Marie Meijer said something into the radio, then turned to me and said, "If someone runs from the building in this direction, we're the ones designated to stop them. Is that okay with you?"

I smiled. This was a lot more action than I'd expected. I no longer felt tired.

Then the SWAT team swung into action. Even from our position, I could hear the pounding on the door and the officer yelling in Dutch. I suspected he was saying something along the lines of "Search warrant. Open the door."

A team member came up from the back of the line with a one-person battering ram. He swung and hit the solid wood door twice, and the booming thumps echoed in the ancient street like explosions. On the second strike, the lock gave way. The door flew open wide, with only the lower hinge keeping it attached to the frame. The team was inside in an instant.

My heart raced as I watched the raid commence. I was worried about the cops, worried about the victims, and bothered that I had no role in it.

I could hear a woman's wailing scream like a fire alarm, then two flash-bangs—distraction devices that we also used in Miami to shock and blind. The loud *boom, boom* echoed through the apartment complex like thunder. Even at this distance, standing just outside Marie's car, I could feel the vibration.

CHAPTER 31

THE NEXT SOUNDS I heard were not flash-bangs but gunshots. *Holy shit.* I could see the muzzle flashes in the windows. Frozen to the spot, I couldn't think about anything but the poor captives, running in fear.

I heard return fire from the automatic MP5s. It was controlled and disciplined, short bursts of two or three shots. I just hoped it was disciplined enough.

Suddenly, people started spilling out of the apartment building, a few tripping and piling up right in the doorway. Once they were cleared, more people poured out onto the street. A lot of people. I realized that the people waiting to be smuggled didn't want to deal with the police either.

Most of them just stopped in the street. But two men tried a different tactic to escape: blending into the shadows. Unknowingly, they ran directly toward us.

Both were young men and ran with an easy gait. The man closest to me was small and muscular, like a gymnast. I squinted in the dark, trying to see if they had anything in their hands.

Next to the car, Marie never flinched. "Let them get closer. And stay on your side of the car unless I call for you." She was calm and quiet. That's how any good cop talked in the face of a disastrous raid. You didn't want to get others excited or distracted.

The men continued to race up the street toward us, no one following them. They must have imagined they were in the clear.

Marie stepped in front of the car with something in her right hand. The men started to slow, looking over their shoulders at the apartment building. Marie called out, *"Politie, stoppen."*

Both men skidded to a halt about six feet in front of her. I'm not sure they even noticed me standing on the other side of the car. I fought the urge to race out and help her, a cop's natural instinct for backup.

One man said something to Marie in Dutch while the other tried to slip between her and the car.

Marie gave them another command; I assumed she was telling them to stand still and raise their hands. The man closest to her laughed and then lunged toward her.

That's when I realized what she was holding in her right hand. It was an expandable baton. We usually called it an ASP, the name of one of the baton's manufacturers.

Marie swung up so swiftly that the baton extended during the motion. She caught the man hard under his extended arm. She spun in a complete circle with the ASP still in her hand. This time, she caught the man on the opposite arm.

I winced at the motion and the sickening sound the ASP made when it struck the man's flesh. I'd been in too many training sessions and seen too many people hit with an ASP not to know that the pain was always excruciating.

The man froze as he tried to decide which arm hurt more. Finally, cradling both arms, he crumpled to the ground.

The man who had been trying to slip past Marie turned to see if he could help his partner.

Marie didn't hesitate. This time, needing a little more reach, she took a quick step and lifted her foot off the ground as she swung the baton. It caught the man across his chin and sent him into the side of the car.

He was smaller and in better shape than the other suspect. Apparently, he was also smarter. When he staggered to his feet, he knew he wanted nothing to do with Marie. He turned and broke into an all-out sprint.

I heard Marie mutter, "Damn." She couldn't leave the suspect she'd brought down.

Now it was my turn.

CHAPTER 32

I RAN AFTER the smaller man as fast as I could. Growing up, I was never the quickest kid on the playground; God had decided to make me too big for that. Way too big. So my whole life, I had compensated by thinking races—or chases—through to the end.

I paced myself. I watched as the man darted down an alley to the left. I took that turn, and I saw him slow considerably as he went around another corner. I tried to fix my position in my mind so I wouldn't get lost. It wouldn't be a good look for American law enforcement if I had to call out for help on an empty street with no idea where anyone else was.

When I turned the next corner, the suspect was down to a fast walk. He approached a section of the block under construction. The sidewalk was roped off, and lightweight scaffolding rose along the side of the building.

I kept my easy pace, trying not to make any noise. Even with all my chases in Miami, I'd never gotten used to running in long pants.

Maybe the man heard me coming, or maybe it was chance, but just as I was about to pounce on the suspect, he looked over his shoulder. He immediately sprang up into the air.

The move took me completely by surprise. Then I realized he had grasped a low bar on the scaffolding and pulled himself up like a monkey. The whole structure shook. It wasn't secured to the building yet.

I called for him to come down.

Shockingly, he ignored me.

I watched as he climbed higher, hoping he'd come to his senses. The scaffolding wobbled more and more.

Then it happened—he lost his grip and slipped off the scaffolding. I wanted to say, *I told you so,* but I didn't have the language skills. *Oh, shit,* I thought, *that fall could kill him.*

I watched him drop the twenty or so feet through the cool night air. Some instinct kicked in and I moved to stand underneath him with my hands outstretched.

He landed in them like a toddler.

His left elbow hit me in my right eye, but the sound he made as he landed told me the blow was unintentional. He was more shocked than I was.

I stood there with a grown man in my arms. After a moment, he said something in Dutch. I let his feet touch the ground gently. He spoke again. I said, "I'm sorry, I don't speak Dutch."

The man nodded and said, "English, good. I wish to thank you. You saved me from falling."

"Actually, I saved you from hitting the ground. You were falling no matter what."

"I am in your debt."

"And now we're going to calmly walk back to where your friend is under arrest. And you're not gonna do something stupid like try to get away again."

The man was in his late twenties, I could see now. He looked me up and down, then said, "If I had realized how big you were, I probably would not have run."

I turned him in the direction I wanted to walk and draped my arm across his narrow shoulders like we were friends. "Let's enjoy this stroll back."

"Do I have a choice?"

"Everyone's got a choice. But your other options in this situation would have you limping for at least a year."

I returned to Marie with the man still at my side. I was impressed that she already had her suspect handcuffed and in the back of her car.

She turned and smiled as soon as she saw me. "I was starting to get worried."

"You told me not to let anyone get away." As I stepped from the shadows into the street, she noticed my eye, which I could feel was swelling shut.

Marie said, "Now we have matching eyes."

CHAPTER 33

A FEW MINUTES later, Marie and I led our two prisoners back toward the apartment building. I wasn't prepared for what I saw. I stepped past the battered door, still hanging at an angle, and got my first good look at an apartment that held large groups of people. Human smuggling made real.

These dazed and scared people, some of them near starving, stared up at us with no hope in their eyes. One young woman looked too exhausted to cry. Her blond hair was a tangled mess and her ribs were showing under a translucent nightgown.

Inside, it got worse. The stench of urine and unwashed bodies assaulted my senses. Add the sharp smell of gunpowder from the flash-bangs and gunfire, and it was brutal. The odor seemed to have a life of its own. It made my eyes water.

No one should ever have to live like this. I was angry at myself for not acting fast enough. It was frustrating that something as terrible as human smuggling was so widespread. I was also angry at my bosses for not taking it seriously enough. Most of all, I was angry at the smugglers.

Three teenage girls in oversize T-shirts wept on

a couch. A young female police officer tried to comfort them. I felt like I was invading their privacy just by glimpsing them in this condition.

Marie was clearly respected among the cops. SWAT team members stepped out of her way immediately. One young uniformed officer who had taken part in the raid escorted both of us upstairs.

Marie looked over her shoulder as we walked. "You can see that this was a relatively big operation. There were twenty-six people housed here and five men running the place. The two we caught are known drug runners from the Rotterdam area. But there were two fatalities in the raid."

We stopped on the third floor. Several uniformed officers stood around the corpse of a pudgy, middle-aged man. He had four bullet holes in his chest and one in his right cheek. A World War II Walther P38 with the slide locked back sat on a table next to him.

The blood from his chest wounds had pooled to a sticky puddle on the hardwood floor. His brown eyes were still wide open. His Nirvana T-shirt looked to be original; it had faded lettering and a few tears in it.

It was hard for me to muster much sympathy for a modern-day slaver.

Marie said, "He fired six rounds. They fired sixteen." Then she led me farther into the room. I felt a wave of sorrow looking down at the next body.

It was a young woman sprawled across a velvet couch. Someone had placed a blanket over her body, but her face was exposed. She was young, nineteen or so. Blood still trickled from the corner of her mouth.

Marie said, "For some reason, the man shot her

in the chest before he opened fire on the arrest team. They think she might have run for the door to get away just as he started shooting. In any case, it's a tragedy."

None of the cops could even look at the dead girl. I knew what they were thinking—that they had failed her.

I felt the same way. I'd seen my share of bodies in Miami, but most of them were criminals involved in the drug trade or in gangs. Somehow, those deaths didn't affect me nearly as much as seeing this one, a young woman whose only crime was wanting to get out of Europe.

In the United States, the media doesn't care much about gang violence in places like Chicago and Miami until a bystander is killed. But the subsequent outrage rarely lasts long enough to galvanize the public into helping the police.

I thought of all the things this young woman might have done with her life. She might have had children eventually. A death like this can ripple through eternity.

After a minute, I stepped over to the edge of the room and sat on a folding chair. My legs felt shaky. Marie pulled another chair close to me and sat down too. "Now you see why I am so obsessed with the smuggling rings. With your help, we can really hurt them."

I looked at her and said, "Hurt them? I want to crush them."

CHAPTER 34

HANNA GREETE SAT with her brother at Mata Hari, a little restaurant on Oudezijds Achterburgwal, right on the canal. She liked the food, but even more, she liked how quiet it was.

Albert bitched about it being too fancy. She knew his real complaint was that they didn't sell pot, although he had already smoked a joint with a pretty Canadian tourist earlier. The three beers he'd downed here had only made him mellower. This was the best time to talk to Albert.

He put a hand on Hanna's and said, "We only lost two girls from our load. Some groups lost as many as ten. We should feel lucky they hit that place instead of the one Gregor runs. Not only would we have lost most of our load, but you know that fat little turd wouldn't have hesitated to flip on us to the police."

It took Hanna a moment to realize her brother was actually making sense. He was a loose cannon and a hothead, but no one had ever accused Albert of being stupid. In fact, if he hadn't been thrown out of school for sleeping with his teacher, he might have had a fine academic career.

Hanna sighed and shook her head. She still couldn't speak.

Albert said, "She's getting to you. That policewoman, Marie Meijer. Are you bothered that she has made it her business to cripple our business?"

Hanna slapped the flat of her hand on the table, startling her brother, and said, "Yes, that's exactly what's bothering me. It's what's been bothering me for months. That smug detective. All we hear from our contacts is that she's leading the charge against our industry."

She looked at Albert. She noticed for the first time a gray streak running through his goatee.

Albert said, "It's easy to focus on Marie Meijer, but we have plenty of other problems to address."

Hanna glared at her brother. "Not until we deal with her. I don't even want to hear her name again. If you need to refer to her, call her Funky-Eyed Bitch or Snake Plissken."

A broad smile spread across Albert's face.

Hanna said, "What is it?"

"First, I like the fact that you can see a little humor in this. Second, you know *Escape from New York* is my favorite movie, and now, every time I see Kurt Russell, I'll smile, thinking about the one night when I was the reasonable sibling."

Hanna said, "It just starts to be overwhelming. You try to make a better life for your family, but there's always someone looking to stop you— the Russians, the police, or someone on your own payroll."

Albert said, "Then let's deal with the detective." He paused, then said, "No, let's deal with Funky-Eyed Bitch first. That should be relatively easy."

"When do you want to do it?"

"We can do a little surveillance tonight. Let's see what happens. But I promise, by the time you're ready to ship those people to Miami, she won't be a problem anymore."

CHAPTER 35

TWO HOURS LATER, Hanna and Albert stood on a street corner in Haarlem, about twenty kilometers outside of Amsterdam.

Albert glanced down the slowly sloping hill to a redbrick road that led to a pleasant-looking three-story apartment complex.

Albert turned to Hanna and said, "How on earth did you find exactly where she lived?"

"Heinrich got the information for me. And he's still quite upset that you threatened him with a knife. I had to pay him more than double what I normally do."

Albert grinned. "Usually the knife gives me a discount. Maybe next time I can make my point more clearly."

Hanna said, "He even found out that she lives with two cats. It sounds like he knows someone at the national police headquarters. Say what you want about Heinrich, he can be subtle and inconspicuous."

Albert pulled his survival knife from under his sports coat. In the lamplight, his eyes seemed to glow. He said, "I can go down there and finish this right this minute."

Hanna shook her head. "We need to wait. We can't do it anywhere around this apartment complex. The cops would be all over us. And I don't want to risk anyone finding out that I have ears everywhere. If we did something like this, there's no way Heinrich would ever give us information again. And there's no guarantee he'd keep his mouth shut."

She turned and looked down at the building. The apartment was on the second floor, and several lights burned. The Funky-Eyed Bitch was home.

"We need to do this in the street somewhere," Hanna said. "That way it won't be traced back to us. With any luck, it could be written off as some kind of random act of violence. Maybe they'll believe some refugee went crazy and stabbed her. I'm just not sure how we might find her later."

Albert said, "I have an idea." He reached into the outer pocket of his sports coat and pulled out a case about the size of a deck of cards.

"What's that?"

"The tracker you told me to buy. I was going to test it to make sure I understood it. This will work perfectly." Without waiting for a reply, Albert started walking toward the parking lot on the side of the apartment building. The very first car in the lot was a Volkswagen Golf hatchback with a police emblem on the dashboard.

He was already on his knees checking the batteries in the store-bought tracker when his sister caught up to him.

"Do you know how to use it? Can it be traced back to us?"

"No, it can't. And we need to practice with this gadget. Once we have the diamonds, we'll want to be sure we know how to track them accurately."

Hanna heard a door shut. She glanced around the corner of the building to see Detective Marie Meijer strolling down the sidewalk toward the parking lot.

Hanna barked in a harsh whisper, "Hurry up. She's coming."

Albert smiled and said, "Last chance. I can kill her right here, right now."

Hanna shook her head.

Albert said, "Got it. Let's get out of here."

Hanna was surprised by the rush she got from doing something as simple as this. Her heart was racing, perspiration forming on her forehead. They stepped onto the sidewalk with their backs to the detective, and Hanna put her arm around Albert's waist as if they were a couple on a date.

She heard the car door open and shut, then the pinging sound of an underpowered engine as the detective pulled away from the parking lot.

Albert brought up his phone and opened an app. He said, "We got her. Let's see where she's headed."

CHAPTER 36

THERE WAS A different vibe between Marie Meijer and me the next evening. The swelling in my eye from the suspect's elbow had receded during the night, but I was still disturbed by what I'd seen after the raid by the Koninklijke Marechaussee. The image of the dead girl stuck in my head. Her pretty face would never smile again.

It's easy for a cop to pretend he's seen it all and nothing bothers him. The reality is that if you see too much, there's nothing anyone can do to save you.

So on the job, I never minimized the tragedy I saw. It kept me human. Connected. I embraced the fact that I could still be shocked. I tried to stay positive, and I genuinely liked people. Most people. Even knowing what I knew, I gave people the benefit of the doubt. Like my dad used to say, people do what they have to do. Of course, he was using that as an excuse for why he was leaving my mother, but I could see how it made sense.

Now we were back in De Wallen, the largest of the red-light districts, and Marie was showing me the building where she believed the human-trafficking ring operated. We walked because it was faster than sitting in traffic, no matter what kind of car you had.

I didn't like seeing the young women in bikinis behind windows. I knew what a hard life prostitutes had, sanctioned by the government or not. The girls in the booths with red lights worked twenty-two hours a day. The booths were closed from six to eight in the morning, then opened again for the business-men to stop for a quickie on the way to work.

I was surprised at the number of tourists, some with children, casually walking down the district's narrow streets. We slipped into a café for a quick break.

Marie took a sip of coffee and stretched her arms. She seemed more relaxed in this setting. She said, "What's your social life like back at home?"

"Dull to nonexistent."

She smiled and said, "I doubt that. A tall, hand-some police officer in a city like Miami? I bet you're busy every night."

We'd shared a lot over the past couple of days, but I wasn't quite ready to get into my home life with her. At least, not the details about my mom. We sat quietly for a while longer, then I finally had to ask her about her eye.

She focused both eyes on me and said, "It's a birth defect. Why? Am I not pretty? Would I be a freak in Miami?"

I held up my hands. "I'm so sorry. I didn't mean to touch a nerve. It's just that you're so confident and your eye doesn't seem to bother you. You even made a joke about our eyes matching. I was just curious."

Marie waved off my apology and said, "I try not to be self-conscious about it. The doctor said the eyelid droops slightly because of damage to a nerve. I used to wear nonprescription eyeglasses to hide it, but when I turned thirty, I realized anyone who was bothered by my eye was not someone I wanted in my life."

I said, "'Think of all the beauty still left around you and be happy.'"

Marie gave me a dazzling smile. "Okay, I'll bite. Who said that?"

I couldn't hide my own smile. "Anne Frank."

"So you have a quote for every situation."

I laughed. "I picked that one up reading about Anne Frank last night."

"Why did you learn all these quotes?"

"My bachelor's degree is in philosophy. I noticed that it freaked out my coaches at the University of Miami when I spouted quotes. No one expects a big tight end to go to class, let alone study. I knew there was no way I was going to go pro, so I studied hard."

Marie gave a dainty laugh. "What does one do with a degree in philosophy?"

"Go to law school."

"And how does someone who went to law school become a police officer?"

That, I was not about to get into. There were too many complicated elements involved. I could've told her that I wanted to make a difference in the world or that I liked the excitement. Instead, I just shrugged and said, "I like my job."

She got that I didn't want to talk about it. "Do you live alone? I bet you have a fancy apartment on South Beach."

"That's almost exactly right. Except that I live fifty miles northwest of South Beach in a house with my mom and my sister."

Marie paused, then said, "That's sweet. I think."

"Sweet, weird—it's a matter of perspective. The fact is they're good roommates and I can trust them. I haven't always had that kind of success in my other living arrangements."

Clearly wanting to move on and not make me uncomfortable, Marie said, "Why don't we take a look at some other neighborhoods?"

It was like police work anywhere. Gather as much intelligence as possible before you act. I felt at home.

CHAPTER 37

IT WAS EARLY evening when Hanna and Albert started following Marie Meijer. Hanna wanted Albert to practice with the tracker. The signal had faded in and out a couple of times during the day, but he was learning how to follow the display on his iPhone.

Albert put his hand on her arm as they turned a corner in central Amsterdam. He pointed across a busy street and said, "She's just leaving that café and her car is parked out front."

Hanna said, "Who's that with her? It looks like a cop."

"He's either a cop or some kind of wrestler. He'd be a handful."

"It's too crowded here. Let's see where they head next. I'd prefer to get Funky-Eyed Bitch by herself." Albert had given Hanna a Browning nine-millimeter pistol. He carried the Makarov nine-millimeter he'd bought at a military-surplus show. He'd had to pay the man extra to buy a working pistol, not just a museum item.

They tracked the couple into the Oost District and found the car parked near Molukkenstraat, a block from the canal.

Hanna said, "Why would they be over here?"

"Does it matter? This is perfect. With all the crazy shit that goes on around here, no one would be surprised by a shooting." He glanced around, hoping to see Meijer. "Remember, your gun is just for extra security. Let me do the shooting. We'll do it when there are no witnesses."

"Are you going to shoot the man too?"

"If he's with her, I have to shoot him. There can't be any witnesses. But I'm pretty good with this thing. I might be able to do it from down the block."

Hanna didn't like the idea of murder, but she could only deal with so many problems at once. Marie Meijer was the driving force of human-smuggling investigations. With her gone, Hanna could focus on the Russians. Just today, they had threatened her again, after Albert had stabbed one of their flunkies in the shoulder. She'd tried to explain that it was a personal argument in a bar, nothing to do with business.

That's all Russians cared about.

CHAPTER 38

WE PARKED THE car on a side street in the Oost District, and I noticed that this area catered to a younger, more vibrant crowd. There didn't seem to be many tourists here, judging by how clean and serene the district felt.

I was so comfortable with Marie now that it felt like I'd known her for years. She had a quick sense of humor, and, more important, she could let things go. She showed no resentment for my question about her eye earlier.

When she took me to a charming place called the Volkshotel, I wondered what she was up to. One of the desk clerks waved to Marie as we entered.

Marie looked over her left shoulder and said, "There's a bar on the roof, Canvas. It'll give us a nice view, and they have several beers that are outstanding."

I had given up trying to decipher the menus, so when we got there, I left my order up to Marie and she didn't let me down.

The IPA was from Belgium and the name unpronounceable. It had to be close to 10 percent alcohol. But it went down easy. Very easy. If this beer had been available in Miami when I was younger, I might not have graduated.

Marie looked over and said, "Do you feel like being honest with me for a few minutes? Have I earned your trust enough?"

I lifted my beer and said, "Fire away."

"How's a smart, good-looking guy like you not married? You wouldn't be able to stay single for ten days on the streets of Amsterdam."

I'd been prepared for a question about my mother. I was even ready to tell her all about the dementia that had stolen Mom from me and Lila a little bit at a time. It was the biggest, most difficult thing in my life. But this question hit home in a different way.

I took a long pull on the beer and said, "It's not a big deal."

That made Marie laugh. "I'm sorry, but when anyone begins a discussion with 'It's not a big deal,' it's usually a pretty big deal."

She was right. "What I meant to say was there's not a good explanation. There's just an old story." I paused to take another sip of beer and choose my words.

"Basically, I was engaged to a girl in law school. I took an internship with a local attorney in Miami, and the flashy son of a bitch stole my fiancée. That's why I'm not married."

Marie was quite serious when she said, "I'm sorry the woman didn't have enough sense to recognize she was with a good guy." She paused, then added, "I was engaged once myself."

"What happened?"

"Who knows? He got scared, I got scared. It just didn't work out."

I said, "At least my way, you end up with an interesting story."

I enjoyed making Marie laugh.

I said, "The worst of it is that I see the son of a bitch around town all the time. And he's married to my ex-fiancée. If the fact that he's still alive doesn't show how much restraint I have, nothing will."

She smiled, patted my hand, and said, "Poor baby."

She meant it, and I felt better. Not a bad evening.

CHAPTER 39

HANNA WATCHED AS Albert jogged across the street to her. Generally, in their business, she handled all the details about shipments and money, and her brother acted as an enforcer. But lately, she was concerned she'd given him too long a leash, and she had been accompanying him on some of his jobs to ensure that he didn't go overboard.

Now he trotted back to her position and said, "They're sitting up in that rooftop bar, Canvas, having a beer. Their car is a few blocks the other way. They'll come out the front and probably take the alley back to the car. We could wait and catch them then."

Hanna said, "And you still don't know who the man is?"

"No. I don't care how big he is—a bullet in the face should keep him pretty quiet."

Soon, just as Albert had predicted, the Dutch detective and her big male friend came out of the hotel and started walking toward her car, stopping periodically to look at things on the walls.

Hanna and Albert fell in behind their two targets, and Hanna wondered what they were looking at. It took her a few minutes to realize they were reading some of the historical plaques on the buildings. The man had to be some kind of tourist.

A few blocks from the car, Albert turned to Hanna excitedly and said, "This is perfect. There's no one around. It's dark. They've slowed down. This is so easy, it's embarrassing."

Hanna said, "Can you do it from a distance? Even with just a handgun?"

"We can stay right here behind this Mini Cooper, and I'll hit both of them. If it doesn't do the trick, I can walk down there and finish them. But this should be no problem at all."

He knelt down next to the British car. There was a blank space where the Cooper emblem should have been. He pulled the Makarov semiautomatic pistol from the back of his waistband and steadied it on the edge of the car.

Hanna crouched behind him and saw that his barrel was pointing at the Dutch detective. Good. Marie Meijer was the main target. Hanna didn't really care if they got the big man or not. He wouldn't be able to identify them anyway.

She could hear Albert steady his breathing and sight down his extended arm.

This was one less problem Hanna would have to worry about.

CHAPTER 40

IN FRONT OF a small brick building, I studied a little bronze plaque that informed me the structure had been built in 1790.

I mumbled, "Holy shit. The oldest house in my neighborhood was built in 1963."

Marie said, "Perhaps you can come back when you have more time. I could show you a lot more than just the criminal aspects of Amsterdam—there's art and history here as well. The Rijksmuseum and the van Gogh museum are fabulous."

I let out a laugh. "Art and history? Are you crazy? I'm from Florida. I want to see sports and pretty girls."

A smile slid across Marie's face. She reached up and gently touched my black eye. "We have soccer, and there's a rugby club on Saturdays that would love to have someone like you. As for pretty girls, that's a matter of your perspective."

I said, "I'm impressed with Amsterdam so far. Who knows, you and I might make some key arrests, and then we can visit every museum in the city."

She paused for a moment, then said, "I hope we can sort out the information I'm getting now about another load of people bound for the United States. We think the traffickers will try Miami again. That's where their contacts are."

"Now *you've* got some pretty good contacts in Miami as well. We'll do whatever we can to stop these criminals." I was serious. Aside from the fact that she'd shown me a good time here in Amsterdam, Marie was a hell of a cop, and she was working a really big case. A case that could shut down a human-trafficking operation. She had intel and a witness who was feeding her tips; that's how we'd saved the kids in Miami, and that's how we'd stop the traffickers. There was no way anyone could pull me off it now.

I heard the gunshot. Then two more. Instinctively, Marie and I both crouched behind a concrete planter for cover.

Amsterdam was starting to feel more like home.

CHAPTER 41

HANNA WATCHED HER brother line up the shot. Yes, this was business, but it was also clearly personal, and killing Marie felt necessary. The detective was too interested in Hanna's operation. The Funky-Eyed Bitch had made it personal first.

Hanna was crouched low behind the Mini Cooper, watching the spot where the detective had taken cover, when a movement near her left shoulder caught her attention.

Albert looked ready to shoot when Hanna whispered, "Wait."

Albert whispered back, "What's wrong?"

"Someone's behind us."

Just as Albert started to turn, Hanna heard a gunshot, and the rear window of the Mini Cooper shattered. Albert grabbed his sister and shoved her away from the car, across the sidewalk, and into the entryway of a small shop.

There were two more shots. The bullets pinged off the bricks surrounding the entryway. A fleck of debris hit Hanna in the eye. She was confused and fighting panic. What the hell was this? Who was shooting at them?

Albert kept low with his gun up, scanning the dark buildings around them.

Hanna said, "Who's shooting?"

He continued to scan for targets. "I'll give you one guess."

"The Russians," Hanna answered. "But why?"

"Take your pick: The money we owe them. The fact that I had to get rough with one of them in a bar. Or that we're competition for them."

"I meant, why *now*?"

Albert was silent.

Hanna had to ask. "Is there something you're not telling me?"

Albert hesitated, then said, "Remember the pretty Canadian tourist I got high with yesterday?"

"Yeah?"

"What if I told you she wasn't Canadian, but Russian? And that after we got high, we fooled around at my apartment. Oh yeah, and that her husband is an enforcer for the Russian mob."

Hanna shook her head. "You're an ass, but at least that makes a little more sense. Now I get why the Russians are trying to kill you."

Albert fired two rounds that looked like wild shots to Hanna. A streetlight across the road shattered, making it suddenly darker. Then two men scurried out of the shadows.

Albert fired three more shots. One of the men fell onto the hard brick road and dropped a pistol as he hit the ground. Albert immediately jumped up and ran toward the fleeing man.

Hanna was impressed by her brother's abilities, but he soon gave up the chase. The escaping man had had a solid head start. Albert turned and walked slowly back toward her. As he passed the Russian lying in the road, Albert extended his right arm and pumped another bullet into the man's back.

Hanna flinched at the sound and at the sight of the man spasming on the ground. Albert's expression never changed as he walked past her and said, "C'mon, we need to get out of here."

CHAPTER 42

MARIE AND I huddled behind the heavy planter, listening to the gunshots. As a Miami police detective, I'd heard plenty of gunfights. I once saw two separate gunfights converge, gang members opening up on people they didn't know or care about.

We stayed in position for a while after the shots ended and the sound of running footsteps receded. When I heard one last shot long after all the others, I knew someone had executed a coup de grâce.

Marie had her pistol drawn, but we both felt secure behind the planter. She had called for help, so it was hopefully on the way. But we couldn't just sit by if innocent bystanders had been injured or if someone was in danger.

Marie said, "I don't think those shots were meant for us."

"Let's not risk it. I heard at least two different calibers and it sounded like people were trading shots. At least until the end."

Marie stood up and said, "You can come with me or wait here."

That really wasn't a choice. I trotted alongside her to the main street. We paused at the corner to scan for any other gunmen. A crowd had started to huddle around someone lying in the street. That told us the fight was over.

Marie bowled into the group with her badge out. She checked the man's pulse, then looked at his face closely. She turned to me and said, "I know this man. He's an enforcer for Emile Rostoff's organization. Or, rather, he *was* an enforcer for Rostoff."

I said, "Any idea who'd tangle with him like this?"

"The better question is whether the Russian interrupted someone. Maybe someone with a gun looking for us."

"What makes you say that?"

"Just a hunch. Don't you ever have an intuition about something?"

"I do. Maybe this means you're really getting to the traffickers."

Marie said, "In that case, it's time to turn up the heat."

I looked at her, now fully convinced that Marie was the total package.

CHAPTER 43

MARIE WAS SUPPOSED to drive me to the airport, but I convinced her to let me see the kids first, since I'd promised them I'd say goodbye before I left. She knew me well enough by now to have built in time for the stop. We parked in front of the main administration building at the child-services facility.

Marie stayed by the car to make a phone call as I rushed inside. I realized in my haste just how anxious I was to see them.

A middle-aged man at the front desk looked over his reading glasses and said something to me in Dutch. I didn't speak the language, but I could understand snotty when I heard it.

I said, "My name is Tom Moon. I brought the kids from Miami."

The man nodded and said, "Ah, Mr. Moon, of course. The children are in class, but if you can wait a couple of hours, they can slip out and say hello."

"I'm sorry, I'm on my way to the airport now."

"No, *I'm* sorry. Shouldn't you have scheduled this better? At the moment, as I said, the children are busy."

I just ignored him and walked straight ahead through the unlocked double doors. The man almost fell off his stool trying to get to his feet and stop me. He followed me down the hallway, yammering at me as we walked. "Don't make me call the police," he said.

I looked over my shoulder and smiled. "I'll save you the trouble. Step outside your front door. There's a cop standing right out there. See if she'll do anything."

Before we could further cement our friendship, I heard a child yell, "Tom, Tom!"

At the end of the corridor, beautiful little Michele stood staring at me. She had a wide grin on her tiny face. She ran down the hall and leaped into my arms.

A moment later, Olivia darted from another room and jumped into the hug without a word. That caused a stir of excitement, and before I knew it, all six of the kids were involved. I felt like I was in a friendly rugby scrum.

After a few minutes of all of us hugging, one of the teachers gave me permission to talk with them in a classroom. *That should please the officious little prick at the front desk,* I thought.

Most of the kids had some piece of hopeful news. Joseph from Poland was very excited that the police had finally talked to him about his missing sister. One of Jacques's relatives from Belgium had invited him to live with their family.

The only one without an update was the Finnish girl, Annika, who was quiet. She looked down, her long blond hair hanging into her face.

I put my arm around her and pulled her close. That earned me a smile.

Annika said, "My mother was my only living relative. The social worker says she'll find a family for me to live with. I'll be okay."

I said, "You'll be better than okay. You're smart and beautiful. You're going to do special things."

"You really think so?"

"Absolutely. You can always call me if you need someone to talk to. And Marie will still be here in Amsterdam."

That brought a broad smile. I felt better. The kids were safe, and that's what mattered. When I had to leave, we had another group hug.

I had to take a quick break to compose myself before I stepped out to join Marie. This goodbye had been harder than I'd expected it to be.

CHAPTER 44

FORTY MINUTES LATER, Marie and I stood facing each other in front of my plane's gate. She checked the crowds moving around us every few seconds. You can't take the vigilance out of a good cop.

She said, "I look forward to hearing from you."

"I'll stay in close touch with you about everything."

She smiled and said, "I promise to check on the kids until all of them are back where they're supposed to be."

"Especially Annika?"

"Especially Annika."

"Thank you." I wanted to kiss her. I wanted to show her how I felt. I swept a strand of hair away from her face and carefully tucked it behind her ear. I knew we had a connection.

I sprang back to reality and said, "We'll probably see each other again soon. This case is going to heat up in more ways than we can imagine. If they do try to run a load of people to Miami, just call me and I'll take care of everything. Maybe we can even scam a trip for you."

"I'd love to see Miami. I'd also like to meet your mother and sister. They sound wonderful."

"My mom's wonderful. I'm reserving judgment on my sister."

Marie smiled again and said, "I hope this visit didn't give you the wrong idea about Amsterdam, considering you caught a fleeing felon and almost stumbled into a fatal gunfight with the Russian mob. We really are a friendly city. Writers say we are a tribute to the ordinary man. You just got to see the worst part of ordinary men."

I said, "There's nothing about Amsterdam I didn't enjoy. Even our crazy first and second dates. And I never thought I'd say this, but I have to get back to the relative safety of Miami."

The man at the ticket counter called over to me. "You're the last one. You need to hurry, sir."

Marie patted me on the chest, then pushed me away. "Hurry, you don't want to miss your plane."

CHAPTER 45

Miami

SOMEHOW, THE PLANE ride back to the U.S. didn't wear me out like the flight to Amsterdam had. Probably because I was able to sleep better when I wasn't worried about six kids.

That doesn't mean I wasn't tired when I fumbled with the key to get into my house in Coral Springs. When I stepped inside, my mom saw me, and a smile washed over her face. I was glad to see her, and she was happy to see me too. She said, "Hey, Chuck." It was casual and friendly. But Chuck was my dad's name. This was not a good sign.

"How was work today?" Mom continued. "We really should have a family dinner because there's so much to catch up on. Tommy has decided to go to the University of Miami, and Lila is the top student in the fourth grade."

I wasn't sure how to handle this. Usually, Mom didn't go into this kind of detail when she slipped into the past. I just stood there, stuck. I was hurt. It hurt every time this funny, intelligent woman who raised me slipped out of reality.

My mom walked toward me with a big smile

on her face. "Well, what do you think? Aren't you proud of your kids?"

I hesitated. "Yes, I am." I waited a moment. "Mom, it's me, Tom. Tommy. Your son."

She looked at me. Confusion swept over her face. She wiped a tear away from her cheek, and I wrapped her up in a hug. Even when I was twelve years old, I was bigger than anyone else in the house, and my mom used to say my hugs were like bear hugs. Now she felt particularly tiny as she wrapped her arms around my waist. She said, "I'm sorry, Tom. I don't know what came over me." She slipped away and hurried into her bedroom.

A few seconds earlier, my sister had walked in from the patio. She was wearing a tank top and shorts, and sweat dripped off her; she'd been doing some kind of exercise outside. "Hey, Tom. Welcome back."

I looked at her and said, "That was weird, right? I mean, even for Mom."

Lila shrugged. She said, "You handled that just right. The doctor says we should try to ground her in reality, that we shouldn't play along if she gets confused about who we are or what year it is."

I shook my head, then looked toward my mom's bedroom.

Lila clapped her hands together and said, "So, how was Amsterdam?"

"You know it was just part of the job."

"Really? No fun at all?"

"I didn't say that." I couldn't help smiling a little, thinking of Marie.

A grin crept across my sister's pretty face. "A girl? Did my brother finally start to chase women again?"

"If I was chasing, I didn't catch. But I did meet an interesting woman."

"Pretty?"

"Beautiful."

"Then you shouldn't let something like the Atlantic Ocean get in the way of seeing her. You deserve it. You're a great guy, and between Mom and your job, you don't have nearly enough fun."

It was the nicest thing my sister had ever said to me.

CHAPTER 46

THE NEXT DAY, I slipped into the task-force offices early. I said a few quick hellos and settled at my desk to get my shit in order. I wanted to hit the ground running, and I started by calling some of my contacts in the Department of Homeland Security. They'd help me keep an eye on ships coming into the South Florida area.

Steph Hall stepped into my small office and gave me a playful little slap on the back of my head. She plopped into the chair by my desk and said, "Rough trip? You look like shit."

"You don't look so sharp yourself," I said. But that wasn't true. She always looked sharp, if a little tired today. This was just how we busted on each other.

"That noticeable, huh?"

I immediately apologized. "I was just kidding."

Steph said, "I'm not. I'm exhausted. My mom came down from Riviera Beach to watch the baby."

I said, "Baby up late? Is she sick? And what about Chaz?"

She waved off my questions. "You know the

DEA. If they wanted you to have a family, they'd issue you one. Besides, he's not the most attentive father in the world."

I had to wonder what she saw in the conceited DEA agent she'd been living with for two years. "What about his parents? Don't they ever help out?"

She shrugged. "They're still coming to grips with the fact that their precious only child is shacked up with a black woman. They're a little old-fashioned."

"You mean racist."

"Either way, they're no help."

I knew Steph wanted to marry the bozo, but the guy couldn't see the gold that was right in front of his face. That was enough to convince me that Chaz was an idiot. The fact that he wouldn't help out with his own kid sealed it for me.

Steph said, "I'm glad you're back. The boss tends to focus on me when you're not here. He had me running around doing all kinds of stupid shit that I'd much rather you would do." Her laugh positively lifted my spirits. She stood up and said, "What do you think about lunch today?"

I nodded and smiled as she walked out of my office.

Two minutes after Steph left, a new visitor surprised me. I heard someone say, "What's happening, Anti?" and I looked up to see Alvin Teague's grinning face.

"What the hell are you doing here, Smooth Jazz?"

"Just checking out the office I intend to move into once I replace you." Then he straightened his tie and added, "I was also hoping to run into Lorena Perez."

That explained it. "Look, Jazz, the only way

she'd talk to you is if you literally ran into her with your car."

"Since when do you know so much about women?"

That was a good question. I pivoted. "I know about smart women, and smart women aren't impressed by a Brooks Brothers suit—"

"Armani."

"Or that shit you call flirting."

Teague looked unfazed. "Tell that beauty I was looking for her and that I said hello." He winked and was gone.

CHAPTER 47

I NEVER LIKED doing briefings in front of my own squad. Cops tend to ignore any information that comes from someone they know. That's why a lot of agencies use outside trainers. To paraphrase Jesus, you can't be a prophet in your own hometown.

A few years ago, I was in a briefing for a narcotics warrant where an undercover detective, Willie Hodge, went on too long about what a little apartment looked like on the inside. That's all it took for Willie to earn the nickname "Cameron"— as in James Cameron, director of movies that run way too long, like *Titanic* and *Avatar*. One slip-up and you could be stuck with a nickname for your entire career. I still call Willie "Cameron." And he answers to it.

Studying philosophy occasionally gives me insights into why people react to certain things the way they do. But philosophy doesn't help me connect to high-achieving cops who are anxious to get out and work.

Now I wanted to find a way to make each of these experienced cops understand how important this case was to me, even if I had to begin with an educational seminar. Human trafficking is not a crime commonly investigated by U.S. authorities, and our laws and understanding of the crime are evolving. Too many cops still equate human trafficking with prostitution. There are overlapping elements, but human trafficking encompasses all kinds of exploitation. And it's not confined to faraway, impoverished places; it's a growing blot on wealthy countries.

I wanted to make sure everyone on the task force realized that human trafficking was all I would focus on until we wrapped up this smuggling ring. I recapped everything that had happened to me in Amsterdam. (Almost everything. I might've left out a detail or two, like smoking pot.)

I could tell it would be a hard sell when the smartest member of the task force, our resident CPA, Lorena Perez, said, "Isn't it mostly just prostitution?"

"I gotta tell you, Lorena, a month ago I might've said yes. We all know how dirty a business prostitution is, how some of the girls work for rough pimps and make almost no money. Prostitution is not a career most people choose if they can avoid it.

"But human trafficking is bigger and ten times worse. Essentially, traffickers are taking people, both male and female, and turning them into slaves. The victims earn almost no money while they're trying to pay off what they think their debt is. Pretty girls are often forced to become sex slaves. Someone's got to do something about this."

To her credit, Lorena nodded and said, "I guess that's why every strip club in Miami-Dade now has only Russian dancers."

"It's one of the reasons. Chill and I had a talk

with Roman Rostoff before I left. He's wrapped up in human trafficking, as well as all the other shit he's into. We may end up tangling with his organization."

That got everyone's attention. Good.

Lorena Perez said, "What are you going to need from us, Tom?" She flipped her dark hair; it looked like she'd spent hours styling it.

"Lots of surveillance until we can interdict the next load of people being smuggled in. I'm in close contact with the Dutch national police. They have a couple of sources giving them information."

After the meeting broke up, Steph Hall caught up to me before I made it back to my office.

"You have such a good grasp of the issues we're facing," Steph said. "But maybe try acting a bit more fun-loving. Not so intense. I've seen you outside of work; I know how you joke with your sister and how you take care of your mom. We could use that guy around the task force a little more."

All I could say was "Understood and noted." I thought about it for a moment, then added, "Thanks. Not everyone is so honest."

"There is something you could do for me to show your appreciation."

I looked at Steph and said, "Anything you want."

"Explain to me how you got the nickname Anti."

It bothered Steph to no end that I'd never given her the backstory on my street name, and it tickled me that it frustrated her not to know. Still, I was almost about to say something when our supervisor asked me to come into his office. I smiled at the look on Steph's face, shrugged, and said, "Sorry, some other time. Duty calls."

CHAPTER 48

I WAS CONCENTRATING so hard that when the phone on my desk rang, it startled me. As soon as I heard Marie Meijer's voice on the other end of the line, a goofy grin spread across my face.

After some small talk, Marie said, "I visited the kids at their facility. Monnie was reunited with her father and they're leaving for Nairobi in two days."

I didn't tell her that Monnie had already sent me a message on Facebook about it.

Marie went on. "They've also made contact with Olivia's mother. She's been frantically searching for the little girl for the past four months. The Spanish authorities thought it was some kind of custody dispute with her ex-husband and never took the matter too seriously. The others are all fine and living like a little family. It's really quite sweet. They're just missing their giant, dim-witted father." She let out a great laugh after delivering her little dig.

I said, "I'm setting things up on this end in case another load of people comes in."

"One of my sources said they're getting ready to move any day. I have surveillance on the Amsterdam and Rotterdam ports. We're also monitoring all the airports in Western Europe with flights to Miami. My source thinks that's where they're headed again."

I said, "Have you heard any more specifics about the time of arrival or method of travel? Just like you, we have limited resources. There's no way I can cover all the ports in South Florida and all the airports."

"I think it's too many people to ride on a single commercial airliner. It would be too expensive. From what I hear, there are more than twenty people ready to be moved. That means it's got to be by boat. We're trying to figure out where and hopefully rescue the people while they're still in Europe." Marie paused, then added, "There's something else."

"What's that?"

"Emile Rostoff is definitely involved. That means his brother in Miami will be too. My source says that the Russian we found in the street had been shot by Hanna's brother."

"Can you arrest him for it?"

"No. No evidence. But that means the Russians will be in no mood to fool around. I wouldn't be surprised if our case ends with the murder of Hanna and Albert Greete."

I let out a laugh. "Sorry. I guess I should sound more concerned. I've had narcotics cases end that way. We say they're 'exceptionally cleared.'"

"I like that term. Either way, it's crucial to find these people being smuggled."

"It sounds like you should come to Miami. We need to work this case together."

"I agree. I'm trying to figure out the details now."

We chatted for a few more minutes, then I stepped out of my office and ran into Steph. "Hi," I said.

"Why are you in such a giddy mood?" she asked.

"How can you tell what kind of mood I'm in from a quick hello in the hallway?"

Steph smiled and put her hands on her hips. "Really? I spend more time with you than anyone else in your life does. Besides, if you're not scowling, you're probably in a good mood. All I'm saying is, keep it up. It's a good look and good for the office."

I was getting the sense that maybe I wasn't as collegial as I could be at work. Thank God for honest people like Steph. Aside from my mom and sister, she might have been the only person in the world I could count on.

CHAPTER 49

WHEN I SAW Anthony Chilleo walking past my office, I grabbed him and pulled him inside.

After we talked for a minute about the task force and my trip, I got to my real concern. "Did anything happen with the Russians or my sister while I was gone? She claims that she didn't even go out during my entire trip."

Chill smiled. "She didn't leave the house after six on any of the days you were gone."

"Holy crap, you didn't do a full surveillance on her the whole time I was away, did you?"

He didn't say a word but pointed to the bag of technical equipment he had given me weeks before. It was still where he'd left it; I hadn't bothered to put it away yet. I knew it held several trackers and other devices.

"You put a tracker on my sister's car?"

"Yep."

I stared at him as I searched for the right words. Then I nodded and said, "Brilliant."

Chill just shrugged. He'd been around a long time and knew every possible trick. Why physically follow someone when you can just check your phone and see where her vehicle is?

But I didn't like to think about how close Lila had come to being a bargaining chip in this deadly game. We were going to have to have a serious chat soon.

I asked Chill, "Do you have anything new on Rostoff?"

"He's been holding off on a drug deal he was making with some Colombians. It must piss him off to know that someone is finally watching him. This is the first time he's ever had a problem he couldn't buy his way out of."

"That means he might get desperate and try to threaten us. Or worse."

Chill let out a snort. "Good luck with that."

I liked his attitude. I sensed that Chill didn't do anything in a half-assed way. Maybe that's why he had been married twice.

I looked at him. "Keep your eyes open. You should probably warn your ex-wife as well."

"It'd be a sad day for any Russians who bother her. A redneck from Ocala with a concealed-weapons permit? I think she'll be fine."

I believed him.

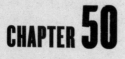

CHAPTER 50

Ostend, Belgium

HANNA GREETE HAD spent a lot of time on this load. Minors tended to listen well, but this group was mixed ages. Hanna had a few teenagers, several Eastern European women, and two Indian men. The total count was twenty-three.

Earlier, at her office, Hanna had supervised as one of her workers sewed the five blood diamonds Hanna intended to sell in the United States into a red Everest backpack. She'd already secured the tracking device in a pocket of the bag and had sewn the pocket shut. The woman had held up the back-pack for inspection. Hanna ran her hands over the strap where the diamonds were hidden. Aside from a few bumps, there was no way to tell anything was concealed inside.

She'd touched the pocket holding the tracker. "It's bigger than I remembered."

Albert said, "It's the same as the one I stuck on Marie Meijer's car. I added a second battery pack so that it will work on the low setting for almost twenty days."

"Why is there a low and a high setting?"

"It has to do with how strong the signal is. We're

losing some strength but gaining many extra days of use. I didn't think you wanted to trust our cargo to switch out batteries halfway through the trip."

Satisfied with that part of her plan, Hanna had to firm up the details that would mean the difference between earning half a million euros or hiding from the Russians for the rest of her life.

Hanna had noticed surveillance at the port in Rotterdam; she'd started looking at alternative ports. She'd finally settled on Ostend, Belgium, near Bruges.

Her brother had put her in touch with the first mate of the *Scandinavian Queen,* a midsize freighter that operated under a Danish flag.

Now Hanna was meeting the first mate at a bar in Ostend. The place didn't even have a name. It was just "the bar near the port." The bare concrete floor showed stains of old fights. Other stains represented where patrons had puked up the thick Belgian beer.

She looked across the table at the tall, weatherbeaten first mate. "My brother says you're reliable and will make sure everyone arrives safely," she said.

The fifty-year-old sailor nodded, then took another giant gulp of beer from an oversize mug. Albert had told her the man had been on the ship for the past seven years.

"For what I'm paying you, I expect reliability," Hanna added. "I should probably expect more than that for the cost."

The sailor put down his mug and looked across the table at her. "You came to me. Not the other way around. I know Albert and trust him, so I agreed. But taking shit from a skirt is not part of the price tag."

He seemed to think that he'd put her in her place, which bothered Hanna. She chose her next actions carefully. She stood up from the table and marched away. With every step, she expected the first mate to call out and stop her. She paused ever so slightly at the door, lifting her hand to the knob slowly.

Still silence.

She stepped through the doorway into the evening air of Ostend. A cool breeze blew from the water. She couldn't have people she paid talking to her like that. She'd have to find another way to move the load.

The specially built storage container she'd bought had already been moved to a facility just outside the port, and the plan was easy. Just before the ship was set to sail, she would have her cargo loaded. The extra-large container, with four air vents and a small toilet built into one corner, could be used over and over.

Apparently, the container would now have to be on a different ship.

As she reached her car, Hanna heard a man say, "Hold on." It was the sailor.

She opened the car door as if she hadn't heard him.

He raised his voice. "Perhaps I was a bit too blunt."

Hanna glanced at him. "Too *stupid* is more like it."

The man looked sheepish. Finally, he said, "I'll do it. I can check on the container every day and bring them extra food. If I do it late enough, when most of the crew is asleep, I can even let them out onto the deck."

Hanna thought about it, then said, "No. I'll hire someone else." She slid into the car.

The sailor stepped closer and said, "C'mon, I'll do a great job."

Hanna said, "For half the money."

"You mean half the money up front?"

"No, nothing up front and half of our original price when the load arrives safely. That's my only offer now. Consider it a tax on being reactionary and sexist."

The man stood there, mulling over the offer. Finally, he said, "Damn, I thought your brother was the tough one."

CHAPTER 51

Amsterdam

MAGDA ANDRUSKIEWICZ SAT on the edge of the bed. If she looked out the window, she could catch a glimpse of the moon. She'd turned sixteen a few months earlier, but to the other girls in the room with her, she was something like a mother.

Sitting next to her on the edge of the bed was a thirteen-year-old Belgian girl who couldn't stop crying. The only common language they had was English, but the other girl's accent was so thick it was difficult for Magda to follow what she was saying. As best she could tell, the girl was homesick. That didn't explain why she was trying to get to the United States, but it did explain why Magda's shoulder was soaking wet from the girl's tears.

Magda didn't know what else to do but put her arm around the girl and tell her everything would be all right. That approach had worked with the other girl crammed into the room with them. She was also sixteen and had been crying earlier, but Magda had gotten her to lie down quietly and close her eyes. The exhausted teenager had fallen asleep almost immediately.

Magda had left Poland with her older brother,

intending to come to Amsterdam. They had met a nice man in Poland who'd said there was plenty of work in Amsterdam and easy transit to the U.S. from the Netherlands' largest city.

The trip was a series of bus rides and hostel stays until they reached Germany. There, in a chaotic Berlin station full of refugees from various nations, they'd been caught up in a crushing crowd, and she'd gotten separated from her brother. Magda didn't have any identification or a working mobile phone, and she was too scared to go to the police.

She waited in Berlin for three days, hoping to find her brother again, searching the streets; she'd even tried e-mailing him from an internet café.

Out of options, she had found a way to get to the United States, thinking she could get in touch with her brother from there. The lady who had set everything up, Hanna, had even given her a new backpack with clothes and a few other things. Hanna told Magda that she could get her into the United States and that all Magda would have to do was work for someone in Miami to pay off the expense. It sounded like a pretty good deal.

The girl Magda was comforting quieted down. After a few minutes, Magda realized she had fallen asleep in her arms. Magda looked through the window to see the moon one last time for the night.

She settled the younger girl on an air mattress, then lay down on her own thin mattress and stared up at the ceiling. It was only then, after trying to comfort the two other girls in the room for most of the evening, that she wanted to cry as well.

Magda wondered who would comfort her.

CHAPTER 52

Miami

I KNEW EVERYONE in Miami, and as more information came from Marie Meijer, that was really starting to pay off.

I had run down a dozen tips and confirmed some details, but we still didn't know exactly how the load of humans was going to come into the United States. And as much as I wanted to know everything about the case and get it done as quickly as possible, I had other responsibilities.

That's why at lunchtime I drove my FBI-issued Ford Explorer at incredibly unsafe speeds back to my home in Coral Springs. I was well aware of the FBI restrictions on vehicle use, but sometimes you just had to be efficient and flout the rules. In my case, *sometimes* was all the time. My sister claimed I had a complex about authority and enjoyed breaking rules. I could never admit to her that she was right, I *did* enjoy it. Breaking rules had become my hobby.

My mom had a doctor's appointment, and I'd decided to take her to it since my sister had already done a lot more than her share of looking after her.

I was also starting to worry about Lila's drinking, but I was still working out a way to talk to her about it.

That's why I didn't mind taking my mother to the neurologist, just across the county line in Boca Raton.

My mom had been acting a little differently recently. I'd really noticed it since I'd gotten back to Miami. It wasn't just being in the moment versus living in the past; she had started to get confused about exactly *where* she was and she wasn't shy about expressing that confusion.

In the car on the way to the doctor's office, my mom asked, "Are you going to bring those kids by the house again? It was wonderful having young people around."

"I don't think so, Mom. They were just visiting."

"I don't suppose you'll be supplying me with grandchildren anytime soon?"

"Not unless I kidnap them. If I go the normal route, it could take a while. First I have to find a woman that I'm attracted to. Then we have to date and fall in love. We should share the same goals with regards to kids. And then, finally, we'd start the process of having one. I wouldn't hold my breath."

"Nonsense. A tall, handsome, educated man like you should have his pick of women."

"Says his mom."

She laughed at that. The laugh lines that formed around her eyes made me smile. It was just like when I was younger, when I could talk to her about anything.

We got to the doctor's office and I checked us in while my mom took a seat in the lobby. There were a few people there, the usual assortment of elderly men accompanied by concerned wives or children. I had seen it all before in the three-year odyssey of my mother's disease.

While we were sitting there waiting, out of the blue my mom said very loudly, "Where are we?"

"At Dr. Spirazza's office."

"Who? Why aren't we at Dr. Goldman's office? I like her."

"Because Dr. Spirazza is a neurologist. He might be able to give us some tips on how to manage your issues."

My mom said, "What issues?" Her voice got louder; it was starting to make me nervous. "The only issue I have now is that I'm not seeing Dr. Goldman."

I could see in her posture and movements that she was getting agitated. I had no real response to it. The man sitting next to her slid over another seat. A woman who was accompanying her father gave me an understanding look. But my mom became more upset.

I held her hand and stroked her arm, but it had no effect. I kept my cool and finally thought of something. I looked at my mother and said, "What's the difference between a jellyfish and a lawyer?"

The question immediately caught her attention and she calmed down. She was intrigued as she considered the options. Finally, she asked me, "What's the difference?"

"One is a spineless, poisonous blob. The other is a form of marine life." It was an old joke, but it made her laugh hard. And then, for no apparent reason, she went back to normal and started quietly flipping through an AARP magazine.

The woman with the older man smiled and said, "You're a pro, aren't you?"

"You can catch my show nightly at the Improv."

Even my mom chuckled at that one.

CHAPTER 53

NO ONE EXPECTS a philosophy major to be terribly organized. And by FBI standards, I was not. That didn't stop me from being effective, but still, sometimes the mess got to me.

It took me an hour to get my office just the way I wanted it. Stacks of papers that had been sitting on the credenza behind the desk were now in either the shred basket or the filing cabinet. The stuff pinned to my bulletin board was updated. I recognized that some of the previous reminders, like a to-do list from two and a half years ago that I'd carried with me from the Miami Police Department, were probably no longer useful.

I'd even used the tiny vacuum cleaner someone had brought in to give the carpet a good once-over.

Steph Hall stepped into the doorway and said, "Wow, I didn't know you had so much room. What's the occasion?"

"No occasion. It was just getting a little messy."

"We all assumed that was the natural order of things with you. The office looks about the same as it did right after you moved in. What are you going to do for an encore this afternoon? Maybe wash your Explorer?"

"Did it last night. It smells like a new car."

"Okay, what the heck is going on? Do you know something I don't?"

"I don't know how busy I'll be once this case gets off the ground. I thought it was a good time to clean things up."

"Uh-huh. And when does the Dutch detective come to Miami?"

"This afternoon." I tried to sound casual, but Steph knew me too well.

"I'm starting to suspect that you and this detective have more in common than the case."

"It's not like that."

Steph raised an eyebrow and said, "With guys, it's always like that. Men have one-track minds. So tell me, is she pretty?"

"Beautiful." I didn't even bother to hide my smile. I checked the clock on my desk and realized I had to head out to the airport soon.

Steph said, "Can I help with anything?"

"You've already done too much. You're the best." I stood and gathered my things.

She said, "Have I done enough to learn why your street name is Anti?"

"I don't know if I'd go that far."

She playfully slapped me on the arm. "Don't be a shit. I could just ask a Miami cop."

"Where's the fun in that?"

Steph bowed her head. "You're right. I'll figure it out. Or I'll get you to spill one day."

"Good luck with that." I let her hear me snicker as I left.

An hour later, I used my connections at Miami

International to get right to the gate as passengers disembarked from the Amsterdam plane.

I didn't want to go overboard, but I had gotten a haircut. I wore a simple sports coat. Marie spotted me as soon as she stepped off the Jetway. I liked the smile that spread across her face.

I reached in for a hug and she put out her hand and we were caught in the awkward no-man's-land between a hug and a handshake. She put one arm around my shoulders and gave me a squeeze.

After we retrieved her single bag, we walked to my car. Marie said, "The newest information I have came from my best informant, who told me that a ship left from somewhere in Northern Europe about a week ago and should be here in the next few days."

"And you can't narrow that down at all?"

"I might be able to once we're closer to the day the ship arrives."

"Just like they can trick you by leaving from any one of the ports in Europe, they could come into the port of Miami, Port Everglades in Fort Lauderdale, or even Palm Beach."

Marie said, "I understand. I just want to make the best case possible."

"I'd like to get a little press on the arrests so that people can see how serious human trafficking really is. Media coverage would probably help the task force as well."

Marie agreed. As we made our way to my car, she said, "What do we do now?"

"I'm going to get you something to eat. You set the standard in Amsterdam for hospitality."

I loved her smile.

CHAPTER 54

IT WAS LATE in the afternoon by the time I got Marie settled in her downtown hotel room. I had planned to take her to the office and introduce her around, but to be honest, I liked my alternative plan better.

She was hungry, so I'd stopped my Explorer near a food truck that was always on Eighth Street just west of the interstate, before the street turns into Calle Ocho, famous for restaurants visited by presidents and the Cuban culture on display.

Marie looked at the truck with the neon letters on the side that said SANDWICHES. She said, "You're only taking me to the nicest places, I see."

The owner, Luis, waved to me as we stepped up to the truck's window. I smiled and held up two fingers. He nodded.

"I don't want you to fill up too much before dinner. Besides, these are the best Cuban sandwiches in the city. He's usually sold out by this time of day."

"What other kinds of sandwiches does he sell?"

"There are no other sandwiches recognized by Miami residents. Try one."

Marie said, "Don't we get a choice of what's on it?"

"No. In Miami, a Cuban sandwich is ham, pork, pickles, mustard, and a little mayo. Otherwise it's not a Cuban sandwich, and most places won't sell it."

When I tried to pay, Luis held up his hands. "Never from you."

I thanked him and stuffed a ten in the tip jar.

As we sat in the air-conditioning of my car, Marie said, "Did he not charge you because you're with the police?"

"Sort of. Years ago, he was robbed and his teenage daughter was pistol-whipped by the robber. There was no way to ID the suspect and Luis was too scared to give us many details. His daughter was a mess. She had two surgeries. It pissed me off," I said. "So I put an offer out on the street for information about the guy."

"What kind of offer?"

"I let the best snitches know that I'd give them a walk on their next crack-possession charge if they came up with the name."

"And did they?"

"The next day I had Ronald Jerris in custody for robbery and assault. It was his fifth arrest that year."

Marie thought about it and said, "An offer to ignore possession of crack? I'd never be allowed to do that at home."

"I'm not supposed to do it here either. But letting a brutal robber get away with beating a teenage girl isn't right. Given the choice between what's legal and what's right, I chose right."

"And now you get free sandwiches."

"Which I'd like to pay for, but it would hurt his pride. But better than a free lunch is that his daughter is entering her third year at the University of Central Florida."

We finished our sandwiches and got on our way. As I drove, Marie sat in the passenger seat and took in all the sights of South Florida. "What city is this?" she asked at one point.

"It's called Coral Springs. This is where people who work in Miami live. At least, people who work in public service."

Marie turned to me. "Are we going to your house?"

"I thought you might like to eat a home-cooked meal and see what an average American family made up of only adults is like." I was taking a risk; I wasn't sure how she'd react to this.

She gave me a broad smile and said, "Will your mom and sister be there?"

"They're busy making our dinner as we speak."

All Marie said was "Excellent."

CHAPTER 55

I TOOK MARIE to my house, despite the fact that I had some concerns. My mom had been pretty good since the incident at the doctor's office a few days ago, but the likelihood of her having an episode increased as time went on, and I was afraid we were due for a bad night.

My apprehension grew as I turned into my driveway and parked the Explorer. I didn't know whether I should warn Marie or just roll the dice and see what happened. "Marie, I probably need to tell you something," I said.

She turned in the seat to give me her full attention. "Of course."

I thought about how to phrase it, but there'd be no point in telling her if my mom was doing well. Finally, I chickened out and said, "I'm really glad you got a chance to come to Florida. My mom and sister are going to love you."

I appreciated the smile she gave me.

I felt like I was about to make entry on a search warrant as we ambled up the walkway. As soon as the door opened and I caught a whiff of the Italian food, I felt better.

My little sister popped out of the kitchen immediately, walked right up to Marie, and extended her hand. "You must be Marie. I'm sorry you have to put up with my bonehead brother. He said you took great care of him in Amsterdam, so we hope to do the same for you."

I stepped next to my sister and gave her a hug. My primary purpose was to gauge the amount of alcohol on her breath. It was tolerable.

Lila took Marie by the arm and walked her toward the kitchen. Lila casually looked over her shoulder and winked at me. That meant everything was okay. At least for now.

I don't know why, but my mom had become something of a gourmet cook since her diagnosis of dementia. As kids, Lila and I got only the basics. We were well fed, but no one would've considered our house a culinary mecca. Now something had clicked, and my mom seemed to understand much more about seasoning; she'd begun making astonishing dishes. I'd asked the doctor about it. He'd just shrugged and said, "I wish I could tell you if it was related to the dementia. The truth is, we have very little idea of what things are triggered by this disease."

Tonight, I was happy and relieved to see that Mom was as gracious and charming as she normally was. Or at least, as she used to be. She ushered the three of us out to the patio, where she had a pitcher of mojitos ready. We settled in for a drink, Marie sitting between me and my sister, and my mom said, "I tried a new lasagna recipe tonight, and we'll start with a salad of arugula, strawberries, and walnuts."

I clapped my hands and said, "That sounds delicious."

My mom touched my arm and said, "Thanks, Chuck."

My heart skipped a beat.

After my mom had wandered back into the kitchen, Marie leaned over and asked, "Why did she call you Chuck? Is that your middle name?"

I decided it was time to explain things. I wasn't embarrassed; I just never knew how to tell people that my mom sometimes lived in a different time and place.

CHAPTER 56

Amsterdam

HANNA GREETE HAD raced around Amsterdam for several days taking care of various tasks so that she could leave for the United States with a clear schedule. She'd planned to fly to Miami to be at the dock when the *Scandinavian Queen* arrived, but now she had to waste time meeting with her Russian contact Alexi at his favorite little pub in the Oost District.

At least in a pub she'd only have to put up with alcohol, not the constant odor of pot.

She tried to be friendly as well as professional when dealing with the Russians, as there was no way to completely avoid them in this business. Today, though, she didn't have the patience for pretense, and as soon as she sat at the small table and faced Alexi, she got right to the point. "I hope this is important. I have never been busier in my whole life," she said.

Alexi was as calm and cool as always. He took a sip of his beer, wiped his mouth with a napkin, and asked, "Are you about to go to Miami?"

"Yes. Yes, I am. And the people I'm delivering there should go a long way toward covering any debts I have with Mr. Rostoff."

Alexi nodded and smiled. "I'm sure it will. But Mr. Rostoff is a little nervous that you're leaving the country. We're going to need some collateral before you depart."

"Collateral? You already loaned me the money. The only way I can pay it back is to go on this trip. You should've asked for collateral when you offered me the loan."

"But we didn't, which is why we're asking for it now."

"What kind of collateral did you have in mind?"

"We were thinking about the diamonds that everyone knows you possess."

Hanna gave him a flat stare and said, "No."

That didn't faze Alexi. He said, "Perhaps we could babysit your daughter. She would be safe and we would have the collateral we need."

Hanna looked at the well-dressed, middle-aged man, trying to assess if he was joking. Finally, she said, "Are you insane? Why would I ever leave my daughter with you? I'm afraid the entire concept of collateral is not going to work out."

"What about your brother, Albert?"

"You're not listening to me. There will be no collateral. Besides, I heard some of your people are very angry at Albert."

"He did kill one of our enforcers. It was most impressive. And we understand that our man was not without some culpability. But this is business. We would guarantee your brother's safety until you returned and a payment was made."

Hanna tried to appear as if she were considering the offer. That was probably her best option to get out of this pub safely. She said, "Let me speak to Albert. I'll see what we can work out. I won't be leaving for almost a week anyway." That little lie should buy her some breathing room.

"We have contacts in Miami waiting to help you. Your success is our success. But there needs to be some trust between us."

"In our business, trust is a rare commodity. Just like collateral, it's difficult to come up with, and no one has much."

Alexi flexed his fingers and said, "I'm the one who stood up for you when you needed money. I saw that you ran a reasonable operation and had the potential to supply us with a lot of people in the Miami area. We are always needing more people in the organization. At least, the kind that you supply. Please don't mistake my faith in you for foolishness. I do not like to be jerked around."

Hanna nodded as she stood up. "Nor do I. This load will go through. My debt to you will be paid and I don't expect any trouble while I'm gone." She had nothing more to say, so she simply turned on her heel and left.

CHAPTER 57

HANNA WAS COMPOSED as she walked away from the infuriatingly calm Alexi, but as soon as he was out of sight, she rushed back to her office. She was not about to risk the Russians deciding they were going to *take* collateral whether she offered it or not.

Janine, Tasi, and Lisbeth—the young women who worked for Hanna—could tell just by her stride what kind of pressure their boss was under. As soon as she burst through the door, all three of them jumped up to see how they could help.

Hanna took a moment and looked at the three young women. She might be tough on them occasionally, but she couldn't put them at risk. There was no telling what the Russians would do while she was gone. She said, "We might be facing some challenges from the Russians. I understand if anyone wants to quit." She looked from girl to girl. "Let me know now. I'll even throw in a full month's pay as severance."

None of the girls spoke up.

"No one wants to jump ship?"

They all shook their heads with varying degrees of decisiveness.

"That may be a lack of judgment, but I'm proud of you all," Hanna said, a catch in her voice. This was loyalty.

Janine spoke up. "What do you need us to do?"

Hanna thought about it. "What I really need you and Lisbeth to do is nothing. Just lay low for the couple of weeks I'll be out of town. Don't come here, no matter what. I'll call you and let you know when it's safe."

Janine's younger sister, Tasi, who didn't have her sister's organizational skills or street smarts but who was as pretty as any twenty-year-old in the city, said, "What about me? Am I okay to work here?"

Hanna looked at the poor, silly girl who didn't have the common sense to know when her life was in danger. "No, Tasi, I'm going to need you to come with me."

"To the United States?" It was clear the girl thought this might be a joke.

Hanna nodded.

The young woman smiled, revealing perfectly straight white teeth. "You need me to help you on your trip?" Tasi couldn't hide her excitement.

Hanna said, "I've decided to take Josie with me. You'll be an excellent nanny."

It all seemed to make sense to the young woman at that point. She bounced up and down for a moment, clapping her hands. All Hanna could think was that Tasi was too naive to stay here alone. And she certainly didn't believe Tasi was capable of keeping her daughter safe. That's why she was going to bring Albert too.

Hanna found her brother in the back room. She

said, "I've decided to take Josie and you with me on the trip to Miami."

Albert looked up from the magazine he was reading and said, "I thought you said there'd be nothing for me to do in Miami. This sounds fishy to me."

"Alexi has asked for collateral if I'm leaving the country. He made some veiled threats against you and Josie."

"Take Josie. That's perfect. Besides, if I don't have to worry about you two, I can eliminate a lot of our problems here in Amsterdam."

Hanna liked his optimism, but she wasn't about to let her crazy brother go running around Amsterdam murdering Russians.

Before an argument developed, Josie walked into the room. Albert adjusted immediately. He was always careful not to let his niece overhear anything about their business.

Hanna looked at her daughter and said, "How would you like to go on holiday?"

The young girl widened her eyes and asked, "Where?"

"Miami, Florida, in the United States."

"Is that near Disney World?"

"How big can Florida be? When we're done in Miami, we'll go to Disney World."

Josie turned to her uncle and said, "Mom won't go on some of the wild rides."

Albert said, "I know, she's not much fun." He winked at his sister, then looked back at Josie. "But I'll take you on any ride you want."

Josie said, "Do you think we'll be able to see an alligator in Florida?"

"I guarantee it. They have whole farms of alligators there. Some of them even do tricks."

Josie tilted her head and said, "That's not true, is it?"

Albert raised his right hand and said, "I swear."

At that, the girl excitedly bounded out of the room.

Hanna looked at her brother. "I guess that means you're coming. I should get Josie to ask you to do things more often."

CHAPTER 58

HANNA DIDN'T WANT to take any chances, so she decided to leave for Miami out of Paris. She, Albert, Josie, and Tasi took the train to France. The entire trip, Albert conducted his version of counter-surveillance by roaming through the cars, making certain no one was following them on the train.

Hanna, Albert, and Josie had fake passports that identified them by different names. Tasi used her regular passport. No one would recognize her name or suspect her of anything.

Hanna wanted to let down her guard for just a moment and enjoy the train ride. She wanted to appreciate the scenery and think about the future. She was starting to believe they had a future. But she just couldn't relax.

Josie and Tasi were oblivious as they searched their phones for information on Florida and Disney World. It made Hanna smile, seeing Josie so excited. It was a childhood Hanna would've liked. All that mattered to her was Josie's happiness.

Albert came back to the car.

Hanna snapped, "Sit down. You're making me nervous."

"Rostoff won't be happy we slipped away from Amsterdam."

"All will be forgotten when we pay him. The Russians will help us in Miami because they need our load. It will all work out. So just sit down and relax."

He plopped into the seat facing the girls and Hanna felt like they were a little family.

Fifteen minutes later, two young men came into the car and sat near the door. They smiled and nodded when Hanna and Albert looked up at them, the only other people in the car. One of the men lowered the wide window, and the noise of the train boomed through the car. Cool air rushed in.

Albert gave Hanna a look.

She said, "No, relax. They're just passengers."

Albert sat for a minute more, then stood up and casually strolled down the aisle. The girls, who were facing forward, were still engrossed in their phones. They couldn't see the new passengers without turning around.

Albert headed toward the loo at the far end of the car. As he passed the men, he said, in Dutch, "How's it going?"

The thinner of the two, a man about twenty-five years old, answered, "Good, and you?"

Hanna heard the slight Russian accent in the greeting. Damn. Albert was onto something.

Her brother turned just as the man stood and popped open a switchblade.

Albert moved like lightning as he parried a blow, then threw his elbow into the young man's clean-shaven jaw.

His head twisted, and a tooth flew out of his mouth and bounced off the seat. A line of spittle with blood in it streaked across the clean tan wall.

Somehow, Albert ended up with the knife in his hand.

Hanna watched, stunned, wondering how she could help. The girls were still in their own little world, and the sound from the open window had drowned out the commotion.

Albert moved again before the second man could draw a weapon. He put the point of the switchblade to the man's bearded throat and took a small automatic pistol from him. Albert turned to his sister, winked, and smiled.

The young man's eyes were wide. The neatly trimmed beard made him look like a boy pretending to be a man. So did the ease with which Albert had disarmed him.

Albert put the pistol to the man's head and gave him an order in a low voice.

The bearded man helped his dazed Russian friend up and Albert escorted the two of them to an electrical and maintenance closet wedged next to the restroom. Albert said something else, opened the locked closet door with the first man's knife, and forced the two inside.

Thirty seconds later, he flopped, exhausted, into the seat next to Hanna.

She said, "How do you know they won't scream for help?"

Albert tapped the pistol in his waistband. "I explained that if they didn't keep quiet until I told them they could come out, there would be plenty of air holes in the door. Young pretty boys aren't used to people fighting back. We'll be fine."

Hanna had known her brother was tough, but this was spectacular. He looked like a movie spy. How could she *not* feel safe traveling with him?

CHAPTER 59

Miami

I'D BEEN BURNING up my contacts trying to keep an eye on everything that came through the ports in Florida. The problem was that Florida, being a long peninsula, had a lot of damn ports. I didn't even bother to consider what would happen if the ship came into a port outside of Florida.

It was easy to get overwhelmed with data and details, and this was where my background in sports came in handy. If I viewed major cases the way I used to view football games, I kept a better attitude and was able to manage each task that popped up a little more easily.

This wasn't a game, but that's how cops have to look at major cases. Every cop has some form of psychological trick to help cope with the stress that gets piled on us from all sides by the administration, the public, and our own natural desire to make arrests in every case. Not to mention the stress that comes from department infighting, though in my experience, the hardworking cops who want to solve cases don't care much about promotions or office politics.

Still, it didn't pay to ignore them completely. As Plato said, "One of the penalties for refusing to participate in politics is that you end up being governed by your inferiors." That's especially true in police work, and I was experiencing it on the task force. Luckily, our supervisor left decisions about assignments up to my discretion.

Chill, Steph Hall, and Lorena Perez were all looking at the Rostoff connection. It bugged me that the smug son of a bitch Roman Rostoff thought he could sit in his fancy office and count his money without facing any consequences for his illegal activities. Maybe that's how it worked in Moscow, but it wouldn't fly in Miami. I didn't care how many Russians lived here.

Now Marie Meijer and I were in my FBI-issued Explorer heading to Port Everglades in Fort Lauderdale. The way Marie took in everything that flashed past as we drove made me feel like I'd brought her to an alien world.

"It's all so green," she said.

"It's the subtropics. That's what happens. Wait until summer and you'll understand why things are green—they get watered every single afternoon."

"Why don't they call this the port of Fort Lauderdale instead of Port Everglades?"

I shrugged. "No one consulted me when they were naming it. It's a big port with the second-busiest cruise terminal in the world."

"Where is the busiest cruise terminal?"

"Miami. Where else? That's part of what's making everything so difficult. There are so many ships coming into the ports daily, not even counting the cruise ships, and it's impossible to investigate them all."

I drove into the port off Seventeenth Street so that Marie could get an idea of the size of it. Even the county convention center was at the port. The cruise terminal was bustling as I eased past a security checkpoint and inched toward the cargo terminal. While not as elaborate as the cruise terminal, this area sprawled over acres of the port.

There were oil and natural-gas storage containers on the property between the port and US 1. I had visited them once during a class on terrorism, and I didn't like to consider the damage that would be done to downtown Fort Lauderdale if a terrorist managed to puncture one of the tanks and ignite the contents.

I didn't mention that to Marie. Tourists don't like to hear about potential terror threats.

I found a spot near the southernmost part of the port. This part of the port wasn't too busy today. In fact, it felt a little isolated. A few cars were parked haphazardly. One crane was working to unload a small freighter farther down the dock, and the sound of metal against metal echoed through the port.

We stepped out of my car and looked at the three ships that had docked since last night. None of them would have been confused with the *Queen Mary*.

The middle ship held about fifteen containers on the bow and dozens more amidships and on the stern. One of the containers caught my attention. A rail-thin man smoking a cigarette was playing with the lock on the front of it.

I nudged Marie and pointed at the ship.

Marie said, "I'm not sure what I'm looking at. It looks like a normal cargo ship to me. I don't see anything unusual."

"The container near the bow of the ship has air vents along the sides. We've got to get a better look."

CHAPTER 60

IT'S HARD TO overestimate the importance of cell phones in modern police work. As I hustled down to the ship with Marie, all I could manage was a quick check with an FBI analyst on my phone; I gave her the ship's name and said that it was docked at Port Everglades. The analyst told me right away that the ship had left from Belgium and had made several other stops before arriving in Florida, and she was working on the registration as I reached the gangplank.

It wasn't a particularly large ship. I guessed it had about fifteen crew members. It wouldn't have drawn my attention if I hadn't noticed that one container; I'd seen enough containers to know they usually didn't have air vents.

As we approached, I slipped on a blue FBI windbreaker and draped a police badge on a chain around my neck so there would be no confusion that I was a cop.

A muscle-bound fortyish Hispanic man wearing a shirt with the shipping company's logo on it stepped onto the gangplank at the other end and walked forward. He raised his hand like a crossing guard and said, "The ship is not open to the public." He held his crossing-guard pose for a few seconds to show off his massive biceps, then added, "Step back. They're gonna unload."

I stared at the man for a moment. "What about this windbreaker makes you think we're part of the general public?" I asked. "And I don't see the crane down here ready to unload anything."

The man stood straight and flexed his chest muscles, a move a bouncer might make to intimidate someone. He said, "Look, *pendejo,* I don't give a shit who you are. You ain't coming on this ship."

"Are you a member of the crew?"

"I'm a security officer for the shipping company. Move away from the gangplank. I'm not going to tell you again."

"Listen, Paul Blart, Mall Cop, we just want to get a quick look at one container, then we'll be on our way. It'll take only a minute or two."

The muscle-head was a couple of inches shorter than me, and clearly not used to having to look up at someone. He pointed at my FBI jacket and said, "Why do you have an FBI jacket but a City of Miami badge?"

I shrugged. I wasn't in the mood to answer questions. I said, "I'm sorry to confuse you, but we're coming aboard, and I mean right now." I stepped onto the gangplank with Marie directly behind me. The man gave a few inches but didn't get out of the way.

He said, "Don't you need a warrant to search the ship?"

"Not for this. I have concerns about someone's safety. It's called *exigent circumstances*. And you'd be smart to step aside."

"What are you, a lawyer?"

"As a matter of fact, I am. But this is police business and someone's life might be in danger." I began marching forward, Marie right behind me. It wasn't until we reached the far side of the gangplank that the security officer offered any resistance. He braced himself at the end of the gangplank as if he thought his big chest and biceps would be enough to stop a determined cop who was six foot four and weighed 240 pounds.

He was wrong.

CHAPTER 61

ALL IT REALLY took was a slight body twist, just like a coach had taught me at the University of Miami. I quickly shifted everything to my left, and the security officer squirted past me. He fell face-first onto the gangplank. I never actually touched him. That was the best kind of confrontation.

I liked how Marie calmly stepped over the man without saying a word.

We wasted no time heading to the bow of the ship and the container with the air vents. I didn't want to think about what it would've been like to cross the Atlantic in something like this. I was scared to see what was inside.

The security officer picked himself up and caught up to us. Like an angry little kid, he said, "I called my supervisor. Only Customs can come on the ship at any time. You're not with Customs. That's about the only police-agency ID you don't have on you."

I said, "Did you call your supervisor over to the ship? I'd like to speak with him or her."

That brought the man up short. "No. She's not on-site. But she said you don't have permission to be on the ship."

All I said was "Noted," and we continued making our way to the bow of the ship.

Before we even reached the container, the thin sailor who I'd seen smoking a cigarette in front of it earlier turned to face me. He was wearing a faded red Def Leppard T-shirt with a frayed edge where the collar should have been. His laminated ID and port card were attached to his belt.

The man spoke to the security officer in English with a thick Dutch accent. "Hey, what's this? The captain said no one was to come aboard until the crane was ready to start unloading."

I pointed to the badge on my chest and said, "Police business. I'd like to look at this container more closely."

The crew member said, "And I'd like to get a blow job from a Hooters waitress. Both of us are going to be disappointed."

I scooted around the man, secretly hoping he'd make the mistake of putting his hands on me. I don't know if it was my size or my official position that gave him a little bit of common sense, but all he did was follow me, complaining in my ear the whole way.

"We can't open any of these containers," he said. "They have special locks. You're wasting your time. You're wasting *my* time."

Marie looked at the door and said, "This lock has been tampered with. It's not even an official transport lock."

I didn't hesitate to pull a rescue tool off the wall. It looked like a thick crowbar with a pointy end.

Now the crewman stood directly between me and the door to the container. He looked serious. I hoped I wouldn't have to fight him or, God forbid, go for my gun, although I would if he or the security officer drew a weapon.

We stood there in silence. Marie sensed the tension and, like a good partner, moved into position to take action if she had to. She was behind the men, neither of whom was paying any attention to her. I'd seen her in action and had no doubt she could stop these two idiots from doing anything stupid.

Sweat poured down the security officer's face. He was nervous. This was way outside his experience.

Finally, the crewman said, "The captain'll have something to say about this."

He looked toward the bow. I stepped past him to the shipping container, avoiding the security guard like I was a hockey player skating past a defender. No one had touched me and I still had the crowbar in my hand.

I paused at the door for a moment. I thought I heard something move inside the container. Marie knocked on the side of the container, and I heard more movement. My heart started to race. I prayed that we weren't too late to save everyone inside.

Then the security officer said, "What's that noise?" It was like a light bulb went on over his head. He realized what was going on and what was at stake. When the crewman started to move toward me, it was the security officer who stopped him.

I nodded my thanks to the security officer, then set the crowbar against the lock. It broke off with the right leverage and my full weight against it.

I pulled one side of the door open. The smell that hit us was ferocious. It turned my stomach and made my eyes water.

Behind me, I heard Marie mumble, "Oh my God."

CHAPTER 62

ASIDE FROM THE stench that was making my eyes water, the first thing I noticed was the strange light inside the container. There were two scratched Plexiglas panels across the top that allowed sunlight inside, but the light that came through the hazy plastic was yellow and gave the entire container a freaky look.

Something flashed out of the corner and made me duck my head to one side. Then a shriek tore the air. I was completely confused.

All at once, things came into focus, and I understood much more clearly. There were no people inside the container. It was filled with exotic parrots and macaws.

I stepped inside and saw feathers raining down from the birds in the top row of cages. A battery-operated light dangled from a cord. The man in the red T-shirt must have just been in to check on the birds.

I tried to get an idea of how many birds were crammed into the container. At first, I thought it was dozens, then I realized it was more than a hundred, all of them extravagant, with lavish colors and powerful vocal cords, or whatever birds use to make noise.

Marie stood just outside the door, which was wise. She said, "These are all African. A number of different species. I'd say they're really, really valuable."

Here I'd been thinking we were about to set twenty or so people free. I turned to ask the thin man in the Def Leppard T-shirt about the container and cargo, but he was already racing for the gangplank.

I looked at the security officer and said, "Can you call someone to stop him?"

The muscle-bound man raised his hands and said, "My job is to make sure no one gets *on* the boat."

"Don't you have the sheriff's office or Customs on your radio somewhere?"

He shook his head. "They made me take their channel off my radio. They said I was too enthusiastic and made too many calls for assistance."

I looked at Marie.

She said, "Isn't this still a crime? I mean, he *is* a smuggler."

I wasn't happy about it, but I started to jog after the man. This day was not going the way I'd thought it would.

CHAPTER 63

BY THE TIME I was off the ship and on the dock, the thin man in the Def Leppard T-shirt was jogging west, away from the water. He headed toward the wide-open fields that housed the storage containers for gas and oil. This was not the kind of chase people saw on police shows or in the movies. Most criminals aren't in particularly good shape, and most cops avoid running after suspects unless they've committed a serious crime.

I kept the man in sight easily enough, but this was not an impressive foot chase. We weren't going terribly fast, and there were no obstacles or traffic. Just as real-life fistfights tend to be messy events, real-life foot chases generally aren't that exciting either. I could have just let him run—the guy lived on the ship, and he'd be easy to find. But secretly, I didn't want to disappoint Marie. This was the kind of story I'd have to embellish a few years down the road. Maybe I'd add a parrot sitting on his shoulder...

Then the chase got even less interesting. The man started to slow drastically, and by the time I was a dozen yards behind him, he was leaning over with his hands on his knees, gasping for air.

Before I could say anything to him, he vomited onto the grass. That made me jump back. I can put up with a lot of unpleasant things; I'd seen more nastiness in my few years working in Miami than most people see in a lifetime. But vomit always made me gag and want to vomit myself.

I did a moonwalk away from the man. He was downwind so I didn't smell it, but the second time he heaved, I almost lost my lunch.

Then the man looked up at me and said in a Dutch accent, "I can't believe you guys figured out what I was doing."

I just shrugged. "It's my job." I needed someone to see me as superior today.

The man started to ramble about how he'd gathered the birds over several months during a trip to the western coast of Africa. He had an agreement with the captain and first mate to split the money. That's how he'd been able to get back and forth to the container so easily. "We needed a big payday here in America," he said. "I already spoke to a pet-store owner in Miami and one in West Palm Beach. Between them, I was going to be able to sell almost my entire shipment." The man sounded wistful and depressed. I let him talk. I hadn't placed him under arrest, and these were voluntary statements. Although I kind of wished he'd shut up.

A few minutes later, an SUV with two U.S. Customs agents rolled up next to us. I identified myself, explained the situation, and told them about the man's confession. The older agent, a tubby man about fifty, said, "We appreciate getting good cases like this, but why the hell didn't a Miami cop working on an FBI task force call us about these concerns beforehand?"

"I was afraid it was just a wild-goose chase. Excuse the pun."

The younger agent, a woman, said, "More like you didn't want to share the credit for any arrest on human trafficking."

Her partner said, "Why didn't you follow protocol? We don't bother you at your office."

I looked over at the scared Dutch sailor and said, "Looks like you don't bother people at *your* office either."

U.S. Customs was not amused.

CHAPTER 64

AFTER ARRIVING IN Miami and checking in at the Miami Gardens Inn, Hanna and Albert rushed downtown. They spoke with several jewelers in the Seybold Building, trying to find a buyer for the diamonds that would arrive in Miami with their load of human cargo. Albert also made inquiries into where he might find a gun quickly.

They were directed to a pawnshop on Seventh Avenue near Twenty-Fifth Street, just east of the airport. Jeff's Pawn and Gun was in a tiny strip mall with multiple vacant stores. The area looked like a ghost town.

Hanna checked the time. The sign on the shop said it was open until eight p.m. They still had half an hour.

Albert strutted into the place like he owned it. This was his area of expertise. Hanna thought it was only fair to give him some leeway in this side of their work, since he listened to her in business matters.

Albert smiled at the thin, older man behind the counter and said, "Howdy, partner. How are you this evening?"

The pawnshop clerk just stared at him over the

frames of his glasses pushed to the end of his long nose. A pack of Camels sat in the front pocket of his plaid shirt. If this was Jeff, whatever money the store made was not due to the owner's sparkling personality.

"You're not on drugs, are you?" the man asked Albert.

Albert looked astonished and shook his head. "Just a visitor. I guess I'm a little too friendly. Sorry."

Maybe-Jeff said, "I can deal with friendly visitors. It's the drug addicts that traipse in and out of here all day that I have no patience with. What can I do for you?"

Albert looked into the glass case and pointed to a black semiautomatic pistol. "Could I take a look at that Beretta?"

The man retrieved the gun and racked the slide to be sure it was empty. "There's a three-day waiting period, and you'll have to show me ID." He looked at Hanna, then back at Albert. "Where the hell are you from, anyway?"

Albert didn't hesitate. "Belgium."

"Good. You don't look like it, but I wanted to make sure you wasn't one of them Muslim freaks always interested in blowing something up."

Albert chuckled and said, "Nope, not a Muslim. And anything I blew up, you would approve of."

That comment earned a quick cackle from the older man.

Albert handled the gun briefly, checking the barrel and the breech. Then he shook his head and said, "Wish I could buy this right now. I'm afraid we'll be on our way to Disney World in a few days. The only ID I have was issued in Europe."

The pawnbroker said, "Yeah, even if they call it a

gun-free zone, you hate to be unarmed when others are packing. More innocent people die in gun-free zones than anywhere else."

"Guess I'll be helpless too. Just want to protect my family." Albert watched the man closely.

Finally, he said, "I got nothing against Belgians. I hear you've loved Americans since the big war. You seem to know your guns pretty well. And I hate how the government is always interfering."

Albert muttered, "Me too."

"I have a way to get you a gun right now, but there's a premium."

"How much of a premium?"

"A hundred percent of the cost of the gun."

Albert held up the Beretta and said, "This gun?"

The pawnbroker nodded.

Albert smiled and said, "Done."

A few minutes later, they walked out of the store with the Beretta and two boxes of ammo. Albert turned to Hanna and said, "America really is the land of opportunity."

CHAPTER 65

HANNA DIDN'T WANT her brother to see the tremor in her hands. She was as nervous as she'd ever been. It was just before nine o'clock and they were sitting at a booth in a bar called Glow inside the massive Fontainebleau Hotel on Miami Beach. The luxury of the place was mind-boggling to Hanna. The bar was on an outdoor deck with a shimmering pool and view of the Atlantic. The people at the bar looked like movie stars. Every one of them, men and women, could have been a model or an actor.

From a business standpoint, it wasn't late, but from a parenting standpoint, it was getting there; she'd told Josie and Tasi they would be back to the hotel before eleven. Hanna didn't like breaking a promise. She tried to set a good example for her daughter.

Across from her in the booth was her Russian contact, a fit forty-year-old who looked more like a lifeguard than a gangster. He had a dyed-blue goatee that gave him an edgy vibe, but he was friendly enough. He spoke with a Russian accent, and he'd told them to call him Billy.

Albert had whispered, "Somehow I don't think that's his given name."

Hanna just gave her brother a stare.

Billy had ordered a round of Mojitos, but Hanna hadn't touched hers. She wanted to get to the meat of the conversation now that they'd gotten through the small talk.

Billy said, "I can take ten girls as long as they're not too ugly or old. My preference is for Europeans. I can make more money with them. The downside is they tend to form relationships with customers and make some of my men jealous." He looked at them from under his dark, thick eyebrows, but he got no response.

He added, "I might be able to take the rest off your hands, but at a discount. The cops have been bothering us recently and nothing is easy. But what I can offer should cover most of your debt to the Rostoff brothers."

Hanna saw what Billy was doing. She had spent five years in this business and knew all the negotiating ploys. Where others had failed or been murdered by the competition, she and her brother had built a decent business. If it hadn't been for some bad luck, she never would've had to borrow the money she was so desperate to pay back now.

Hanna said, "By my calculations, it will cover the whole debt."

Billy smiled. "Let's get the people in first, then we'll see where we are with money. There's a charge for using our contact in Customs, and there are a few other fees."

Hanna didn't want to ask what the other fees were.

Then Billy said, "I heard you might be interested in selling some high-quality diamonds."

That took Hanna by surprise. "How did you hear about the diamonds?"

Billy chuckled. "My dear, I speak with my partners in Amsterdam at least twice a week. If they know about it, I know about it. I also know that, late this afternoon, you visited three jewelers in the Seybold Building. Nothing remains a secret there. By tomorrow, every jeweler in the city will be interested in your diamonds. I was just hoping to beat the rush."

"Let's worry about dispersing my load of people first. Once that's settled, I'll be happy to talk about other issues."

"Where and when does the load come in?"

This time, Albert, who had been sitting quietly next to his sister in the booth, said, "That's not information we wish to share before they arrive. I'm sure you understand."

Billy flexed the muscles in his jaw. He understood, and that was the problem.

Hanna took control of the conversation again. "I need to arrange transportation and housing before I can do anything else."

Billy smiled and said, "If you want, you can call me directly as soon as they arrive. I can have transportation ready to take much of the load off your hands right away. That should keep your expenses down."

Hanna considered the offer. It would certainly be easier if someone else arranged for vans and hotel rooms. They were also running short on cash, and with that thought, she made her decision.

Hanna reached across the table and shook Billy's hand. "I will be calling you sometime in the next three days."

Billy gave her a charming smile and said, "I look forward to it."

CHAPTER 66

I SAT IN a conference room at the task-force offices with Marie Meijer and Steph Hall. Both of them looked fresh, while I looked like I hadn't slept much. Because I hadn't.

Marie's informant in Amsterdam had said to expect the ship to dock somewhere in the Southeast sometime tomorrow, but that was all the information available. Marie said, "It comes from a well-placed informant, but they say they're getting only bits and pieces. They pass the information on to me as soon as they get it."

Steph shook her head and said, "That rules out undertaking any kind of rescue on the high seas, which was a long shot in the first place. But we've got to free those people as quickly as possible. There's no telling what sort of conditions they're being held in."

That's why I liked working with Steph Hall—she understood what was important. All the arrest stats in the world didn't help someone who died while being trafficked.

Lorena Perez said, "I've been looking at some financial info we've gotten on Rostoff. Most of it appears legit. He donates a shitload of money to a Miami Beach councilman and charities associated with Miami Beach. He's getting a humanitarian award there next week."

I said, "Great. Everyone thinks he's a prince while in reality, he ruins lives."

Lorena said, "His main muscle, Billy the Blade, lives in Fort Lauderdale. He doesn't owe anything on his condo or his Corvette."

Lorena was matter-of-fact when she passed on information. She wasn't an accountant, but she knew how to figure out relationships by following the money. She was good on surveillance too. No one suspected that a beautiful woman with big hair and perfect makeup was actually a cop.

I stood up. "I hate to say it, but it's time I have a discussion with the boss about what we're going to do."

Steph said, "Good luck."

"You're not coming with me?"

"Oh, *hell* no. It's depressing to go in there. He sucks the life out of me. If I ever get that skittish, I hope someone shoots me."

"You'll be lucky if someone doesn't shoot you for other reasons long before that."

She tried to hide it, but she laughed. That gave me the courage I needed to march into the supervisor's office. Still, I felt like I was walking the green mile.

To me, the supervisor's office seemed antiseptic and fake. He had certificates and newspaper articles framed and hanging on the wall. Everything had a place. There was no mess on the desk. In police work, I considered that the mark of someone who was not doing enough. I don't care how OCD you are, if you're busy in law enforcement, shit gets messy. Both figuratively and literally.

I stood in the doorway until the supervisor looked up from the computer screen. I always got the impression he was a little annoyed when he had to speak to someone personally instead of reading a report.

He said from his desk, "Can I help you?"

It was hardly a warm invitation, but this had to get done. I stepped into the office and sat down in the chair directly across from his desk. I quickly explained the developing situation and finished up by saying, "All we have to do is identify the right ship, then make a tactical entry. Possibly get a search warrant to go through the containers as rapidly as possible. We don't want to risk the lives of the people being trafficked."

I sat in awkward and uncomfortable silence while my supervisor considered everything I'd said. After almost a minute he said, "So that's all we need to do. Just identify the right ship out of the hundreds that enter our Florida ports every day, go to a magistrate with this pile of info coming from God knows where, then risk the lives of FBI personnel as well as civilian port workers by assaulting the ship. If that's all we have to do, then I'm thrilled with your plan."

"When you say it like that, it sounds almost impossible."

"How should I say it? I'm the one responsible for everyone's safety on this task force. And everyone's actions."

"Are you saying we should do nothing?" I kept my voice under control. Just barely.

He shrugged. "For now, keep gathering more

intel. The information coming from Holland is sketchy at best. You're talking about using multiple agents on surveillance for several days. Plus, I'm still clearing up some of your mess from that wild-goose chase down at Port Everglades. I've had more than a few calls from bigwigs at Customs who say you insulted their agents and agency. Is that true?"

"Insulted or enlightened. It's a matter of interpretation."

The supervisor said, "The Customs agents at Port Everglades would disagree with that."

"Sure they would. No one wants to admit that it was a Miami cop who discovered a whole container of illegal tropical birds. And that the smuggler ran halfway across port property before anyone from Customs even bothered to waddle out to a car and see what was going on."

The supervisor said, "So you see my point. Do more background and let's see how things shake out before we commit too many resources to this human-trafficking case. We already have the one arrest of the Dutch guy at the airport."

The lawyer in me was ready to debate the purpose of law enforcement in general and this task force in particular. Instead, I took a shortcut.

I said, "That's fine. No problem. I'll just call the Miami Police. Their SWAT team has a lot more experience than the FBI's anyway. They'll swoop in there and grab those people. That way we won't risk any resources from the task force." I had to fight to keep the smug smile off my face.

After considering this for ten seconds longer than I'd thought he would, he said, "Don't call the Miami police. I can justify this as part of the task-force activity. I was just worried because intercepting a ship can be tactically difficult. I don't want to risk lives unnecessarily."

"I don't know anyone who does. I'm sure we can handle it within the task force. Some surveillance, and we'll get a DHS agent on the case with us. Most important, we'll make sure to get some stats for the task force."

I could tell by his smile that stats were his real goal.

CHAPTER 67

WE DECIDED TO focus on the port of Miami. It was a risk, one that was tearing at my insides. I couldn't sleep. I barely ate. If we were wrong, there was no telling what would happen to the people on the ship.

Marie brought up an excellent point. "Hanna must have contacts in Miami, no? We know she had a contact here when she tried to smuggle the children through the airport. I have a stomach feeling she'll do it again."

"Gut feeling," I said.

"Isn't the gut the same as the stomach?"

I let it go.

As a Miami cop, I'd done a ton of surveillance at the port. Once, while waiting for a ship that was supposed to have a load of hash from Turkey, I witnessed a snatch-and-run. A young white guy grabbed a woman's purse and sprinted out of the port toward the American Airlines Arena. I was the only one around, and the ship I was waiting on hadn't docked yet, so I chased him.

Come to think of it, maybe I do chase after suspects more than your average cop. Probably an instinct carried over from my U M days on the field. He was fast at first, then lost some steam. I almost cornered him near Sixth Street, but he jumped over a fence and had a clean getaway in front of him. Then he stopped on the far side of the fence and turned back to me.

He said, "You're Moon, right?"

"Yeah."

He laughed. "Anti–Ray Lewis. I can see why the 'Canes never made a decent bowl while you were playing. See ya later." And he was gone.

Every time I'm at the port, I daydream about catching that guy. Even though he had a point.

I tried to imagine what it might be like to live in a shipping container for over a week. It gave me the willies. We had to get this right. I didn't want to see another dead girl someone had been trying to smuggle. I didn't care if I was kicked off the task force for not making arrests. Right now, I just wanted to find those people.

I never realized how many ships came and went out of the port. I had a DHS supervisor on call. I explained about a possible leak coming from Customs.

The DHS supervisor, a guy named Rick Morris, said, "You watch too much TV."

I chuckled and said, "I hope so. But I also work in Miami. Anything's possible."

With the trouble I'd had from Customs over the past few days, I thought it would be best not to call Rick until we had a hot prospect.

The waiting was killing me.

CHAPTER 68

THE SUN DIPPED in the west and all the lights in the port came on. You could argue that a full day of surveillance with no results was a bust, but all it really meant was that we'd be doing it over again tomorrow. That's the life of a cop.

Marie had found the day fascinating. She liked seeing how the port operated and hearing stories about police work in and around Miami.

She asked me, "How long will you stay on the task force?"

I shrugged. "Who knows? I have to produce or they'll just rotate me off. I know someone from the Miami PD who wants my spot."

"You need arrests to stay?"

"They don't keep me for my charming personality."

"What if we don't make arrests but are able to save the people being trafficked?"

"I'll be thrilled."

"Even if you get moved off the task force?"

"I'll still be a cop."

She smiled and squeezed my hand. She looked toward the water.

Two ships had just docked. I checked with my DHS contact and he said they had both sailed from ports in Europe. After a moment, he narrowed it down, said one had come from the Netherlands, the other from Belgium.

After I convinced him to come down to the port, I turned to my partners and said, "Let's walk down to the ships. The one on the left is from the Netherlands and the other one is from Belgium. These are the best prospects we've had."

We didn't want to blow the surveillance in case neither of these was the right ship, so we stood back from the dock looking at them both. Steph asked, "Is one of them more likely than the other?"

Marie said, "I haven't heard anything more specific from my informants. But both ships fit the profile we've been looking for."

I was torn. If we jumped on one of the ships, word would get out. Sailors talked, and now, with cell phones, they were in instant communication with one another all over the world. I didn't want to expose the surveillance early, but I couldn't risk leaving people locked in one of those shipping containers one minute longer than they had to be.

If we picked the wrong ship, the crew on the other ship could flee and we'd have no suspects. I felt a knot in my stomach as I worked through the different scenarios. I wasn't even factoring in the chance that someone aboard either ship might be armed and try to stop us.

There was no way we could do this without causing a major stir. It would throw the port into chaos for at least two hours and the news media would swoop down on it in minutes.

I looked around at the port crews and Customs

people walking right past us about fifty yards from the two ships.

One Customs inspector with dark hair paused and checked his phone right in front of us. There was absolutely nothing remarkable about him— except his ID. His name was Vacile, which sounded familiar to me.

My eyes involuntarily followed the unremarkable Customs inspector.

Then it hit me. I remembered where I had seen his name. He was the inspector at the Miami airport. I'd noticed at the time how the trafficker purposely moved to Vacile's line for entry to the U.S. We'd just thought it was a case of a lazy inspector. DHS had said they'd follow up on it as a personnel matter.

This couldn't be a coincidence.

We had to risk it. I wasn't about to lose a load of people just to make some arrests. We had to do something, and now.

Whatever ship Vacile stepped onto was the ship we were going to search.

CHAPTER 69

I PULLED OUT a small pair of binoculars that generally saw action only during Miami Dolphins games and used them to track the Customs inspector named Vacile.

He spoke to a few people but kept moving, so no one was with him when he started poking around containers sitting at the front of the suspect ship.

My heart started to beat faster. This could be it. There was so much riding on what we did next that I felt a flutter of anxiety. I couldn't stop thinking about the people locked on board. We had to get to them.

By now, Lorena Perez, Anthony Chilleo, and Rick Morris, the DHS supervisor I'd been talking to on the phone, had gathered near the ship. I explained how I'd recognized Vacile from the airport. Morris, an in-shape, middle-aged man with a slightly graying crew cut, said, "That's a pretty thin story to ruin someone's reputation over."

I said, "Do you know this guy personally?"

"Never heard of him." He glanced down at his phone. "But I'm looking at his personnel file and he doesn't have any complaints. Coincidences happen

all the time. That's why they're called *coincidences*.
Like how it was a coincidence that I was the internal
affairs supervisor on call when you said you needed
help. If you had called the next day, then, by coincidence, I'd be at my college reunion right now instead
of here. See what I mean about coincidences?"

He was right. It was a long shot. "'Coincidence is
God's way of staying anonymous,'" I said.

Only Steph knew to ask, "Okay, who said that?"

"Albert Einstein."

The DHS agent said, "So your probable cause is
based on a dead physicist's comments about God?"

I was losing my patience, and I raised my voice.
"Look, Rick, people might die. This is a literal
life-and-death situation. C'mon, don't be an administrative geek now. Be a cop. If we ignore this
and do nothing and people wind up dying, we're
responsible for the death of every one of them. Tell
me, is that something you could live with?"

Rick shook his head and said, "Let's go."

CHAPTER 70

THE TIME HAD come. Hanna Greete felt like a bundle of exposed nerves. Everything was an assault on her senses. She tried to stay quiet as she and Albert waited near the port of Miami. All of her hard work came down to the next few hours. If anything happened and they weren't able to pay off their debts, all was lost. There was no other way to look at the situation.

They could see the ship they were waiting for, the *Scandinavian Queen,* docked next to another ship in the easternmost section of the port.

Two long passenger vans rumbled into the loading zone behind Hanna and Albert.

Hanna twisted on the bench and saw Billy, her Russian contact, pop out of the front passenger seat of the first van. He wore a dark suit and had his thinning hair slicked back. She hid her surprise.

He was his usual cheerful self. Billy clapped his hands together as he walked toward them. "And how are my Dutch friends on this beautiful evening?" He had a wide grin.

Albert leaned in close to his sister and mumbled,

"This can't be a good sign." He reached under his shirt. Hanna placed a hand on her brother's arm.

She said, "Wait. Let's hear what he has to say."

"Whatever he says, it will mean he's screwing us out of our money. This isn't the Vatican we're dealing with. These guys don't care about our troubles."

Hanna stepped forward and asked Billy, "How did you know it was time to come to the port?" Her aggressive tone didn't seem to bother the friendly Russian.

Billy held up his hands but kept a smile. "You're not serious, are you?" Billy said. His accent sounded almost elegant. "You don't think our mutual contact won't call us first? Surely you can't be that naive."

Hanna eyed the other Russians coming out of the vans. They all had hard edges, even the lone woman, who was tall, with straight dark hair. Serious expressions, alert eyes, and the quiet restlessness that came with expecting trouble.

Hanna said, "We're paying for the service; we expect to be the ones who get the benefit from it."

"Vacile may take money from you, but he's a loyal Russian. He texted me as he was about to enter the ship."

Hanna noticed the Russians near the vans were keeping a close eye on Albert. Her brother was aware of their interest.

She hoped this didn't turn into a bloody fight.

CHAPTER 71

THE FIRST THING I noticed as we carefully approached the ship we'd seen Vacile enter—the *Scandinavian Queen*—was a security guard standing at the top of the gangplank. The lanky young man looked from the ship to the dock. *Not this shit again,* I thought.

I slowed everyone down a little way from the ship and said, "I've had to deal with a shipping security agent once already this week. I'd rather we didn't have to muscle our way past this guy. Any ideas?" I looked around the group.

Without any hesitation, Steph Hall said, "I got this." She hid her badge, unbuttoned two buttons on her shirt, looked over her shoulder, and gave me a wink.

Lorena Perez said, "Really, you think that's gonna work?"

Steph said, "He's a dude under twenty-five. It'll work."

Chill said, "Probably would, but what if I try something else first?"

Steph looked annoyed for a moment, then said,

"I'll defer to your experience." ATF agents went undercover on a regular basis.

I moved a little closer to the ship in case there was trouble. I was really doing this for the benefit of the young security officer on the boat. If he did something stupid, I didn't want Steph or Chill to break one of his legs and toss him in the water.

Chill made a little show of wandering around like he was lost. I liked how he stooped over slightly to give the impression he was older than he was.

He stopped by the gangplank and called up to get the security guard's attention. The guard looked down at Chill, who said something in a quiet voice.

The guard yelled back, "What was that? I can't hear you."

Chill leaned against the gangplank handrail and coughed like he'd been a lifelong pack-a-day smoker.

I was impressed. He sold me on the coughing fit even though I knew he was a runner.

Chill hacked a little louder and motioned to the young security guard to come close.

The man didn't hesitate. He scurried down the gangplank like a lab rat waiting to eat cancer-laced candy.

Chill looked over at us with a sly smile. There really wasn't any substitution for experience.

Once the guard was next to him, Chill composed himself and mumbled thanks. He straightened up a bit and said, "I'm okay now. Thanks for coming to help."

The young man beamed. "No problem. Are you sure you're okay?"

Now Chill began a subtle but effective interrogation of the security agent. First there was the usual stuff, like "What's your name? Where are you from?" Then he got to the real question: "How many people are on the ship right now?"

The young man did a double take and said, "Wait, what?"

It was like Chill had changed from a caterpillar to a butterfly. He slipped the badge he wore on a chain out from under his shirt and grasped the young man tightly by the upper arm. Chill changed his tone and said, "How many people are on board?"

"I—I—I don't really know."

Now Rick Morris, the Customs supervisor, stepped up to the young man and said, "Answer the question, jack-off."

Chill looked at him sharply and said, "I got this, Rick. Back off." He turned his attention back to the suddenly terrified security man. Chill put his hand on the young guard's shoulder and said, "Tell me who you *think* is on board."

The young man stuttered again and finally was able to blurt out, "The Customs inspector just came on, and the first mate is on board. I think a lot of the crew already slipped off for the evening."

Now our entire group gathered around the security guard. Chill slid the young man's radio out of its harness and said, "I'll give this back when we're done."

I stood in front of the young man and looked down at him. "You're gonna need to sit right here and not talk to anyone or call anyone until we come off the ship. Is this clearly understood?"

The young man nodded and sat down on the concrete bench near the ship.

We all carefully stepped onto the rickety gang-plank, trying to limit the noise. Sounds echoed in the still night. I could hear a car horn out on Biscayne Boulevard. We fanned out near the bridge. I got a weird vibe from the almost empty ship, which reminded me of something from *The Walking Dead*.

The first thing Rick said was "That's weird. If there's a Customs inspector on board, there should be a Customs person at the gangplank and a couple in the wheelhouse. Something's not right."

Steph gave him a flat stare and said, "No shit."

CHAPTER 72

I WASTED NO time once we were on board. Every minute was vital; we had to get to the people in the storage container. I'd worry about arrests and charges afterward. If this Customs inspector, Vacile, was helping human traffickers, he was about to have the worst night of his life.

I just started marching toward the bow, cutting between the towering storage containers on the metal deck that showed signs of rust and wear. I felt like I was in Monument Valley.

It was spooky. I didn't even *hear* anyone else on board. Stepping carefully, I minimized any sound. Everyone behind me was just as careful. My heart raced as I considered all the things that could go wrong. That's what I always did before any kind of operation, whether it was a search warrant, an interview, or something as important as this.

I heard muffled voices as we approached the front. A tall, older sailor, probably the first mate, was talking amiably with Vacile. The Customs inspector was about forty-five years old; he had a potbelly, and his blue uniform didn't complement his shape. The two men stood in front of a single container. There were air vents along the top. It was obvious what we were looking at.

I stepped out of the shadows and came in full view of the two men.

The sailor barked at me, "No one is allowed on board."

I immediately recognized his accent as Dutch.

Marie stepped forward and spoke sharply to the man in Dutch, which caught him by surprise. It also tipped off Vacile that it was probably time to go.

He backed away slowly and bumped into Rick, our own Customs contact, who was clearly not happy.

Rick grabbed Vacile by the shoulders and said, "I'm Rick Morris. I'm an honest Customs supervisor, and you're not gonna move another inch until we've sorted this out." He calmly reached down and removed the inspector's service weapon from its holster.

I looked at the first mate and said, "Open this container." When he hesitated, I shouted, "Right now!" The man jumped but still made no move toward the lock.

The sailor said, "I don't have a key."

Acting on impulse, I reached over and banged the side of the container. There was a commotion from inside. I could hear shouting and people moving around.

Rick sprang forward with a passkey but couldn't get the container open. This was taking too long.

I looked around in desperation and saw another tool like the one on the ship with the smuggled parrots. I pulled it off the wall and shouted for Rick to move out of the way.

I swung the tool like a knight slaying a dragon,

starting above my head and using my full 240 pounds to bring it down. The sound of the captive people yelling gave me strength.

I hit the lock perfectly on the first swing. The impact ran up my arm, but the door creaked open.

This time, I recognized the smell that hit me immediately. It was human waste. And something else.

CHAPTER 73

HANNA AND ALBERT glided along with Billy and his crew of tough-looking Russians. Hanna tried to speak to the lone female, the tall thirty-something woman with straight dark hair, but either the woman didn't speak English or she didn't want to engage with Hanna. Which was a bad sign for what might happen later.

Hanna glanced at her brother. Her concern was obvious to him; he was the person who had always looked after her. He smiled and nodded in an effort to calm her down. It was like when they were children; no matter what was going on, Albert would always say, "It'll all work out."

She wished she had his confidence. All she could think about was what would happen if they lost this load too.

Billy, the friendly Russian, looked over his shoulder at Hanna and said, "See, a nice quiet evening at the port. We'll walk out of here with everyone and no one will ever notice. You can't put a price on that kind of security."

Hanna sensed new fees coming her way. She cut her eyes over to Albert again. He had his hand near where his newly acquired pistol was concealed under his shirt. At least the Russians hadn't guessed that he was armed.

Hanna didn't like the wobbly gangplank or the loud noise their hard shoes made when they walked up the metal ramp. She was surprised no one came to investigate. The first mate she'd hired had done a good job.

Hanna realized the Russians had subtly changed positions to surround them; now she and Albert were in the middle of their group.

Thank God Albert was with her, Hanna thought.

Not even Billy was speaking anymore as they worked their way forward on the ship.

As she stepped between two shipping containers, Hanna saw a group of people standing around a familiar shape: the specially built container she'd bought.

Her heart stopped. She recognized Marie Meijer.

Before she could say anything, the tallest of the Russians drew a pistol from the back of his pants. Billy slipped away from the front and eased between other containers.

Albert inched to the rear of the group and drew his own pistol. No one but Hanna saw it in his hand.

CHAPTER 74

I STOOD BY the shipping container's open door and stared at the group of twenty or so pitiful people inside. Several girls were weeping. A couple of people darted out of the fetid container and onto the ship.

The scene inside the container shocked me, and that's saying something for a veteran of the Miami Police Department. Almost all cops reach a point when they think they've seen it all and can no longer be surprised by people's behavior or scenes of violence.

I'd witnessed children shot in the streets. I'd once held pressure on a wound in the abdomen of a nine-year-old girl in Liberty City, desperate to stop the blood that was pumping out. She had unwittingly stepped into a gunfight between two local gangs and caught a nine-millimeter round just below her rib cage.

I'd picked her up and carried her like a doll, keeping one hand pressed down hard on the wound in her abdomen. I ran till I thought my heart might burst to where the paramedics said they'd meet me, a block away from the gunfire.

I rode with her in the ambulance because she didn't want me to leave her.

I stayed with her until she was taken into surgery, and then I waited at the hospital to explain to her stepfather what had happened.

I sat with my uniform covered in the little girl's blood. I could barely keep it together. Nurses offered me coffee and tried to talk to me as I waited.

Her stepfather finally showed up and asked me what the hell was going on.

I explained what had happened and told him that the surgeon was hopeful he could save the little girl.

All the man said to that was "This ain't gonna cost me nothing, is it?"

That whole situation had shocked and bothered me for weeks after. And it didn't touch what I was looking at now.

The stench of human waste and vomit coming from the shipping container made my eyes water. A rat scurried out of it. Before I could tell the people inside they were safe, I heard movement behind me. It caught everyone's attention.

I looked around to see a group of people I didn't know. I focused on a blued semiautomatic pistol in the hand of a tall guy wearing a dark sports coat.

Lorena Perez shouted, "Police, don't move!" and drew her department-issued Glock. But it had no effect on the man with the handgun. She let loose three quick rounds.

The sound of the gunfire among the containers was deafening and disorienting, like thunder inside a small room. The noise was everywhere, swarming my senses. I stumbled forward and tried to pull the container door shut to protect the people inside.

But that wasn't going to happen. There was no way those prisoners would let the door shut on them again, not even if people were shooting right in front of them. A mass of the people still inside the container slammed the door open.

I backed to the side of the container and drew my service pistol. People from the unknown group had guns up and were firing. Steph and Rick Morris were returning fire.

I needed to know Marie was safe. She was unarmed. What had I been thinking, bringing her here? I raised my pistol. There were no obvious targets, but a few shots crossed between the two groups.

My heart was pounding in my chest from the adrenaline rush and the shock of being shot at. I looked over my shoulder. There were a few people cowering inside the storage container and several others lying still on its nasty, garbage-covered floor.

Marie leaped forward and slammed her body into a man trying to get to the container. She knocked him back, but he quickly regained his balance and swung the butt of his pistol into Marie's face.

Her head snapped and twisted.

I needed to help her.

Two things happened quickly: three rounds pinged off the vent I was using for cover, forcing me back down, and Marie took another blow, this one a punch from the man's other hand.

I stared in horror as he brought his pistol up and pointed it at Marie. I raised my pistol for a tricky shot, hoping to at least distract the man.

But Marie was quicker. She kicked and darted to one side. Her foot connected with the man's knee and he fell, and she followed that up with a kick to the man's head.

Teeth flew and blood painted a pattern on the side of the container.

A tall woman scooped up the injured man, and the two of them disappeared into the maze of containers.

There was one more rush of fire, then, like the aftermath of most gunfights, an eerie, all-encompassing quiet. Part of it had to do with my ears ringing from the sudden loud noises. Part of it was the fact that there was very little activity at this time of the evening in the port of Miami.

And part of it, I knew, was that there were people down on both sides of the fight.

CHAPTER 75

AS SOON AS she heard the first shots, Hanna realized exactly what Albert planned to do. He wanted to use this as cover to shoot Billy the Russian. He wasn't going to wait for a police officer to do it.

Hanna flinched as Albert shot one of the Russians in the back. The man just dropped. Nothing like in the movies. He just fell forward, silent and still in the midst of chaos.

Albert wasted no time. He grabbed Hanna by the wrist and tugged her along as they fled the shooting.

Albert managed to say, "I think that shit Billy is headed for the gangplank. We better not see him on the ship."

Hanna risked a quick glimpse over her shoulder. They'd already gotten far enough away that all she could see was a few flashes from pistols. It was amazing how much the sound of gunfire was reduced when you got a few dozen yards and a couple of shipping containers away from it.

Hanna recognized a couple of the younger women running past them, headed for the front of the ship. They were girls she had housed in Amsterdam.

She'd thought these girls would've trusted her. It must be the gunfire. Hanna didn't like the idea that they would betray her and run when they knew they still had to work off the cost of their transportation. The people she transported usually wanted to trust someone. And they'd known the travel would be hard.

She planted her feet to stop Albert from dragging her along.

He looked at her, astonished. "Are you crazy? We've got to get out of here."

"We need the red backpack. Either Magda has the pack or it's back in the container."

"Back there, where all the gunfire is? Where the police are waiting for us? No, thanks. We need to keep running."

Hanna glanced over the side of the ship and saw the girl she was looking for. And she had the backpack over her shoulder. She yelled at Albert, "Right there. Magda's right there."

"And running faster than we could ever hope to," Albert pointed out. "Don't worry. The tracker is in the backpack. We'll let things settle down here and then we'll be able to find her easily. At least we can salvage the diamonds."

Hanna followed her brother off the ship. The chaos from the ship had spread to the docks. People were running in every direction. No one knew if this was a terrorist attack or a drug-gang shootout.

Hanna followed Albert's lead as he immediately slowed to a fast walk. They headed directly off the port grounds. She was going to take a serious financial hit on this fiasco.

CHAPTER 76

IT TOOK ONLY a moment for me to regain my senses and realize I had to act immediately. I wanted to chase the shooters, but there were too many people who needed help right in front of me.

I swept the area for gunmen. Once I determined it was clear, I holstered my pistol. Two men from the group that had confronted us were dead.

One of the men had been shot in the back, but I didn't know if it was an accident or if someone from his group had gotten tired of him. For safety reasons, I took the pistols from the bodies and secured them.

A moment later, I was at Marie's side. She was on the deck and bleeding badly from cuts on her face. I could barely recognize her under all the blood. It pooled and dripped off her nose like a cheap faucet.

She said, "I swear, it's not that bad. Some of the blood isn't mine. Check on the girls in the container."

A moment later I was in front of the storage container. The smell turned my stomach. A haze seemed to have settled over the few people still in the container. Piles of garbage filled the back corners. Junk-food wrappers, empty water bottles, and used toilet paper overflowed from one small garbage can to form a small mountain. Cockroaches scattered when I stepped inside.

A bucket used as a toilet was visible through a flimsy plastic curtain. I had a hard time imagining what the nine-day trip from Europe had been like for these poor souls.

Steph was checking the pulse of a man on the ground. He was ashen and his eyes looked up lifelessly at the rusty walls of the container. One leather loafer was missing from his left foot.

Steph looked up at me and shook her head.

I said, "Hit by a stray bullet?"

Steph said, "No. We have four dead in here. It looks like they all died from illness or heat exhaustion." She indicated another man on the ground and two girls against the rear wall. There were three young women, alive, huddling together near the door to the container. Steph went to comfort them.

I went over to the rear wall. The two girls looked like they had been dead a couple of days. They had been placed next to each other and covered with a plastic tarp.

Both the girls looked like young teenagers; they had long hair and pretty faces. Faces with eyes that would never see home or family again. It was heartbreaking.

I thought about how these poor people had lived for the last nine days and I got mad. Fury washed over me like a wave. I couldn't remember the last time I had been this pissed off. And I knew just who I could focus my anger on.

I stepped out of the container with my hand

on my pistol and said, "Where is that goddamn Inspector Vacile?"

Lorena Perez just pointed.

Across the cluttered deck, our best source of information lay flat, half of his face missing. Blood had gushed from the gunshot wound on his left cheek. Based on where he'd landed, I guessed he'd been shot by the men who surprised us. I wondered if it was done on purpose to keep him from talking to us.

I stepped over to Lorena. She wasn't injured but she didn't look too good. Her hands were shaking and she was leaning back against a storage container.

I put my arm around her shoulder. "You saved our asses. You okay?"

She looked up and nodded but didn't say a word. I'd seen it before. The aftermath of police shooting could be devastating. She'd done her duty and proved she had talent.

Anthony Chilleo was holding pressure on the wound on Rick Morris's arm.

I said, "Chill, how bad is it?"

"I'll survive," the Customs supervisor said.

"We've got help on the way. Nothing we can do for the others," Chill said.

I searched the two dead men's pockets, found some ID, and said, "They're Russian."

Chill mumbled, "Shocker."

CHAPTER 77

HANNA SLAPPED THE wall in frustration. "Why can't we get a decent reading on the tracker?"

Albert didn't take his eyes off his phone as he tried again to refresh the location of the tracker sewn into the red backpack.

They'd spent two hours near the port looking for Magda with the red backpack.

During a quick break, sitting on the seawall in Bayside with the trendy shops behind them all closing down for the evening, Hanna turned to her brother and said, "Why did you shoot a Russian in the back?"

Albert looked at her as if she were speaking Martian. "What do you mean? Why *wouldn't* I shoot him? They were trying to rip us off. It was our best chance to rid ourselves of the Russians here in Miami."

"Did you see what happened to Billy?"

"No. It was too crazy. We're lucky we got out of there alive." Albert focused on his phone as he tried to bring up the tracker again.

Hanna said, "It's getting late. Let's head back to the hotel."

As soon as the cab pulled into the Miami Gardens Inn, Hanna saw that the lights to their first-floor room were off. There was no way Josie and Tasi had gone to bed this early. There should have been a glow from the TV set, at the very least.

They rushed to the door, Albert with his pistol out.

Hanna fumbled with the key in the low light, then shoved the heavy door open and immediately flicked on a light so that Albert could scan the room.

The first thing she noticed was the blood spattered across the sheet on the foldout bed.

The second was a bloody handprint on the bathroom door.

Hanna's whole world started to spin as she tried to comprehend what had happened. She cried out, "Josie," praying to God she would get some kind of response.

There was just dead silence.

CHAPTER 78

HANNA FOUGHT THE urge to scream. Nothing had prepared her for the scene she was witnessing. She cried out again, "Josie!" Then she heard a sound coming from the bathroom.

She and Albert rushed to the bathroom door. The smell of vomit was overwhelming. She pushed the door open and found Tasi kneeling next to the toilet with blood pouring from her nose and lips. She had two puffy black eyes. Josie's babysitter had been beaten so badly, she was sick to her stomach.

Hanna didn't like to see the young woman in such distress, but she couldn't waste any time. "Where's Josie?"

Tasi started sobbing, then leaned over the toilet to throw up again. The retro pink toilet made the blood and vomit stand out more. Even the kitschy palm-tree wallpaper seemed ominous now.

Hanna gently took Tasi by the shoulders and made her turn from the toilet. She said, "Tasi, what happened? Where is Josie?" She spoke slowly and clearly, as if she were talking to someone who didn't understand Dutch.

Tasi took in gulps of air. Haltingly, she said,

"A man tapped on our front door. He said he was a maintenance worker. I opened the door just a crack." Tasi broke down and cried for a moment. "There was a woman there too, and she started kicking me in the stomach and the face. I was crying and couldn't see but I heard Josie yell as the man dragged her out of the room."

"When did this happen?"

"Less than an hour ago."

"What did the man and woman look like?" Albert asked.

Tasi coughed and spit some blood into the toilet. She collected her thoughts and said, "The woman was tall with dark hair. The man had a goatee. It was dyed blue."

Billy. Hanna would murder him right now if he were in front of her. She asked Albert, "How do you think they found us?"

Albert was silent for a moment, then said, "I know exactly how they found us."

Five minutes later, Albert and Hanna were in the cluttered reception area of the Miami Gardens Inn. Ancient magazines, paperbacks with torn covers, and old VHS movies lay haphazardly on a shaky bookshelf. The clerk who'd checked them in looked up and said, "Good evening." His Russian accent set Hanna on edge. Albert was already over the edge.

Without saying a word, Albert grabbed the young man by the shirt collar, dragged him over the counter, and threw him onto the hard floor. He'd stuck his pistol in the young man's ear before Hanna even realized he'd drawn it.

Albert spoke slowly and clearly in English. "I don't want you to make a mistake you'll regret the rest of your life." He shoved the pistol into the man's ear harder. "I'm going to ask you a question. If you lie, I'm going to put a bullet through your head. Do you understand me?"

The young man nodded vigorously.

Albert said, "Let me see your phone."

The clerk carefully reached into his pocket and pulled out a new iPhone. Albert made him open it, looked at a few numbers, and said, "Whose number is this?"

The young man hesitated and Albert pressed the gun harder into his ear. The man yelled, "Wait, wait, I don't know his name! He runs a lot of the strip clubs. He told me to keep an eye out for you guys. I just did like I was told."

Albert remained unnaturally calm and said, "Where did they take the girl?"

"I don't know. I swear to God, I don't know." The clerk started to cry, and sweat poured down his forehead.

Albert said, "FaceTime him."

"What?"

Albert smacked his cheek with the barrel of the pistol. He didn't feel like explaining. The young man quickly hit Redial. After a couple of rings, an image came on the iPhone. It was Billy.

Friendly as always, Billy said, "Ah, Albert. I wondered what happened to you guys. Glad you made it away from the ship safely."

"Where's Josie?"

Billy kept smiling. He said something to someone else in the room.

Albert made sure the pistol in the clerk's ear was framed in the phone properly. "Tell me where my niece is or you'll be cleaning up this asshole's brains for a week."

Billy said, "The young man that works at that nasty little hotel? I don't know him. Go ahead and shoot. I couldn't care less. But you might be able to use the five hundred dollars cash I gave him. Perhaps you should check his pockets. But shoot him if you want."

The young man sucked in some oxygen and started to shake.

Then Billy said, "If you'd like to be reasonable, I'm sure we could work out a simple trade. The diamonds for the girl. That's the only thing I'm interested in talking to you about."

Hanna grabbed the phone and said, "Is Josie okay?"

Billy chuckled and said, "Don't worry, mama bear. We're taking good care of your baby bear." He turned the camera briefly so Hanna could see Josie sitting in a chair with a Kleenex in her hand.

Billy said, "It's late. We'll talk some more tomorrow. It's a simple deal. Diamonds for the girl. It will make up for that disaster at the port." The image disappeared and the line went dead.

Albert gave the clerk a hard look, then he patted his pants pockets. He reached in the right pocket and pulled out the wad of cash.

Just as Hanna opened the door, Albert turned and screamed, "Bang!"

The young man flinched and then burst into tears.

CHAPTER 79

I SAT BY Marie's side at Jackson Memorial as a distressingly young ER doctor put nine stitches in her left cheek. She'd been right; most of the blood was not hers.

After Marie had been sewn up, she turned to me and asked, "How do I look?" Her sly smile broke the tension and I laughed.

"Beautiful." I wasn't kidding. But even with the scrapes and stitches, she was ready to get back to work. After the visit to Jackson Memorial, we searched the streets of Miami for the people who had fled from the ship. We managed to find six young women, two young men, and two older women. Most were wandering around the port area. Two were at a shelter.

Once back in the station, we began taking statements from the victims who spoke English. Their accounts of traveling over the Atlantic in the shipping container were harrowing.

About five days into the trip, they said, the older of the two men from India had fallen asleep and never woke up. The younger women, who spoke the same language and appeared to be friends, said they believed that the younger Indian man had had some sort of cardiac event when he discovered the other man was dead.

The two dead girls, they said, were from somewhere in Belgium. One of them had started getting sick a few days earlier, and the other girl, who never spoke to anyone and whose name they didn't know, began throwing up as well. They had both died about a day ago.

It was heartbreaking. Marie, for all of her toughness, had a hard time dealing with it. She clearly felt like she had personally let them down.

I gave her a few minutes. She composed herself, but it wasn't easy. Cops aren't robots, and few civilians can comprehend what police officers see on a regular basis. It's a miracle that there aren't cops breaking down all the time.

I said, "It's not your fault. It's the traffickers and people like Rostoff. They don't care about anything but money."

"It's just so sad," Marie said. "Society has forgotten these people. I've seen it in Amsterdam. Young girls think they can make their fortune by coming here, but it's all lies. I wish we could do something to hurt predators like the Rostoff brothers. The death penalty would be too good for them."

I nodded and said, "We'll do something. I can't let Roman Rostoff sit up in that luxury office like he's an earl."

Marie took a moment to wipe her tears and blow her nose on a paper towel. Then she looked at me with bloodshot eyes and said, "Let's get back to work."

I don't even know what time I got home that night. When I woke up in the morning, after only a few hours' sleep, I was still exhausted. The smell of pancakes and bacon drew me out of bed. I felt like I was a character in a fairy tale wandering into a trap.

My sister, looking very professional in a dark, fitted dress, was in the hall, getting ready to head to the school where she worked as a speech pathologist. She tilted her head toward the kitchen and shrugged. That's when I realized it was my mother cooking. This was phenomenal; she almost never cooked in the morning.

My sister and I sat down at the small dining-room table and before we could say anything, my mom plopped down two plates piled with eggs, pancakes, and bacon. She looked like a waitress at a Denny's.

Why couldn't it be like this every morning?

I asked a few of my normal questions, trying to figure out if she was in our current reality or a former one. She seemed fine. She called me Tommy and asked Lila some specific questions about her job.

Finally, I had to say, "Mom, what's going on? What's with all the food?"

She eased down into the chair next to me and took a sip of her coffee. "You think I'm not aware of what's been happening, that I just live in my own little world and expect you guys to cater to my every need? It's terrifying. Not because I'm losing my grip on reality, but because of everything I'm putting you through."

Lila reached across the table and grasped my mother's hand. They both had tears in their eyes. I almost did the same, but I wanted to hear what else my mom had to say.

She flicked a tear off her cheek and said, "You

both do so much for me, I just wanted to do a little something for you."

Lila stood up and hugged her. "We do it because we love you, Mom."

"And I'm doing this because I love you. No one realizes how much a mother loves her children. She really will do anything for them. I'm just sorry you have to do so much for me now."

I stood up and kissed her gently on the forehead. There was nothing else I could add to this conversation.

CHAPTER 80

BEFORE I PICKED Marie up at her hotel, I stopped by the Miami Police headquarters to put the word out about what had happened at the port. The oddly shaped five-story building on Second Avenue had seen its share of history. Over the years, Miami had witnessed all kinds of riots, shifting demographics, mass immigration from Cuba, and even a visit from the pope. Through it all, the police department—at least the building—never changed. And even the department's critics always knew they could run to us when things in the neighborhood got out of control.

Most people had no idea how things really worked on the streets. I remember a crack dealer named Walter Slates from back when I worked patrol just west of the downtown. He'd shoot a bird at me every time I drove past in my cruiser. He made fun of my record with the University of Miami's football team.

That's why, when he approached my patrol car one day, I was suspicious. He said, "I need help."

I took the bait and asked him what the problem was.

"The goddamn Colombians say they gonna kill me. Ain't nothing like the Cubans. The Cubans'll listen to you. The Cubans are reasonable. But these Colombians is crazy. I need protection."

"So all of a sudden you don't hate the police?"

"Never really hated the police. It's just fun to screw with you. Even if I did hate the police, I don't hate no more. Can you help me?"

We helped him. Walter Slates turned his life around. He now works for Florida Power and Light somewhere up near West Palm Beach. He made it a point to come by and thank me a few years ago.

I knew that by putting the word out at the station, I could count on tips from contacts on the street. The beat cops heard we hadn't found all the people who'd been in the container, and it took them only about an hour to round up the rest. Now we had almost all of them. Except one. A blond Polish girl named Magda who spoke some English.

Finding that girl was our only goal this morning.

Instead of hello, the first thing Marie had said to me when I met her in the lobby of the downtown Marriott was "I just got off the phone with my best informant. Hanna and Albert Greete are in Miami, looking for a girl who fled from the boat. She has a backpack with a fortune in diamonds hidden in it."

"Let me guess—it's the one girl we haven't found yet. Magda from Poland."

"Exactly."

"Does she know she has the diamonds?"

"I don't think so. I heard they're supposed to be sewn into the strap."

We got busy checking shelters and streets near the port and downtown.

Around midmorning, I grabbed a doorknob that turned out to be covered with grease. Someone had smeared the knob with goo as a joke or as a way to put people off, but in any case, I now had bicycle grease all over my right palm.

Marie was speaking with a woman who ran a homeless shelter and I was looking for a paper towel to wipe my hand when I noticed someone coming in my direction.

There are a lot of men wearing suits in Miami, but not many with goatees dyed blue. It was Billy the Blade, Rostoff's muscle. I immediately realized he was doing the same thing Marie and I were. He didn't know how many people we'd rescued from the ship and he was probably hoping to recover some of his investment right now.

I turned to face him, and after a few seconds, he looked up and noticed me. That's one of the benefits of my size—I can be very obvious when I want to be.

I'd obviously caught the Russian by surprise. It took him a moment to put on his usual smile. Then he strutted toward me in his expensive cream-colored Brooks Brothers suit.

Billy kept his broad smile as he said, "Detective, did you already get kicked off your task force? You have to work the streets of Miami again?"

I gave a little chuckle and said, "I think you overestimate your boss's influence."

"I'm not sure it's possible to overestimate Mr. Rostoff's influence."

"The better question is why *you're* working the streets of Miami."

"We're not far from my office. I just thought I'd go for a walk and get some fresh air. By the way, how's your lovely sister?"

He'd pushed the right buttons. I decided to keep my mouth shut.

Billy said, "We're not that different, you know."

I held up my left hand—the clean one—and said, "Hold it right there. We could not be *more* different. You're a predator, plain and simple. You're a dirtbag here just like you were in Russia. Leopards don't change their spots."

"Believe what you want, but the truth is that you'll die poor while I live near the beach in Fort Lauderdale."

"Maybe, but you'll die a lot younger than me."

"Is that a threat?"

"A fact. Go ahead and try to point out the old gangsters in Miami. There aren't any. Even the Colombians don't last much past fifty, and that's if they're lucky."

Billy shook his head and said, "Drugs are a dangerous and dirty business."

I leaned in a little closer. "Can I give you some friendly advice?"

"Sure, why not?"

I gently placed my right hand on his shoulder and said, "Your boss is going to go down. You don't have to be on the ship when it sinks."

Billy let out a laugh. "This isn't Russia. There are many rules the police must follow here. I don't think you can harass us for no reason."

I just smiled as I removed my hand. I admired the perfect grease handprint on his otherwise pristine cream suit. "You have a nice day, Billy."

"Same to you, Detective." He turned and left.

I could see my handprint on the suit even from a block away. I knew we had to find the missing girl before the Russians did.

CHAPTER

MAGDA ANDRUSKIEWICZ OPENED her eyes with a start. It wasn't until she glanced up and saw the blue sky past the rough metal roof that her body relaxed slightly. The long ride to the United States in the shipping container with the others had been horrifying. Especially when people started dying. Even the girl she'd worked so hard to comfort in Amsterdam had fallen sick and died the day before they'd arrived in Miami.

Magda wasn't sure if she'd ever be able to sleep indoors again. She'd fled the chaos around the ship where people were shooting and kept running. She'd run and run until she'd realized just how big the city was.

She'd tried to get into a homeless shelter, but it was full for the night. It was warm in Miami, though, and a woman there had told her that she could sleep in the alley behind the shelter. Then the woman had given her two turkey sandwiches. Magda had eaten one immediately and saved the other for the next day.

Now, after a few hours of snatched sleep, Magda had no idea what to do. When she'd waited in

Amsterdam, the woman named Hanna had arranged everything. Here, she knew no one. And after the way they had traveled, Magda no longer trusted Hanna.

She had found herself a little nook between some boxes and a dumpster. After the stench in the container, the scent from the dumpster was like a forest in springtime. A metal roof covered her hiding spot and would keep her dry if it rained.

Several others had come and gone during the night, mostly older men. No one bothered her, which was both a surprise and a relief.

Just before she'd fled the ship, Magda had grabbed the red backpack by instinct, and she was now using it as a pillow. It held a change of clothes and a light jacket.

She sat up and began eating her second turkey sandwich. An older black man wearing a red beret leaned against a wall a few meters from her. He seemed to be staring at her. It made her nervous.

The man must have realized he was upsetting her because he said, "I'm sorry, I didn't mean to scare you. It's just that your sandwich looks good. I'm not allowed to go inside no more because they once caught me with alcohol. That's one of the big rules here. No alcohol and no weapons. I wish I'd paid more attention."

The man had a friendly quality to his round face. Magda liked his beret. Without thinking, she tore her sandwich in two and offered half to the man.

With a broad smile, he stepped over to her and took it, then held it up as if he were about to give a toast. The words PROPERTY OF THE AMERICAN AIR-LINES ARENA were stenciled on his windbreaker.

The older man went to eat his sandwich, and she

tucked herself farther into her nook. She was scared and tired. She prayed to the Blessed Virgin to keep her safe and help her find her brother. She was starting to doubt her own judgment. No way she should have traveled across the Atlantic in a nasty shipping container. She worried about the other people who'd been with her. Where had they all fled?

She finished her sandwich, then laid her head on the backpack, hoping to drift off to sleep for a while. She hummed a lullaby her mother used to sing to her and Joseph when they were little. It had been a long time since she'd felt safe and happy. She missed Joseph. They had been separated during the trip from Poland.

A few minutes later, she heard a new voice. It was louder than any of the others she had heard in the alley.

She peeked between the slats of a pallet next to her and saw a middle-aged homeless man with a white film over one eye speaking to a man in a fancy suit.

CHAPTER 82

MAGDA HAD A bad feeling about the man in the fancy clothes. When she looked more carefully at him, she saw that his goatee was dyed blue, and he had a grease smudge on the shoulder of his cream-colored suit. Just the way he scanned the alley made him seem like a predator. She thought he spoke with an accent, but her English wasn't good enough for her to identify where he was from.

He was talking to a homeless man who had spent the night in the alley using an empty milk carton as a pillow.

The man was smoking a cigarette and sitting on a pallet that had TROPICAL SHIPPING burned into its side. He rocked back and forth slowly, like he was on a ship.

Magda smelled the smoke from his cigarette. It barely masked the man's own body odor.

The man in the suit asked him, "Have you seen any young women around here? Not regulars. Some girls who would've shown up last night."

"Heh, heh, we all want young women," said the homeless man. He was balding, and the little hair he had on the sides of his head shot out in crazy patterns. He laughed. His foggy eye moved in unison with his good eye. The homeless man squinted. "Hey, I know you."

"I don't know how. I don't volunteer in this shithole."

"You work at the club over on Fourth Street." The ash on the homeless man's cigarette slowly grew. A seagull landed near him and pecked at a French fry on the ground.

The man in the suit said, "So what?"

The homeless man said, "You told me to get lost one night. You weren't very nice about it." His voice sounded scratchy, like an old record, but he got his point across: he was mad.

"Did you have the thirty-dollar cover charge?"

"I didn't try to get inside the club. I was just sitting on the sidewalk."

The man in the suit nodded and said, "Oh, panhandling."

"Working."

"Bums scare the customers. We have a certain image."

"You were nasty to me. Why should I help you now?"

The man in the suit reached into his pocket. "For the reward. You help me find some girls I lost last night and I give you a wad of cash."

The homeless man shook his head. "Bullshit. I don't trust you." He looked around at several of the other men; they were ignoring the whole conversation. "I don't think you'd ever pay. So now it's *you* who has to leave. This is *my* alley and I don't want you bothering me." The man stood on unsteady legs from the stacked pallets. He was much smaller than the other man.

The man in the suit just stared. He cut his eyes around the filthy alley to see if anyone intended to help the cocky homeless man.

Then the homeless man barked, "Go." He reached up with his left hand and shoved the man. The long ash from his cigarette broke off and floated down onto a crumpled McDonald's coffee cup.

The man in the suit seemed astonished that someone would speak to him like that, but he recovered quickly.

Magda watched silently as he punched the man with the bad eye. Everyone in the alley looked away. But Magda saw it all. And she knew the man in the suit was searching for her.

The man stayed on his wobbly feet and glared at his attacker. That set the man in the suit off again. He shoved the man onto the stacked pallets, then leaned in and slapped the homeless man hard across the face. "Who the hell do you think you are?" he screamed as he punched the man over and over.

Magda stared, terrified. She looked over and saw the friendly black man in the red beret. She hoped he wouldn't tell anyone she was there.

The man in the suit punched the poor homeless man six times in the face. Blood poured out of his nose and lips and, finally, one of his ears. It left a wild, dark pattern on the patched asphalt of the alley.

He slid off the pallets and lay on the garbage-covered ground, whimpering. Flies were already swarming around his bloody face. One fly stuck in the thick blood on the man's cheek.

The man in the suit cursed at him and kicked him in the ribs several times. When he was finished, he glared around the alley at the other men sitting on broken plastic chairs or stacked boxes. It was a challenge to see if anyone else wanted to cross him.

He disappeared around the corner, and a moment later Magda started to cry.

CHAPTER 83

AFTER MY RUN-IN with Billy, Marie and I continued searching downtown Miami. I had avoided the calls from my boss, but when Stephanie Hall called, I answered.

Stephanie said, "Are you working?"

"Downtown now."

"You've got to be crazy. Do you know how many policies you're violating by coming in the day after a shooting?"

"Miami PD policies or FBI policies?"

"You are the most infuriating man I have ever met."

"Are you telling me *you're* not working? Because if you say you're sitting at home, I won't believe you."

There was a pause. "Maybe I'm at the office with Chill. But we're keeping a low profile. We'll come down to you right now. I checked on Lorena a few minutes ago. She seems to be doing fine."

"I checked on her too. She's definitely doing better than the Russian dude she plugged before he could massacre the rest of us. She better not catch any shit over this."

Steph said, "She won't. It's you I'm worried about."

"Why me?"

Steph said, "I heard the boss talking to some DHS bigwigs. They don't like you. Sounds like you've disrespected them several times in the past few weeks."

"Actually, it's only been this past week. Unless they want to count their screw-up at the airport."

"So you're not worried about it?"

"The only thing I can think about right now is making sure everyone from the shipping container is safe. I put the word out with all the Miami PD and every snitch I ran into on the street that we're still looking for a Polish girl named Magda."

When I finished the call, I turned to Marie, who was just ending a call on her own phone. She looked up at me and said, "My informant in Amsterdam who gets information from Miami says that Rostoff's Russians kidnapped Hanna Greete's daughter from their hotel here in Miami."

"It must have something to do with the way Hanna bungled the offload."

"And what happened with the diamonds."

I noticed excitement in her voice. She usually spoke English slowly and clearly, but now her Dutch accent was pronounced. Police were the same all over—they got excited when they thought they were about to make a decent arrest.

I said, "So the reason I ran into Billy was that he's looking for the diamonds."

"Yes."

"We've got to find that girl Magda first. No matter what."

Marie said, "My informant also says there may

be a tracker in the bag. Even with it, Hanna hasn't been able to locate her."

"Then why haven't the others found her already?"

Marie shrugged.

I said, "Trackers can be finicky. If it's a cheap one, even a metal roof can block the signal." That gave me something to think about.

Around Third Street and Fourth Avenue, when we were checking another one of the homeless shelters, I ran into one of my earliest informants, a tall, lean black man named Titus Barrow, whom everyone called Bulldog.

I pointed him out to Marie and her first question was "Why do they call him Bulldog?"

"You'll figure it out when we talk to him."

Bulldog was standing at his regular corner. He generally sold pot to tourists and crack to his regular customers, although that wasn't a hard-and-fast rule; it was more of a guideline.

As soon as he noticed me, he straightened up and tossed a baggie into the scraggly bushes next to him.

I said, "Don't make me search those bushes, Bulldog."

He mumbled, "Shit, man." Then he turned and squatted to recover the plastic baggie. He handed it over to me without any more complaints.

I think that's when Marie realized how he'd gotten his street name. His lower jaw jutted out and his bottom teeth rested on his upper lip when his mouth was closed, and although he was a thin man, he had drooping jowls.

Bulldog said, "You in narcotics now, Anti?"

"Don't need to be a narcotics detective to spot a shitty dope dealer."

"What's this really about?"

I liked that he was smart enough to realize I didn't give two shits about a minor street dealer. I said, "If you want me to toss this baggie down a sewer, then help us find a missing girl."

Bulldog gave me an odd look.

I said, "The description we have is that she's about sixteen, white, pretty, and blond. She has a thick foreign accent. She's in a world of shit and I need your help."

"I'm your man. What neighborhood you think she in?"

"Maybe downtown near the port. You got my number."

"I'll get everyone I know in on this."

"I expect nothing less."

Now I had a small army helping me find the missing girl.

HANNA WAS DESPERATE to find her daughter. She couldn't even think about what Josie might be going through. She didn't believe the Russians would hurt Josie as long as they thought Hanna was getting them what they wanted. She had to find the Polish girl and the backpack—today.

She and Albert had cruised the streets near the port in an expanding pattern. She just didn't have enough contacts in Miami to reach out for help.

Albert paced nervously next to her. His hand rarely left the butt of the pistol he'd bought. Near the interstate, in an area that clearly wasn't visited by tourists, they checked homeless shelters. They had just walked through a shelter for homeless youth. The woman who ran the place wasn't friendly, but she was efficient. She marched them through the nine rooms used to house young people, four of them per room. She spoke with a drawl that made it difficult for Hanna to understand her.

The woman said, "We get new kids most every day."

Hanna noted the grimy walls and small, thin mattresses laid on the bare floor. It was spare, but probably better than sleeping in the street.

The woman said, "We don't ask no questions. That's why kids come here."

Hanna thanked her, and she and Albert left.

Outside, a young man with tattoos around his neck and upper arms rushed up to them and said, "I heard you asking about a missing girl."

Hanna showed him a photo of Magda on her phone. "Where can we find her?"

"Is there a reward?"

"Yes. Cash."

"How much?"

Hanna rummaged in her small purse and thumbed through the wad of cash Albert had taken from the hotel clerk. She looked up at the young man and said, "Five hundred dollars."

The tattooed kid turned his head in one direction, then the other. He played with the metal stud sticking out of his lower lip. He reached in his pocket and paused.

When his hand came out of his pocket, it held a knife. He raised it to Hanna's face. As he moved, the young man said, "Give me the cash. Maybe I'll find the girl later."

Before Hanna could answer, Albert had his hand around the kid's throat. He mashed the barrel of his pistol hard against the young man's temple.

Without a word, the young man dropped the knife and took a step back. Albert faced him and said, "Tell me the truth. Have you seen the girl? Do you know where she is? Anything other than the truth will be the last thing you ever say. Understand?"

Albert pushed him against a wall. The young man

was shaking. The pistol was still pressed against his temple.

The young man swallowed hard, then gathered the courage to say, "I swear to God, I never seen that girl before. I just needed money."

Albert said, "Then give me a reason not to blow your head off."

The kid said, "There are a bunch of other homeless shelters. That's where I'd look."

Albert pulled the pistol back to smack the would-be robber in the face, but Hanna caught his wrist and said, "We have other things to do. C'mon, Albert."

CHAPTER 85

THEY TOOK THE tattooed kid's advice and started searching south of the port. It was now stretching into the afternoon, but Hanna was far too panicked about her daughter to give up.

On almost every street, Albert constantly swiveled his head, looking in every direction. He was afraid they were being watched.

Hanna said, "Who would be watching us?"

"I don't know. The police. The Russians. This is not paranoia."

"You're right. It's gone past paranoia. I agree we can't trust anyone, but the police don't know we're here, and the Russians already have Josie." She hadn't meant to raise her voice so much, but she was losing patience with her brother.

Behind one homeless shelter in downtown Miami, they noticed an alley where several people were lying on blankets or sitting on pallets. Hanna couldn't pass it by. When she stepped into the alley, the first thing she saw was a man who had been savagely beaten recently. He was holding a bloody towel to his forehead. His nose looked like it had been broken. Both of his eyes had swollen almost shut. His lower lip was split and clearly needed stitches.

No one there seemed too concerned about the man's injuries.

Hanna looked down the wide alley at the make-shift beds and chairs lining the walls. A rat crossed the uneven asphalt with no fear of the humans. The smell of urine and alcohol washed over her. She gave an involuntary shudder. She looked up at the six-story building with cheap air conditioners jammed into its windows. This was not where the rich people of Miami lived.

A round-faced older black man wearing a red military beret with the emblem ripped off looked up at her from his seat.

She stepped over to him and said, "Excuse me, we're looking for a missing girl." She held up her phone with the picture of Magda.

The man studied the photo on the small phone, then nervously glanced over at the man with the bloody face. Then he looked up at Hanna and said, "Why are you looking for her?"

The question surprised Hanna.

Albert snapped, "Why are you asking? Have you seen her or not?"

The older man studied the photo for a moment, then said, "No young women come here. You might want to check over on Miami Avenue. That's where most of the runaways go."

Albert stared at the old man, trying to intimidate him.

The man in the beret gestured at the bloody man and said, "A nasty Russian dude has already been here looking for her. She's a popular young woman. Good luck."

Hanna nodded her thanks.

CHAPTER 86

MIAMI IS A compact city with an easy street-numbering system. It's not until you're looking for someone that it seems vast.

In the middle of the afternoon, my phone rang. The name that came up on my screen was BULLDOG.

I looked at Marie and nodded as I answered the phone. "Talk to me."

Bulldog said, "Meet me over on Biscayne between Fifth and Sixth where the hot-dog vendor in the bikini sits."

"Did you find her?"

"Toss that baggie now." He let out his signature laugh. It sounded like a small pig grunting.

Bulldog was there waiting for us when we got to the meeting point. When I saw him, I said, "If this is some kind of prank—"

Bulldog held up his hand. "I get it. You don't trust me much. I done you right this time."

"How'd you find her so fast?"

"I know people. Kinda like you, but I don't scare them shitless just by showing up."

"Where's the girl?"

Bulldog said, "Behind them pallets. She's safe and

sound. My man Reggie, the older dude in the red beanie, looked after her. He said all kinds of people been by asking for her today. One of them was a nasty Russian who slapped around one of the other homeless guys."

Marie walked past us straight to the rear of the alley. She weaved between makeshift beds, old chairs, and broken furniture.

I waited with Bulldog so as not to scare the girl. It looked like Marie was coaxing a frightened cat out of a tree. It took a while before I saw a hand reach out and touch Marie's outstretched hand. A moment later, Marie couldn't restrain herself and gave the girl a hug.

Apparently, that was all this girl needed. She wrapped her arms around Marie and began to sob. The girl started to speak quickly in what I thought was Russian but then realized was Polish.

Marie calmed the girl down and brushed her blond hair out of her pretty face. The girl picked up a red backpack and walked toward me. Marie slipped an arm around the girl's shoulder.

Marie introduced us and I said, "Nice to meet you, Magda."

Magda turned to Bulldog's friend Reggie, who was sitting in a sketchy green plastic chair with one of the legs cracked. In heavily accented English she said, "Thank you for not telling Hanna I was hiding in the back of the alley."

The man said, "Thank you for the turkey sandwich." He looked over at me, then back to her. "Everyone knows who Anti is. He'll treat you right," he said.

That was the best compliment I'd ever gotten. I handed the man a twenty and said, "Thanks for looking after her."

CHAPTER 87

TEN MINUTES LATER, Magda was sprawled on a beanbag chair in the witness room at the Miami Police Department. No one had seen us bring her in, which was how I'd wanted it.

I wasn't going to let social services take this girl off to some cold facility. Unlike interview rooms, these rooms had a touch of home. There were photos on the walls here, pictures of people riding bikes or going to the beach. Each wall was a different, calming color, not the industrial white or tan found throughout the rest of the building.

A green couch someone had brought from home stretched across the back wall. Magda had gone straight for the beanbag, and Marie leaned in close from a standard hard wooden chair. Most of the pizza I'd bought was gone from the open box on the folding table.

We'd immediately connected Magda's surname, Andruskiewicz, to Joseph, the young pianist in the group of children we'd rescued at the Miami airport.

The raw emotion on Magda's face when Marie told her she knew where her brother was made everything I had done in this case worthwhile. She started to cry and laugh at the same time. By now her eyes were bloodshot, but she kept smiling and asking about Joseph and the others who'd been in the container with her; they were like family to her now.

Marie assured Magda she'd be able to speak to her brother shortly. First, we needed to know more about her ordeal so we could construct a case around her statement.

Magda calmed down and talked to us through occasional sniffles. "When I saw the container, I got scared. It didn't look safe. Hanna kept leading more and more people inside. By then, it was too late to back out."

Marie interrupted with a few questions, looking for details.

Magda said, "I cried the first day in the container. A lot of us did. But toward the end, it got so much worse." She had to stop and blow her nose.

She identified Hanna Greete and her brother, Albert. That, along with some of the information Marie had gathered, was enough to make a decent case against them. But I was after bigger game.

I'd been careful not to inject myself into the interview too much so far. Now I asked, "Did you meet any Russians during all this?"

She shook her head. Then she said, "Perhaps. I'm not very good with English." She paused, gathered her thoughts, and said, "I'm not very good with *accents* in English. There was one man. He beat a homeless man. Beat him badly. Blood everywhere."

"What did the attacker look like?"

She gave a vague description, but when she mentioned the blue goatee, I knew who it was. I told her, "He'll get what he deserves soon enough. You're safe now. You'll be back with your brother before long."

Marie handed the teenager a cell phone and coaxed her to speak. Magda said, "Hello?" Then: "Joseph?" I heard the catch in her voice as she realized who she was talking to. She spoke rapidly in Polish, alternating between laughing, squealing, and weeping.

This was the kind of day I lived for.

CHAPTER 88

I HAD THE whole team meet me east of Biscayne Boulevard in the parking lot between a Holiday Inn and Bayfront Park. The H and I in the first word of the motel's sign had faded. It had been like that for so long, some of the street people called it the "Olday Inn." It was known for cheap rooms in an expensive city.

Stephanie and Chill pulled up about the same time and we met next to my car.

Neither of them wore completely civilian clothes. Tactical pants and polo shirts covering the guns on their hips would fool most of the public, but criminals, street people, and other cops could always spot a plainclothes cop.

Lorena Perez had had to sit this deal out. She was on a ten-day leave while the shooting on the ship was investigated, standard practice in most police agencies. I'd called her earlier in the day, and I could tell she wanted to be out here with us. I would've liked to have her. She'd proven how tough and tactically sound she was last night.

I remembered my first shooting. Shit, I still dreamed about it.

I'd pulled over a shitty, beat-up Dodge Charger for running a stop sign. That kind of stop, it's simple: You give a lecture and let 'em go, unless they have attitude. For attitude, you might give the guy a ticket, although it's not like anyone ever pays 'em. There's a competition in parts of Miami to see how many tickets a single person can rack up. (The current record, sixty-one, is held by a lawn-service worker in Allapattah.)

As I approached the Charger, I noticed how dark the windows were tinted. I couldn't see a thing in there. Before the alarm traveled to my brain, someone poked a TEC-9 out of a cracked-open window.

You've heard of an *Oh, shit* moment? I literally said, "Oh, shit," as I fell back, drawing my service weapon as I went down. I don't know how many times the asshole in the car fired. I'm not even sure how many times *I* fired. I just pulled the trigger on my way to the ground. Forensics later found three slugs in a parked car and one in a tree behind me.

The car squealed away, but three hours later, a twenty-two-year-old convicted carjacker showed up at Jackson Memorial with a bullet deep in his shoulder and a wounded left ear. The surgeon later told me it was almost a perfect circle in his lobe, like the wide-gauge ear-piercings kids have. The surgeon was amused. He'd seen a lot of bullet wounds, but this was the most entertaining.

Good for him, but personally, I've never found bullet wounds or gunfights entertaining.

I was on leave for only three days before I was cleared of the shooting, but it left me shaky. For almost six months after that, I was nervous whenever I approached a car. It didn't help when the shooter pleaded guilty and got only a year in the county jail. There are always side effects to a shooting for a cop. And the effects are cumulative.

I hoped Lorena snapped back quickly. Like any nice Cuban girl born in Miami, she had plenty of family around her. The same family that had begged her not to go into police work in the first place. I once met her father, a dermatologist who lived in Weston. He didn't seem like he would ever give up trying to convince his daughter that it wasn't too late for her to become an accountant.

I briefed Chill and Steph about finding Magda, now safe at the station with my friend Tosha watching her, and told them that Miami Police had located all the other people from the container.

Chill said, "What now?"

"We can make a case against the traffickers from Amsterdam, but it's the Russians I want to tie up in this mess. No way we can let them skate," I said.

"Can't let that prick Rostoff get away with shit like this."

I agreed with him.

"How do we find the Dutch traffickers?" Steph said. "They could be anywhere."

I smiled. "We make them come to us." I grabbed a backpack from inside my car and started walking toward the band shell in Bayfront Park.

I intended to let the cheap tracker and wide-open sky do some legwork for us.

CHAPTER 89

HANNA AND ALBERT brooded on a bench near Miami Dade College's downtown campus. Hanna had just checked on Tasi, who was recovering from her injuries at a hotel in Little Havana. Earlier in the morning, they had left her lying on a king-size bed with ice bags on her face.

Hanna had never seen her brother hang his head before, but right now, his head was drooping toward the sidewalk.

Hanna thought about Josie and started to cry. Her brother put his arm around her shoulder and pulled her tight to him. He said, "We'll get her back."

"How? We need that backpack."

"I have several plans ready. By the time I'm done with Billy and his friends, there won't be many people left in Miami who speak Russian."

Hanna shook her head. "I can't risk Josie. We're going to negotiate." She stared hard at her brother and said, "Understand?"

Albert nodded.

Hanna thought about her own teenage years, about the abuse she took from her father. Albert would always step between the two of them. She didn't know how many beatings her brother had taken for her, but it was more than she could ever pay back. And he was still willing to risk everything for her and her daughter.

This had all turned into a tremendous mess, and Hanna had no idea how to fix it. She decided that if she hadn't found Magda and the bag by tonight, she would meet Billy the Russian in person and see what she could give him in exchange for her daughter. It was a sobering and terrifying prospect.

Hanna wondered what she could offer Rostoff instead of the diamonds. They would probably take Albert, just so they could exact revenge. She wasn't going to sacrifice her brother. But she would sacrifice herself if need be.

She didn't like the idea. She'd go back to work as a prostitute, as she'd done in her early twenties, to pay off her debt to the Russians. She'd do it happily if it meant Josie was safe.

Hanna considered all the selling points she could make during the negotiation. If the Russians took her as payment, they'd have an experienced woman who could handle herself in different situations. Plus the Russians would eliminate their competition in Amsterdam. The Russians were always looking for an edge in business. She could make the argument that this would give it to them.

Albert perked up on the bench next to her. He nudged her and held up his phone. "Look, look. We're getting a clear signal." He held the iPhone out so they could both look at the tiny map with a flashing blue dot that had appeared on the screen.

Hanna sat up straight and said, "Is that the tracker? Where's the signal coming from?"

Albert said, "Close by." He raised his eyes and

looked across the street, then north toward the American Airlines Arena. "She's real close. Maybe over in that park."

He stood up and started moving in that direction, holding the phone out in front of him.

For the first time in a couple of days, Hanna felt real hope.

CHAPTER 90

I SAT ALONE at a picnic table just in front of the park's concert band shell, Biscayne Bay behind me. Marie waited in my car because this was not the right time to have her in public and meeting people. I'd been careful to place my team in the right spots. I kept up a calm demeanor, but I had no illusions about what could go wrong. It wasn't just my safety—the whole team could be at risk. If the Russians showed up, we'd probably be outnumbered and outgunned.

A few cars rolled along Biscayne Boulevard. It was the perfect place to sit and watch for surprises. The red backpack sat on the table with nothing blocking the signal from the tracker. My pistol sat in my lap under the table, though I hoped it didn't come down to fast gunplay. I wanted to be ready just in case. This was all my plan, from start to finish. No one else could be blamed if it went wrong. That was exactly how I wanted it.

It was a beautiful Miami afternoon with a breeze off the ocean. The sun was starting to dip behind some of the taller buildings, and I thought I could see some buzzards roosting on the state building downtown. It was one of the more famous quirks of the Magic City; no one had ever explained why the buzzards preferred that building.

I felt a trickle of sweat run down my back. It was nerves, I knew. A good cop doesn't ignore little signs like perspiration. I took a breath and thought about how this might play out.

I'd never dealt with Dutch criminals before, but from what I'd heard about Albert Greete, he was a badass through and through. In Miami, I could usually spot badasses. They weren't the guys in muscle shirts with big biceps; those were the showy loudmouths. The truly dangerous people in Miami were quiet and watched everything. They noticed when other people were nervous or tried to signal partners. The quiet, dangerous people never gave you a second chance.

If this Dutch dude Albert and his sister, Hanna, were like that, I had plenty to worry about. And that's why I had kept Marie out of sight.

Then I spotted them. They weren't hiding their approach. A man and a woman in their thirties walking across the parking lot, weaving between the cars.

The woman, Hanna, was very attractive, with brown hair and a lean, athletic body.

Her brother looked exactly like I'd expected him to—jeans, a loose shirt to cover a gun, and eyes that were fixed on me. He was shorter than me but in good shape, with broad shoulders and thinning hair. He was not intimidated.

Behind them, casually waiting by parked cars, were my partners and Marie Meijer.

Now the brother and sister were absolutely

focused on me. They saw the backpack in plain sight and clearly wanted to discuss it. That meant Albert wasn't checking his surroundings and didn't see Steph and Chill start to follow him at a distance.

Hanna appeared calm as she approached. Maybe it was because she realized I was waiting for them.

When they were five yards away, they stopped directly in front of me. There were no civilians anywhere in the park. Looking at it tactically and as a police officer, I'd say the setting was perfect.

Hanna said in accented English, "You're the man we saw with Marie Meijer in Amsterdam. So you're a cop too."

I waited in silence for a few moments, then said, "My name is Tom Moon. I'm a Miami police detective." I kept a close watch on her brother as he gave me the stink-eye. I could tell Albert was used to people crumbling under his stare. *Welcome to Miami, pal.*

Hanna said, "At least you don't work for the Rostoffs."

Her brother added, "Or do you?"

I let out a laugh. "I would gladly trade you two if I could arrest Roman Rostoff."

That seemed to satisfy them.

Hanna said, "So what do we do now?"

"Before you do anything stupid, I should probably point out that there are two armed federal agents behind you."

Albert's head snapped around as he swiveled to look behind him.

Chill smiled and waved with his left hand; his right hand held a Glock nine-millimeter.

Steph held her own Glock along the seam of her pants.

Albert turned so they could see his hand was on his gun too.

Just another day in Miami.

CHAPTER 91

I STARED AT the two Dutch human traffickers. I was not particularly shocked that everyone standing around me held a gun. I was holding one too, just not as obviously. On the bright side, no one had been shot yet. That was a plus.

A flutter of nerves ran through me. I had to look at my overall plan and take a few risks.

Hanna said, "No one would benefit from a gunfight. I have only one goal—to save my daughter."

Steph Hall said, "Then tell your brother to drop his pistol. Have him put down the gun and we'll talk."

I was glad we had Marie stashed in one of the cars for now.

Hanna looked around at each of us, trying to decide what to do, for what felt like an hour. Her brother, meanwhile, was sizing us up, assessing whom to shoot first and what would be his best escape route. There was something about Albert that set me on edge, though I guessed he would hold off on using the gun. I assumed he didn't want to risk his sister being shot.

I took a breath, trying to keep calm in case I had

to start shooting. I gripped my pistol tighter; it was still hidden from view under the table. I calculated how long it would take me to raise it.

Both Chill and Steph showed great tactical sense by standing off to the side in case I did exactly that. It was just another example of our team starting to jell.

Albert raised his left hand and opened his fingers wide as he said, "What if we compromise?" He held his pistol in his right hand with only two fingers and slowly tucked it into the waistband of his jeans.

Normally, a cop would never let that kind of bullshit go. But this wasn't a normal situation and these weren't our typical Miami knuckleheads. I was sensing a possible inroad to the Rostoff organization if we played this right.

I kept the gun in my hand as I calmly said, "Tell me what happened to your daughter."

Hanna surprised me by stepping over to the picnic table. She sat on the bench directly across from me. She had a pretty face and piercing brown eyes.

She said, "My daughter, Josie, was kidnapped last night from a hotel near the airport. The kidnappers will exchange her for some diamonds that are in that pack. I don't think we have any other options. We couldn't get her back if we were on the run for killing three police officers. That is, if we even managed to walk away from a gunfight. You have to believe me—the only thing that matters to me is getting my daughter back."

I thought about that for a moment, then said, "Do you know the people who took your daughter?"

"The man I've been talking to is named Billy—"

I said, "Does he have a goatee that's dyed blue?"

Her face told me we were dealing with Billy the Blade.

CHAPTER 92

I LISTENED TO Hanna with an open mind. Steph Hall holstered her pistol.

Albert looked at Steph like Wile E. Coyote looked at the Road Runner. He had no interest in becoming friends.

Hanna finished explaining about the diamonds and her daughter and the Russians. We sat in silence for a few moments. Then I said, "We could help you get your daughter back."

"This man, Billy, is no fool. I know he'll kill her if he has any hint the police are involved. The only way to get her back is to trade the diamonds for her. If you let me do that, I will turn myself in, I'll testify against Billy, I'll do anything. But I have to get my daughter back first."

She was direct and to the point. It left me stumped. I wanted Hanna's daughter returned safely too. I hadn't forgotten that Hanna was a human trafficker who'd ruined the lives of dozens of people and allowed at least four of them to die, but that didn't mean her daughter had to die as well.

I thought about it, and I was thankful no one felt the need to fill the silence with useless chatter. But

I kept an eye on Albert. He was a wild card who might be a little crazy.

I looked from Steph to Chill. I bet they were great poker players, because they didn't give me a hint of what they were thinking.

Finally, I slid the backpack across the table to Hanna. The look on her face told me how shocked she was.

She wasn't the only one.

Steph said, "Wait a minute."

"Take it and go," I told Hanna. "Get your daughter back."

I tried not to chuckle at the confused expression on Albert's face. A hard-core criminal like him wasn't used to a helping hand from the police.

I sat in silence as we watched the brother and sister walk west across the parking lot, the backpack slung over Hanna's left shoulder.

I knew the conversation with my partners was going to be interesting.

CHAPTER 93

STEPH HALL PLOPPED onto the bench across from me. Outrage was written across her face. "Are you insane?" she practically shouted.

I shrugged and said, "Possibly. I'd have to blame it on my DNA."

Chill, standing in front of me, said, "Not cool, Anti. We worked hard for that arrest. We deserved it."

"You know as well as I do that Billy the Blade is not gonna fool around. He wouldn't think twice about slitting that girl's throat. Hell, I've seen his handiwork over on Hallandale Beach." I looked at Steph and Chill as I let them think about what might happen to that girl. "I had to let Hanna leave with the backpack. I'm sorry, but the FBI would only screw up the rescue. None of you can tell me a girl's life is worth a few diamonds."

Steph regained her composure and said, "You don't have the authority to give away evidence and let human traffickers leave."

"And yet that's what I just did."

Chill said, "It's not even legal."

I shook my head and said, "No, it's not necessarily legal, but it's the right thing to do."

I motioned for Chill to join us at the picnic table. Now I had my annoyed coworkers sitting around me. They were not in the mood to hear me explain my reasoning, but I guessed I'd earned enough credit for them to let me speak.

I said, "Everything is going according to plan."

Steph said, "Your plan was to give away a fortune in evidence and let our main suspects go?"

I said, "How did they know to come to the park to find the bag? Because they have a tracker sewn into the backpack." I pulled out my iPhone and brought up a display. "Do you think that's the only tracker in the world? Chill gave me a bag of electronics that included trackers a few weeks ago." I held up my phone to show them the little map with the flashing signal. I said, "Looks like they're still on foot. The tracker should lead us directly to the Russians. We might be able to wrap this whole thing up after they get the girl back."

Steph stood up quickly and said, "We have to start following them. It'll take a few minutes to get the surveillance organized."

I unclipped the compact Miami police radio from my belt, mashed the button, and said, "Smooth Jazz, do you have eyes on the target?"

Alvin Teague's voice came over the radio. "They're about to get into a blue Chevy rental car and I have the tracker on my phone. I have detectives in each direction on Biscayne. This'll be the easiest surveillance in history."

I looked up at Steph, who was staring at me with an open mouth. All I could say was "Teague may be a pompous ass, but he's one hell of a good cop."

I would enjoy the memory of that look on her face for the rest of my life.

CHAPTER 94

HANNA GREETE WAS still in shock that the big cop had handed over the backpack without even asking for a bribe. Albert checked to make sure the diamonds were still in place. The police hadn't even bothered to open up the strap. The diamonds were still there, a ridge under the fabric.

Hanna had only one goal—to get Josie back safely.

Now she and Albert sat in La Carreta, a Cuban restaurant on Eighth Street in Little Havana. Albert had eaten some kind of ham sandwich. She had picked at chips that looked like they were made out of bananas and stared at her phone.

Finally, she called Billy, afraid of what he might say.

Billy answered the phone with his usual exuberance, shouting, "Hello, Hanna!"

"How quickly can you meet us?" Hanna asked.

"Do you have the diamonds?"

"Is Josie safe?"

"How could you think I would do anything to this sweet little girl? But don't forget, I know I can live without the diamonds. Can you live without your daughter?"

Hanna didn't mean for there to be silence on the line, but she had no response. Just the way he'd said that sent a chill through her body.

Billy said, "I can meet you in one hour in South Beach. On the sidewalk across from the Clevelander Hotel, near the beach."

"Put Josie on the phone. I have to know that she's safe," Hanna said.

"You won't take my word for it?"

"Put her on the phone." Hanna purposely kept her tone even and spoke very slowly so there would be no misunderstanding. After a long silence, Hanna heard a whimper on the other end of the phone. "Josie? Is that you, sweetheart?"

"Mama?" Then there was a bout of sobbing.

"Are you okay, Josie?" Hanna waited while someone spoke to her daughter away from the phone.

Josie came back on, sniffled, and said, "Help me, Mama. The man with the blue beard says he'll use his knife on my throat if you don't meet him." She started to say something else but the phone was snatched from her.

Hanna gasped, trying not to picture what Billy might do to her daughter.

Billy came back on the line and said, "I look forward to seeing you in an hour."

"Bring Josie."

"Of course. I wouldn't deny a mother the chance to watch her daughter's throat slit if things don't go exactly as planned. If the diamonds aren't in my hand in one hour, you'll never see your precious daughter again."

He said goodbye, never dropping his friendly tone.

Hanna hung up and looked at her brother. "We have one hour to meet them over on South Beach."

She couldn't read the look in Albert's eyes.

CHAPTER 95

HANNA ALMOST LEFT her brother in Little Havana.

She said, "I need to know you won't do anything crazy, Albert."

"Define *crazy*."

She growled in frustration.

South Beach was only a few miles from downtown Miami, but it felt like a different world. The crowds of pedestrians along Ocean Drive seemed much younger than the people along Brickell or Bayshore Drive.

The Clevelander Hotel sat on the corner of Tenth and Ocean Drive in the Miami Art Deco District. Hanna had heard of the old five-story hotel, but she'd just read an article in the Miami paper that said the only thing the Clevelander was known for now was loud music by the pool and a TV sports show called *Highly Questionable* that was taped in the hotel every afternoon.

Albert drove past the hotel so they could both get a look at the area, but there were too many people to see much, so Hanna told him to drop her near the Clevelander.

"Albert, I'm not kidding, I want you to stay in the car. I'm not going to risk Josie."

Albert said, "And I'm not going to risk both of you. If something goes wrong, I have to be close enough to act."

Hanna knew it was useless to argue with her hardheaded brother, and she appreciated how much he worried about her. She started to slip out of the car, then paused, leaned across the console, and kissed Albert on the cheek. "You're a good brother and a good man. Josie and I both love you."

She was out of the car before Albert could say anything. She didn't want to make it sound like she was saying goodbye, but, just in case, she was.

The backpack rested over her left shoulder. She could feel the diamonds sewn into the strap.

Hanna darted through a break in traffic on Ocean Drive. A red Ferrari swerved to avoid her. Groups of young partyers just starting out their night laughed and shouted as they passed her. She wondered if it was this loud all the time. If you were looking west, away from the ocean, this could be a sunnier, wider Amsterdam.

She twisted her head, scanning in every direction, but she didn't see Billy or any of his henchmen. There were still a number of people sitting on the beach as the sun set over the city behind them.

She cut down a path and saw, through a gap between the bushes and the sand, Billy sitting at a picnic table. Hanna couldn't help looking over her shoulder to make sure Albert hadn't followed her. She caught a glimpse of him across the street, still sitting in the rental car.

He was watching her every step.

She approached the picnic table and Billy. As

she got closer, her heart soared at the sight of her daughter, Josie, sitting next to Billy. Josie's hands were folded on the table and her eyes were cast down. But she appeared unharmed.

The smile Billy gave her made her angry. When they'd first met, Hanna had liked his easygoing style. Now she realized it just masked a sociopath. When this was all over and she had Josie safely in her arms, she might let Albert kill this Russian son of a bitch.

CHAPTER 96

I KNEW ALVIN Teague would be able to conduct a quiet surveillance of Hanna Greete and her brother. I had my own issues to deal with.

Marie had a ton of questions, so I filled her in on everything. She looked at the road and said, "I might have been a complication at a meeting like that."

As soon as I'd crossed the MacArthur Causeway to Miami Beach, following the general path of the tracker I'd put in the red backpack, my phone rang—my office. No way that was good news. I decided I couldn't avoid my supervisor any longer. Hopefully, if I walked him through this carefully, he wouldn't get too nervous. I answered the phone with a friendly "Hey, boss."

The voice on the other end did not belong to the FBI supervisor in charge of the international crimes task force. That was clear.

The first thing I heard was a man with a harsh Brooklyn accent almost screaming, "Don't give me that 'Hey, boss,' bullshit. This is Martin Lobbeler, assistant special agent in charge of the FBI. I'm your supervisor's boss. The asshole who has to listen to your presentations and local-cop view of events. You know, the presentations I usually ignore."

"Yes, sir. What can I do for you?" I needed to keep this professional.

"One thing I don't need is a cowboy like you coming in and working after a shooting. Do you know how it looks for the Bureau to have to hold a press conference about a shooting? You've pulled a lot of shit, including not keeping your supervisory special agent in the loop. And I don't need a local cop stirring up shit with other federal agencies."

"Like which agencies, sir?"

"Like DHS."

"Sir, I'd like—"

"I thought you were supposed to be smart. They told me you had a law degree from the University of Miami, but you're not acting smart. I'm going to be talking to your chief tomorrow. You'll be back in uniform writing tickets."

I couldn't help myself. "In that case, be prepared for a shitload of parking tickets on your car." So much for professionalism. "I'm trying to make a good arrest and I'm sure not getting much support from jerk-offs like you."

I was about to hang up when my supervisor's voice came on the line. He spoke quietly, probably trying to keep the ASAC from hearing. "Calm down, Tom."

"But that idiot ASAC just told me I'm off the task force right when we're in the middle of an operation."

"He said he'd talk to your chief *tomorrow.* Today you're still a member of the task force and a sworn Miami police officer. I expect you to use your best judgment the rest of the day. Do what you think is right, and we'll see what your chief has to say tomorrow. Am I understood?"

I sat in my car, silent. Had my meek and mild supervisor just given me a green light to move forward on this operation? That was sure what it sounded like to me.

Carefully I said, "I hear what you're saying. I'll call you when we resolve the current situation. I think you'll be happy with the progress we've made on the case."

My supervisor said, "You mean the human-trafficking case that I will attribute to Steph Hall if necessary?"

"That's exactly the case I mean." This guy was full of surprises. He already had a way of accounting for the arrests even if I got fired from the task force. That's all I wanted right now. Just a little leeway to do the right thing.

I could always practice law if I had to.

CHAPTER 97

I MET UP with the others in a parking lot behind the Regal Cinema on Lincoln Road. I kept quiet for a minute. I was surprised at how much the angry ASAC's threat bothered me. I really did love working on this task force. But there was no question that the only thing I cared about now was saving Hanna's daughter from the Russians and dropping a big net on as many human traffickers as possible.

An FBI ASAC was not usually involved in operations. For the most part, the ASACs were administrators, and like all administrators, they could be a help or a hindrance. I didn't like him saying that I was a cowboy. Just because I didn't follow the FBI rules didn't mean I was a cowboy. I didn't risk my partners' lives and I always made clean cases that held up in court.

Steph and Chill came up to my car as I was on the radio with Alvin Teague. "Do you have eyes on the target, Smooth Jazz?"

"Ten-four. There's no one we can't follow in the city."

"Especially when you have a tracker on them."

"I barely even looked at it."

"Right. And I was a great football player in college." I purposely said it over the radio so anyone who was helping me would get a good laugh. Now I got more serious and turned to my partners in front of me.

"As soon as Hanna has the girl, we'll swoop in. Smooth Jazz and the other Miami cops know to look after the girl and her mother. That leaves us able to focus on the Russians."

I looked at Marie. "You don't have tactical gear or a gun. I don't want to risk—"

She held up a hand. "I know, I'm a civilian here. Just like you were in Amsterdam. Yet, by chance, you still got involved in our operation when the suspects ran. I'll use common sense. I'll help with the daughter if I'm needed."

I nodded. She'd made it easy for me.

Chill had a half smile on his face. I knew the ATF agent liked the idea of the three of us going against the Russians. I knew he had an ax to grind with Rostoff. I just hoped he didn't do anything crazy.

On the radio, Smooth Jazz said, "The woman is out of the car and crossing Ocean Drive almost in front of the Clevelander. It looks like the male driver is staying with the rental car. She's looking for someone on the beach side of the road."

I grabbed the radio. "Be there in two minutes. Can you keep eyes on the female? She's the one who'll meet the Russians."

Alvin Teague said, "You forget who you're talking to? I can keep eyes on anyone."

I needed to hear that confidence about now.

CHAPTER 98

HANNA GREETE'S LEGS trembled as she headed down the gentle slope of the green area between the street and the beach to the picnic table where Josie was sitting quietly next to Billy the Russian.

Mosquitoes buzzed around her as she approached. She caught a glimpse of couples on the beach gazing out at the Atlantic. This would be a lovely place if it weren't for these crazy Russians.

She had no qualms about giving up the backpack and the diamonds in exchange for her daughter. Her human-trafficking endeavor might not have gone the way she'd planned, but right now all she wanted was Josie safe.

Billy stood up like a gentleman when she reached the picnic table. He held out his hand to show Hanna he wanted her to sit on the bench across from them. He was also telling her not to do anything stupid.

Hanna fought the urge to embrace Josie and forced herself to sit down across from the smiling Russian. She didn't look at Josie because she didn't want to reveal the wave of emotions swirling through her. Her baby was safe. At least for now.

Billy sat and stroked his blue goatee while his brown eyes assessed her. They sat in silence for a few moments. A Mustang revved its engine along Ocean Drive. The occasional sound of the band around the pool at the Clevelander Hotel floated in the humid air.

Billy said, "Hanna, so happy you could join us."

Hanna didn't say a word. She was terrified. She kept her hands in her lap so the Russian wouldn't see them shake. It was all she could do not to break down and scream. She had to stay calm for her daughter. She glanced at Josie, and the look in her eyes told Hanna she was traumatized. It was the first time ever that Hanna had wished she had a gun. If she'd had one, she would've shot Billy in the face.

Her eyes flicked up quickly to where Albert sat in the car. She had been right not to let him come with her to this meeting. But she had to admit there was a certain degree of security in knowing he was close by.

The short strip of greenery here, with the bushes and a few palm trees, changed the atmosphere from up on the strip. In other circumstances, it would be calming. The waves gently rolled onto the beach, making a steady noise that competed with the band at the Clevelander.

Billy smiled at Josie and ran the back of his fingers along her cheek. It made Hanna's skin crawl.

Billy said, "Do you have what I want?"

Hanna just nodded.

"With you?"

She hesitated. If he knew the diamonds were in the backpack she'd carefully set on the ground behind her, he might decide to eliminate both witnesses right there. Now she wondered if she'd made a mistake by coming here without Albert.

Billy's response to her silence was to yank Josie closer to him. He laid an open Buck knife on the table and smiled.

Hanna said, "There's no need for violence. The diamonds are in the backpack."

Billy laughed and clapped his hands. "You've given us quite the runaround."

Hanna didn't answer. She saw two men in suits step off the sidewalk and head toward them. Two more men appeared from behind her, and then a fifth man in a black suit started walking toward them. Billy's loud clap had signaled them.

The man in the black suit was a little older than Billy, about forty-five. He didn't show the deference to him the others did, and he came right up to the table. He addressed Billy in Russian and they argued briefly about something. Then the man marched away toward the beach like a sulking child.

Hanna said, "You annoy everyone, not just me."

Billy turned to Hanna and said, "You'll thank God if all I do is annoy you."

He was hard to fluster.

Billy said, "Give me the backpack."

"Give me my daughter."

Now Billy lost his good humor and leaned forward. "What have I done to make you think this is a negotiation? That knife could be in her eye before you say, 'Don't do it.'"

Hanna reached behind her and lifted the pack. Even under the weight of it, her hand shook wildly. She tossed it onto the picnic table.

Billy stared, a grin on his face.

Hanna ran her finger along the ridge of diamonds to show him they were in the strap.

Billy mumbled, "Clever." He looked up at his men, then at the backpack again.

Hanna said, "Josie, let's go." She stood up to emphasize that she was done talking.

Billy held up one hand and said, "I'm sorry, you can't leave just yet."

Hanna slowly sat back down. "Why? I have nothing left to give you."

"We need your brother."

That caught her by surprise. She just stared at the handsome Russian. Finally she said, "Albert? He's not part of this. I had the diamonds and I just gave them to you. Our deal was that you would give me my daughter for the diamonds."

Billy cut his eyes to the man standing behind Hanna. He shook his head and said, "No, I just said I had to have the diamonds or you wouldn't *see* your daughter again. You can see her. She's safe. If you want her back, I need your brother in her place."

"You can't expect me to sacrifice my brother."

Billy shrugged. "You can sacrifice your daughter if you prefer. Your choice." He gave a quick laugh and said, "Too bad your name's not Sophie."

Hanna said, "He won't come after you if you let us go. I swear to God."

"I'm not worried about your brother coming after me. I'm untouchable here in the U.S. But he's caused all kinds of problems in Amsterdam. We're one big organization. Roman and Emile Rostoff are brothers. You didn't really think we'd let Albert return to Amsterdam, did you?"

Hanna shot him a nasty look. "This was your plan all along."

"Part of it, yes. I knew we'd have to deal with your brother."

Her mind raced, searching for options. For the first time since this whole ordeal started, she realized she had none.

CHAPTER 99

HANNA FELT THE panic rise in her throat. This man wanted to ruin her life. He was going to murder her brother or her daughter. How was it possible that he had her in this position? He wasn't some sort of feudal lord. He was a Russian gangster.

Billy was looking at Hanna as if he expected her to cry. He couldn't have been more wrong. She wasn't sad; she was furious. Furious and scared for her daughter. There was no combination more potent for a mother.

Hanna said, "You won't let us go, even though you have the diamonds?" It was hard to say the words in such an even tone.

Billy said, "I am quite sorry. I wish it could be different. Until your brother shows up, you and your daughter will remain my guests."

"I don't want to leave here with you."

"What you want is of no concern to me. Your failed attempt to smuggle people not only didn't pay off your previous debt, it cost us additional resources *and* our most valuable law enforcement contact. Your debt to us is now quite significant."

"Even with the diamonds? That's nonsense."

Billy didn't smile when he looked Hanna in the eye and said, "Speak to me that way again and your daughter will go through life without a left ear."

Hanna couldn't keep her eyes from drifting down to the knife Billy had set on the table. Suddenly, she felt like she had no control over her own actions. There was no conscious thought as she moved.

She reached down and grabbed the open folding knife on the table. The blade looked nasty, all sharp angles and gleaming steel. She brought the blade up and swung it at Billy's face as fast as she could.

The muscular Russian was quick. He jerked his head back, and the blade missed him by an inch.

Hanna swung at him again, but the result was the same. A smile spread across his face. That stupid, infuriating smile.

Hanna couldn't stop herself—she drove the sharp blade into the top of his left hand. She felt the steel pass through his flesh and tendons and then stick firm in the wooden table. Blood spurted up from the wound like a tiny oil-well gusher.

Billy's eyes bulged and he let out a wail. It hurt Hanna's ears, but it was satisfying to know she had hurt him so deliberately.

The two men closest to Billy rushed to his aid.

Hanna shouted in Dutch, "Run, Josie! Run!"

Her daughter didn't need to be told twice. She jumped off the bench and turned to run.

One of the dark-haired young men moved from Billy and grabbed Josie. She didn't make it three steps.

That's when Hanna heard the first gunshots.

CHAPTER 100

THIS WAS LIKE a lot of operations I'd run in my career. We were making the most of our limited resources and I was working with the local police without telling my supervisor. Everything was going about like I'd expected it to.

Rolling down Ocean Drive in my Explorer, I strained to see where Hanna had gone with the backpack. That was what the Russians wanted, or at least the diamonds inside it. That's what I was looking for. That's where I'd find the Russians.

The last I heard, Hanna's brother was still sitting in the rental car somewhere near the Clevelander Hotel. I could hear bits and pieces of music from the band around the Clevelander pool. Everything in South Beach picked up near dark.

Marie pointed to the road and shouted, "There!"

I saw him. Running across the street was Albert Greete with a pistol in his hand that he was aiming toward the beach. I heard gunshots. *Holy shit.* This crazy Dutchman was running through traffic shooting at someone.

I mashed the brakes and felt the car behind me crash into my bumper. That was the least of my problems. I popped on the blue lights and bailed out of the car.

Marie came out of the car with me but had the sense to wait by the vehicle.

Just as I pulled my service weapon, panic set in among the pedestrians. It started as a low rumble, then progressed to screams. Vehicles screeched to a halt and I heard the unmistakable thuds of cars smashing into other cars. A BMW swerved into a light pole.

A family with two little kids coming off the beach stepped right into the line of fire. My heart stopped when I saw the little girl's face. The beefy father grabbed the kids and fell to the ground, covering the children. That was some good tactical sense. He had to be a Miami native.

People on the beach were running as well, topless women and buff men who had no idea where they were going. It looked like a disaster movie, but only I knew all the terrible things that could really happen in this story.

When I got closer to the beach, I saw Albert exchanging fire with big men dressed in suits— Russians, I assumed. I couldn't see Hanna, but I knew where I was headed.

I dodged a Land Rover as I came off the street and cut across the sidewalk. I intended to intercept Albert.

It was showtime.

CHAPTER 101

HANNA DIDN'T CARE what happened to her; she just wanted to buy enough time to get her daughter away. The sound of gunfire had frozen everyone in place momentarily. Even the man who grabbed Josie had stopped midstride to look over his shoulder.

Billy had quit wailing and was now staring at the knife sticking through his left hand. Blood was still pouring out of the wound, but it wasn't shooting up in the air like it had been a moment before.

The young man just to the side of Billy, dressed in a slick gray pin-striped suit, started to pull the knife out of Billy's hand.

That's when the man's head exploded. Like a bomb. Blood spattered over everything near him. Billy was suddenly covered in brains and blood. The combination of the knife stuck through his hand and the blood everywhere briefly stunned him.

Somehow, he managed to grab the knife in his mutilated hand with his uninjured hand. It took three good tugs before the knife came free of the table and released him.

Billy reached across the table for the backpack.

Hanna snatched it away. Why not? Things couldn't go any worse for this deal. She spun away from the picnic table holding the bag. Albert was only about twenty feet ahead, just crossing the sidewalk.

He fired almost point-blank into a big Russian thug in a blue suit. Even five quick shots to the stomach didn't stop the man; he took another step and grabbed Albert by the neck.

Albert struggled with him for a moment, then broke free, took a step back, and fired a bullet into each of the man's knees. Finally the man dropped to the ground. So much blood was coming out of the wounds that the sand couldn't absorb it all, and it spread around his body.

Hanna needed to get Albert, grab Josie, and disappear with them. There wasn't much else to do at this point.

As she started to run to her brother, Hanna heard someone shout, "Police, don't move!" She looked toward the street and saw the big Miami cop, Tom Moon, rushing down the slope toward the picnic table. She hoped Billy would be the first person he grabbed. She looked over her shoulder for the bloodied Russian but didn't see him.

She turned back to Albert, who was aiming his gun at another Russian. Then she saw a blur as someone came from the side and knocked into her brother.

It was Billy.

Albert rolled and came up on his feet to face Billy. That's when the Russian brought the knife in a wide arc right across Albert's throat.

Albert stood there for a moment, motionless. Then the gash on his throat opened wide, and he reached for it with his left hand. A moment later, he toppled into the sand.

The gun he'd bought here in Miami was still in his right hand.

Billy held the bloody knife and turned toward Hanna. He didn't ask for the backpack.

She knew exactly what he intended to do.

CHAPTER 102

I TRIED TO control my breathing while scanning for the closest threat. Tourists and partyers from the Clevelander were scampering in every direction. I'd managed to block out the clamor of screams, car horns, and approaching sirens. My hand holding the Glock in front of me was steady.

I rushed toward the last place I'd seen Hanna. I knew that anyone in a suit was a threat. One man was already down by the picnic table with the majority of his head missing. Blood and brain matter covered the table and one of the benches.

There were two other Russians near the beach, but I saw Steph Hall and Chill rushing toward them shouting, "Police, don't move!"

I trusted them to handle the two Russians. I turned to the next target. Even though it was hard to see his face because of the blood streaked across it, I knew it was Billy. His build and stupid blue goatee gave him away.

The body next to him wasn't dressed in a suit. I saw it was Hanna's brother, Albert.

In almost the same instant, I realized Billy had a knife in his hand and intended to use it on Hanna.

I didn't have a clear shot at Billy, not with Hanna between us. She was dodging back and forth. I raised my pistol, then lowered it, looking for the right angle. Finally, I realized there was only one way to do this.

I lowered my head and charged forward, hoping my size and the element of surprise would win the day.

I took one step to the right to avoid Hanna, then crashed into Billy like a pickup truck. My left hand reached out to hold his right wrist and keep the knife away from me.

The sound he made when I careened into him told me I'd knocked the breath out of him. We tumbled into the sand and I managed to lose my pistol. This close together, it didn't matter. I held on to his right hand with all of my strength. I grabbed his left hand; it felt odd and slick. Then I realized it was covered in blood, and more blood was pumping out of a wound in the middle of his hand.

He rolled and slipped away from me. We both jumped into a crouch and faced each other. The look in his eyes told me he was scared. He'd lost some blood and had seen his deal go to hell, and now he was probably thinking about what he'd have to tell Roman Rostoff.

I might be able to use that fear.

I scanned the beach around me, searching for my pistol. As I glanced to my left, I took a hard punch to the right side of my face. It made me stagger. Blood started pouring from my nose.

Before I had my full senses back, Billy kicked me hard in the stomach. Now we were both short of breath. I stumbled back and caught a glimpse of Billy running straight at me. With his goatee, the blood on his face, and his eyes open wide, he looked like some kind of demon.

Just as he hit me, I fell backward on purpose and rolled with it. It was the first time in my whole life that that little move worked. He ended up rolling right over the top of me and landed with a hard thump on some sea oats in the sand.

I sprang to my feet, and when Billy got up on his knees, I pretended his head was a football and punted him as hard as I could. The top of my foot connected with his blue goatee. His head snapped up hard. A tooth flew up in the air and disappeared into the sea oats.

Billy grunted as he flopped over onto his back. All the fight had gone out of him. Quickly, I fell on top of him and patted him down for more weapons. He didn't even carry a gun. I guess that's how he'd gotten the nickname Billy the Blade.

It took me only a few seconds to handcuff him and retrieve my pistol.

Chill and Steph were holding their prisoners on the sidewalk about fifty feet from me. I shot Steph a quick thumbs-up to let her know I was okay.

Hanna was sitting next to her dead brother, weeping.

I pulled Billy to his feet so he was standing right next to me, a shell of the well-dressed confident jerk I had dealt with before. His face and suit were covered with blood. His hair was no longer neatly slicked back but stuck up in every direction, revealing his scalp. His face was caked with blood and sand, and his left hand needed immediate medical attention.

I said, "You're done. Kidnapping, murder, human trafficking—your days of living near the beach are over. I might die poor, but I guarantee you'll die in prison."

Billy said, "Wait, can't we work this out?" He spit blood and fragments of teeth into the sand.

"Billy, are you trying to bribe me? I don't mind being poor."

I thought the muscular Russian was going to cry. It was oddly satisfying.

CHAPTER 103

I HELD A shaken Billy upright. His whole world had just collapsed. I needed to give him time to understand that. I needed *him*. He could sink the entire Rostoff organization. I felt the tremor of fear as I held his arm.

Billy said, "I can't go to prison. That's why I fled Russia. I'm sure we can work something out."

I had him. "The only way we can work anything out is if you give up your boss. You make a statement right now to me about Roman Rostoff and maybe I can help you."

"I can transfer any amount of money into any account. Immediately," Billy said.

I snorted. "This isn't the movies. It's not Russia either. That shit doesn't usually work here. That's why I didn't say you could walk, only that I might be able to help you."

Billy considered it and finally said, "How can you help me?"

"Tell us all about the Rostoff organization. I know I can get a prosecutor to work with us. You'll do time, but it'll be in some country-club federal lockup, not a hellhole state prison like Raiford."

Billy stared at me with an unreadable expression. Blood seeped from a dozen places on his face. He was a beaten, broken man. Finally, he mumbled, "Mr. Rostoff will kill me."

I had to think fast. "Unless we arrest him first. We have ways to protect you."

Billy looked down at the ground. I wondered how many people he had killed to protect his boss. This wasn't an easy decision for him, but it was the best time to hit him with the proposal.

I just stood there in silence, letting him consider his options. It took longer than I'd thought it would. He started to speak a couple of times, then stopped. At last he nodded and said, "Okay."

I felt like I had just found a hoard of gold. I finally had a chance to land the big fish: Rostoff.

I heard Steph Hall shout, shaking me out of my daydream. I turned my attention away from Billy. Steph aimed her pistol at someone coming from the beach.

It was another Russian asshole in a black suit. He must've heard Billy and me speaking from the other side of the sea oats. My right hand moved quickly while I held on to Billy's arm with my left hand. He raised a pistol and at the same time I drew my Glock; we were like gunfighters in the Old West.

The man in the black suit got off three rounds before Steph opened fire on him. I popped off two more rounds. Between the two of us, we caught him in the center mass of the chest, and he went down onto the sand in a heap.

I felt Billy pull away from me, and for a moment I

thought he was trying to escape. Then I realized the man's shots hadn't been directed at me—Billy had three holes in his chest. He sank onto the beach.

My best shot at taking down Roman Rostoff was gone.

CHAPTER 104

AFTER THE INCIDENT on the beach, it was a crazy few days. I was suspended while the FBI investigated the shooting. All the Russians had been armed, and the media painted law enforcement in the best possible light for a change.

I remember the relief I felt when Alvin Teague walked back to the scene with Hanna's daughter, Josie. Marie was with them. She had been instrumental in protecting Josie and calming her down. Once she'd spoken Dutch to the girl, Josie realized she was safe.

Teague had managed to cover the surveillance, help save the girl, and make it sound like a normal day at the Miami PD. Like I said, Smooth Jazz might've been a pompous ass, but he was a hell of a cop.

I attended Hanna Greete's first court appearance. I was still suspended, but there was no law that said I couldn't follow the proceedings closely as a civilian. The judge was a former federal prosecutor named Alice Jackson, someone I had dealt with a few times. She gave me a quick smile when I stepped into the back of the courtroom.

Hanna looked much different in the simple tan correctional scrubs she wore to face the judge. Her public defender, Chad Laine, asked for bail. I thought Judge Jackson might laugh out loud.

The judge looked over some paperwork and finally said, "Based on the crimes you're charged with, your lack of residency, and your lack of ties to the community, there will be no bail at this time."

Laine, a tall charmer in a cheap suit with a Florida Gator pin on his lapel, stood and said, "If I personally vouched for my client, would that influence the court?"

Judge Jackson smiled and said, "Yes, it would. It would make me think you were a good attorney who really cared about his client."

"What about in regard to bond for Ms. Greete?"

"Don't be ridiculous. She's a citizen of the Netherlands who appears to have entered this country only for a criminal endeavor. In addition, the indictment details the deaths of four people smuggled into the port of Miami."

The attorney hung his head.

Judge Jackson said, "Good effort, Counselor. I'd like to help out a fellow Gator, but I have no choice in this matter."

Josie had been allowed to return to Amsterdam in the custody of her babysitter, Tasi.

When the hearing was over, I stood at the rail between the public seats and the prosecutor's table. I said hello to the prosecutor and thanked her for her hard work.

The deputy U.S. marshals started to lead Hanna back to the holding cell. As they passed me, she looked up and said, "Thank you for letting us save my daughter."

That's not what I'd expected after such a demanding investigation. Now I felt like the Amsterdam connection on this case was closed. That didn't mean we were done. Though it did mean that Marie Meijer would be going back to Amsterdam, accompanying Magda so she could be reunited with her brother, Joseph.

Three days later, I found myself at the Miami International Airport with Steph Hall saying goodbye to Marie.

Marie had been chatty on the way to the airport, updating me about what she'd been hearing from the kids. Even the children still at the facility in Amsterdam seemed to be adapting well, though Marie said they all asked about me.

We were quiet a moment. I said, "Did this investigation work out the way you'd hoped?"

"We broke up Hanna's smuggling group. That's all I wanted. I'm sure I'll get onto the scent of another group soon." She looked at me closely. "What about you? Did the case work out for you?"

I smiled. "We saved some kids. That's all I ever want to think about."

Marie and I stood close together near the gate while Steph spoke with Magda a dozen feet away. Marie surprised me when she hooked her finger around mine and leaned in closer. "I hope this isn't a permanent goodbye," she said.

I smiled. "No way."

"Are they letting you stay on the task force?"

"Looks like it. It's tough to discipline someone who the *Miami Herald* calls a 'hero cop.'"

"Why do you say it like that? You *are* a hero."

"I'm lucky, that's all. So many things could've gone wrong. Or, I should say, even more wrong.

But the FBI liked the press, so I'm still on the task force."

"Will you find another case connected to Amsterdam?"

"Probably. I'll try."

"I'm glad."

Then she surprised me again by taking my face in her hands and kissing me long and deep. When we stopped, the smiles on our faces said it all.

That was it. There was nothing I could say that would top that kiss. The last call for boarding came over the speaker. Magda joined Marie and they got on the plane.

I turned to Steph, who was grinning at me. I said, "We're just friends." I winked and started walking. I could hear Steph snicker as she followed.

CHAPTER 105

THAT EVENING, I was trying to figure out my life. It had been hard watching Marie leave. But I knew I'd see her again soon.

My home life had improved. Sure, I still took a step close to my sister to smell her breath for alcohol every evening when I came home, but my mom had started taking a couple of new prescriptions, and her condition had improved. She was much more in the moment and called me by my real name most of the time.

I finished eating a meat loaf my mom had made as we chatted about her hobbies. Mom was quite animated for a change. Then the conversation turned to my romantic life, like it always seemed to.

My mom said, "Are you going to see that lovely girl Marie again?"

"I hope so. You know she had to go back to Amsterdam."

"Too bad. She was smart and beautiful. That's a combination that's hard to find anywhere." She looked over at my sister, who was in the kitchen, and then back at me and added, "Except in this family."

I laughed. I appreciated my mother's keen sense of humor, these precious times when she was lucid and in the moment. I said, "Did you do anything interesting today?"

"I played piano for Chuck."

Oh no! My heart sank. I cut my eyes over to my sister in the kitchen. We'd lost her again. I didn't understand the broad smile Lila had on her face.

My mom said, "Then Chuck showed me some stretches and sat with me until Lila got home from work."

Lila was still smiling. I excused myself from the table and stepped into the kitchen. "What's with the grin? You look like the Cheshire cat."

Lila giggled and said, "I've been waiting for this conversation for a couple of days."

"Why is that?"

"The nursing company has been sending a new aide over in the afternoons, a young guy named Chuck." She laughed.

I mumbled, "'The only thing I know is that I know nothing.'"

Lila said, "Jean-Paul Sartre?"

"Socrates, but at least you're playing the game now." I smiled.

"After years of your quotes, I had to pick up some of it. I even quoted Plato on the playground at school the other day."

"Oh yeah? What quote?"

"Something like 'You can discover more about a person in play than conversation.'"

"Close enough. I'm impressed." For the first time I noticed Lila was dressed up. "What're you up to tonight?"

"Going out with some friends. I'll save you the

trouble of spying on me—it's three girls, you know them all, we're not going to any of the clubs you told me to stay away from, and I have to work tomorrow so I won't be drinking much. Happy?"

"Not as happy as I'd be if I could direct your entire life, but it's a start."

My sister kissed me on the cheek, then kissed my mom good night. When she got to the door, she turned and said, "You're being surprisingly reasonable about this."

"You're an adult. I trust you. Just use your head." I wasn't worried, although I couldn't help but touch the phone in my pocket. The tracker Chill had put on her car was still there. I didn't intend to use the tracker. Unless I had to.

I did more than enjoy the quiet evening with my mother. I *appreciated* it. She was interested in what I was working on and what the next steps in my career were going to be. It wasn't until I talked to her about the task force that I realized how much I wanted to stay on it. It was where I was meant to be.

I had one more item to take care of on our human-smuggling case. It was something I was looking forward to. Nothing I would bother my mom with, but the idea of it made me smile.

CHAPTER 106

IT WAS EIGHT fifteen in the evening, and I had timed our arrival perfectly. Steph and I were dressed in professional clothes, nothing flashy. This ballroom at the Fontainebleau in Miami Beach held two hundred of the area's wealthiest and best-connected residents. Rich people liked to show off their clothes and be seen at charity and award events like this one. Even though everyone knew it was all bullshit.

I slipped in the rear door with Steph Hall. A Miami Beach lieutenant, wearing his dress uniform, did a double take when he saw me. He got up from his table in the back and came over.

The tall lieutenant, who was a little older than me, said in a low voice, "Anti, what brings you here to civilization?"

"Business. What's going on with you, Sauce?"

"Usual." He looked up at the stage, where Roman Rostoff was behind a podium delivering his prepared comments in reasonably good English at a slow clip. "Some people don't look too closely at people's backgrounds when they give out awards."

I turned and said, "Steph Hall, this is Lieutenant

William Stein. Sauce, this is my partner at the FBI task force."

The lieutenant said, "The task force that brought Miami-style violence to South Beach last week?"

I took a little bow and said, "The same."

We all chuckled.

Steph said, "How'd you get the nickname 'Sauce'?"

The good-looking lieutenant gave a charming chortle and said, "That's a secret you have to learn over time." Then the lieutenant realized my business might have to do with Roman Rostoff. "Anti, are you here to stir up shit?"

I just smiled.

He glanced at the stage again and said, "Anything you can do to that ass-wipe is good for all of us. I'll just pretend I never saw you. I've got three more years before I can pull the plug. I don't want to answer any uncomfortable questions about why I let you roam through here."

"You got it, Sauce."

Steph and I were careful not to be obtrusive as we walked along the side of the cavernous ballroom.

At the front of the room, I stepped behind some partitions. They hid me from the audience, but I could see the entire stage. I reached in my coat pocket and pulled out some papers. That's when a tall young guy with a ponytail, the one who'd run with Billy the Blade, stepped right in front of me. The last time I'd seen him, he'd made veiled threats about my sister, and I'd crushed his testicles in my hand. It looked like he thought he was going to get some revenge.

I stared at the tattoos going up his neck and could have sworn he had another bud on the end of the tattooed vine that spread onto his cheek.

I said, "I'm sorry, what was your name again?"

He growled, "Tibor."

"Right, sorry. So, asshole, want to get out of my way? I have business with your boss. Official business."

"And it's my business to keep my employer safe," Tibor said.

"'Fortune truly helps those who are of good judgment.'"

"What?" He screwed up his face in a way that made me smile.

"A man named Euripides said that about four hundred years before Christ was born, and yet it applies to you tonight. Use good judgment and step out of the way."

"Or else what?"

"My cold-blooded partner will deal with you." I liked the look on his face as Steph came up and put the stun gun on his bare neck.

I said, "Move, and she zaps you with thirty thousand volts." I stood and enjoyed his silence. I needed to enjoy more things in life. This was a good start.

I stepped around him as Steph ordered him to lie on the ground. She took the gun from his holster.

I strutted right across the stage in front of everyone. Roman Rostoff was forced to stop midsentence. He stared at me. I enjoyed the way he looked past me to see how I'd gotten by his bodyguard.

I gave him a smile and a wink as I joined him at the podium and patted him on the back like I was proud of him. The people in the audience had no idea what was going on. They just stared at the big guy who couldn't afford a designer suit.

I handed the sheaf of papers to Rostoff.

He looked at me and muttered, "What?"

I made sure to speak clearly so that the microphone would pick up everything. "This is a federal subpoena for records related to all of your businesses and bank accounts." I stood for a moment while he just held the papers and stared at me. "For a change, there are plenty of witnesses to the service of this subpoena. The subpoena requires you to personally appear at the FBI office with the records requested."

Everyone in the entire room was silent. Including Rostoff.

I leaned into the microphone and said, "That's right. Your Humanitarian of the Year is being investigated for money laundering, human trafficking, and his role in the shootout on Miami Beach last week. Also for about a thousand business violations relating to tax fraud and licensing issues." I let that hang in the silent room for about five seconds, then said, "Enjoy the rest of your evening."

I stepped off the stage and headed toward the exit. Stephanie Hall joined me, allowing Tibor, the bodyguard, to stand up. She dropped his pistol in a garbage can as we walked out the door.

Yeah, I was going to enjoy that one for a very long time.

EPILOGUE

Amsterdam

JANINE, ONE OF Hanna Greete's former assistants, sat at a desk in a small office in Amsterdam. The cramped office in a warehouse wasn't nearly as nice as the apartment they'd worked out of when Hanna was in charge. But Hanna was in jail in the United States now, and Albert was dead.

Janine had made the most of the opportunity. She knew all of Hanna's contacts. She and her sister, Tasi, simply moved to Oostpoort, away from the city center and tourists. Janine had kept the business going, albeit on a much smaller scale. But if she kept expenses down and only had to worry about Tasi and herself, she could make a fine living.

She doubted the police paid much attention to small operations like hers. And that detective with the national police, Marie Meijer, was probably so happy to have caught Hanna that she'd taken a vacation.

Since Janine had passed so much information on to Marie, the police had dropped fraud charges against her after she'd been arrested in Zaandam. Janine's information had led to Hanna's arrest. Now she was taking over Hanna's former life.

Sitting in the small office still made Janine feel like a queen. She answered her ringing phone and heard the voice of Bertram Hellot; he owned an apartment building that housed girls she was planning to move to the U.S. He told her that one of the girls had gone out and not come back. That wasn't supposed to happen.

Janine didn't mince words. "Find that girl by tonight or I'll have Max cut off your balls and I'll wear them as a necklace. Is that understood?"

"Yes. I'm looking for her right now."

Janine smiled at the former gang member's frantic tone. As it turned out, she had learned a lot more from Hanna than she had realized. Now she understood why Hanna had enjoyed bossing people around.

A knock on the thick wooden door startled her. No doubt the landlord looking for rent, as it was the beginning of the month. Sometimes, when she was short on cash, Janine would send her sister to answer the door. Tasi would flirt with the landlord to distract him. Tasi was there in the office, but today Janine had the cash.

She opened the door with a smile. It faded instantly when she saw Marie Meijer standing there with four uniformed police officers.

The detective with the national police nudged Janine back and barged into the office.

Marie said, "Did you really think the information you gave me on Hanna's operation granted you immunity for all crimes? Even after we dropped your cheap check-fraud charge?"

Janine said, "I don't know what you're talking about."

Marie smiled. Her drooping eyelid lifted up ever

so slightly. "That sounds convincing, except that we found your safe house in Diemen. Bertram Hellot has been working with us."

Janine said, "But I helped you!"

Marie said, "To avoid jail. I never agreed to let you ruin more lives by continuing to traffic in people."

Janine thought about that, then said, "What do you want?"

"Do you know Emile Rostoff?"

"No. Not personally."

Marie nodded. "Too bad. That was your only chance." She turned to a uniformed officer and said, "Take them both."

Janine started to cry as she and Tasi were handcuffed and led out of the office.

ABOUT THE AUTHORS

JAMES PATTERSON is the world's bestselling author and most trusted storyteller. He has created many enduring fictional characters and series, including Alex Cross, the Women's Murder Club, Michael Bennett, Maximum Ride, Middle School, and I Funny. Among his notable literary collaborations are *The President Is Missing*, with President Bill Clinton, and the Max Einstein series, produced in partnership with the Albert Einstein estate. Patterson's writing career is characterized by a single mission: to prove that there is no such thing as a person who "doesn't like to read," only people who haven't found the right book. He's given over three million books to schoolkids and the military, donated more than seventy million dollars to support education, and endowed over five thousand college scholarships for teachers. For his prodigious imagination and championship of literacy in America, Patterson was awarded the 2019 National Humanities Medal. The National Book Foundation presented him with the Literarian Award for Outstanding Service to the American Literary Community, and he is also the recipient of an Edgar Award and nine Emmy Awards. He lives in Florida with his family.

JAMES O. BORN is an award-winning crime and science-fiction novelist as well as a career law enforcement agent. A native Floridian, he still lives in the Sunshine State.

ALEX CROSS ENTERS THE FINAL SHOWDOWN WITH THE RELENTLESS KILLER WHO HAS STALKED HIM AND HIS FAMILY FOR YEARS.

TURN THE PAGE FOR A PREVIEW OF THE NEWEST ALEX CROSS THRILLER.

FEAR NO EVIL

COMING IN NOVEMBER 2021.

CHAPTER 1

Washington, DC
Late June

MATTHEW BUTLER COCKED his head to one side, considering the big-boned blonde in front of him. She was handcuffed and shackled to a heavy oak chair bolted into the concrete floor beneath bright fluorescent lights.

If the woman was anxious about her predicament, she wasn't showing it in the least. She was as chill as the yoga outfit she wore. No sweat on her pale brow. Beneath her warm-up hoodie, her chest rose and fell calmly, each breath measured. Her shoulders were relaxed. Even her eyes looked soft.

Butler adjusted the strap of his shoulder holster.

"I know they've trained you for this sort of thing," he said in a voice with the slightest of Western twangs. "But your training won't work against me, Catherine. It never does."

A fit, balding man with a hawkish nose, Butler had workman's hands and wore black jeans, Nike running shoes, and a dark blue polo shirt. He crossed his thick forearms when she smiled back at him with brilliant white teeth.

"Whoever you are, you are going to be destroyed

for what you're doing," Catherine Hingham said. "When they find out—"

Butler cut her off. "You know, in my many years as a professional, Catherine, I have come to rather enjoy the delicate process of breaking into hearts and minds. They are very much interlinked, you know—hearts and minds—and I have found that one is almost always the key to the other."

"Langley will annihilate you," Hingham said, studying Butler as if she wanted to remember every line in his face.

"Your operators won't help you today," Butler said, gesturing at a pile of blank paper and a pen on the table before her. "Tell me the truth and we can all move on with our lives."

"I'll say it again: You have no jurisdiction over me."

Butler chuckled, gestured around the room. "Oh, but in here, I do."

"I want to see a lawyer, then."

"I'm sure," he said, sobering. "But we're talking about a serious threat to our national security, Catherine. A few rules of engagement can and will be broken in order to thwart that threat."

"I am not a national security threat," she said evenly. "I work for the Central Intelligence Agency, with the highest clearances, in support of my country's freedoms. Your freedoms as well."

"That's what makes your traitorous actions so hard to understand, Catherine."

Her face reddened and she shifted in her chair. "I am no traitor."

Butler took a step toward her. "The hell you're not. We know about the Maldives."

Hingham blinked, furrowed her brow. "The Maldives? Like, the islands in the Indian Ocean?"

"The same."

"I have no idea what you're talking about. I have never been to the Maldives. I've never even been to India."

"No?"

"Never. You can talk to my case officers about it."

"I plan to at some point," Butler said, taking another step toward her. He reached down to touch the back of her left hand before letting his finger trail across her wedding band and modest engagement ring. "Does he know? Your husband?"

"That I work for the CIA?" she said. "Yes. But he has zero idea what I actually do. Those are the rules. We play by them."

Butler sighed as he gently took hold of her left pinkie with his leathery hand, thumb on top.

"Do you know the surest way to sever the connection between the body and mind, and therefore the heart?"

"No," she said.

"Pain," Butler said. He gripped her little finger tight and levered his thumb sharply downward until he heard a bone snap.

CHAPTER 2

CATHERINE HINGHAM SCREAMED in agony, fighting against her restraints, then yelled at him, "You cannot do this! This is the United States of America and I'm a sworn officer of the Central—"

Butler broke her ring finger, then waited for her to stop screaming and crying.

"You have eight fingers left, Catherine," Butler said calmly. "I will break them all and if you still do not tell me what I want to know, I will have your five-year-old daughter brought here and I will begin breaking *her* tiny fingers one by one until you confess."

The CIA officer stared at him in disgust and horror. "Emily has cerebral palsy."

"I know."

"You wouldn't. It's…monstrous."

"It is," he said and sighed again. "And yet, because there is so much at stake, Catherine, I will break your little girl's fingers. But only if you make it necessary."

The CIA officer continued to stare at him for

several moments. He gazed back at her evenly until her lower lip trembled and she hung her head.

"The costs," Hingham whispered hoarsely. "You have no idea what a child like Em…" She could not go on and broke down sobbing.

"The heart wins again," Butler said. He pushed the pile of blank pages in front of her. "Start writing. The Maldives. The numbered accounts. Their connections. All of it."

After a few moments, Catherine Hingham calmed enough to raise her head. "I need witness protection."

"I'll see what I can do," Butler said and held out the pen to her. "Now write."

The CIA officer reached out with both handcuffed hands shaking. She took the pen. "Please," she said. "My family doesn't deserve what will happen if—"

"Write," he said firmly. "And I'll see what I can do."

The CIA officer reluctantly began to scribble names, addresses, account numbers, and more. When she'd moved to a second page, Butler had seen enough to be satisfied.

He walked behind the CIA officer and nodded to a small camera mounted high in the corner of the room.

A gravelly male voice came through the tiny earbud Butler wore in his left ear. "Mmmm. Well done. When you have what we need, end the interview and file your report, please."

Butler nodded again before moving in front of Catherine Hingham. She set her pen down and pushed the pages across the table at him.

"That's it," she said in a hoarse voice. "Everything I know."

"Unlikely," Butler said, using the nail of his index finger to lift up the first sheet so he could scan the information she'd provided on page two. "But this looks useful enough for now. It will give us leverage. Was that so hard, Catherine?"

She relaxed a little and said, "Okay, then, I've given you what you wanted. Now I need a doctor to fix my hand. I need witness protection."

With his fingernail, Butler scooted the confession pages to the far right of the table. "You're a smart woman, Catherine. Well educated. Yale, if I remember. You should know your history better. We don't protect traitors in the United States of America. From Benedict Arnold on, they've all had to pay the price. And now, so will you."

The CIA officer looked confused and then terrified when Butler took a step back and drew a stubby pistol with a sound suppressor from his shoulder holster.

"No, please, my kids are—" she managed before he took aim and shot her between the eyes.

CHAPTER 3

FROM THE TIME we'd met as ten-year-olds, John Sampson, my best friend and long-term DC Metro Police partner, had been stoic, quiet, observant. Since his wife, Billie, had died, he'd become even more reserved and was now given to long bouts of brooding silence. I knew he was still wrestling with grief.

But that late-June morning, Big John was acting as wound up as a kid about to hit the front gates of Disney World as he bopped around my front room, where we'd laid out all our gear for a trip we'd been talking about taking for years.

"You think we'll see a grizzly?" Sampson asked, grinning at me.

"I'm hoping not," I said. "At least, not up close."

"They're in there, big-time. And wolves."

"And deer, elk, and cutthroat trout," I said. "I've been studying the brochure too."

Nana Mama, my ninety-something grandmother, came in wringing her hands and asked with worry in her voice, "Did I hear you say grizzly bears?"

Sampson glowed with excitement. "Nana, the Bob Marshall Wilderness has one of the densest concentrations of grizzlies in the lower forty-eight states. But don't worry. We'll have bear spray and sidearms. And cameras."

"I don't know why you couldn't choose a safer place to go on your manly trip."

"If it was safer, it wouldn't be manly," I said. "There's got to be a challenge."

"Glad I'm an old lady, then. Breakfast in five minutes." Nana Mama turned and shuffled away, shaking her head.

"Checklist?" Sampson said.

"I'm ready if you are."

We started going through every item we'd thought necessary for the twenty-nine-mile horseback trip deep into one of the last great wildernesses on earth and for the five-day raft ride we'd take out of the Bob Marshall on the South Fork of the Flathead River. An outfitter was providing the rafts, tents, food, and bear-proof storage equipment. Everything else had to fit into four rubberized dry bags we'd use on the river after he dropped us off.

We could have signed up for a fully guided affair, but Sampson wanted us to do a good part of the trip alone, and after some thought, I'd agreed. Six days deep in the backcountry of Montana would give Big John many chances to open up and talk, which is critical to the process of coping with tragic loss.

"How's Willow feeling about our little trip?" I asked.

Sampson smiled. "She doesn't like the idea of grizzly bears any more than Nana does, but she knows it will make me happy."

"Your little girl's always been wise beyond her years."

"Truth. Bree liking her job?"

Thinking of my smart, beautiful, and independent wife, I said, "She loves it. Got up early to be at the office. Something about a possible assignment in Paris."

"Paris! What a difference a career change makes."

"No kidding. It was like the gig was tailor-made for her."

"Maybe we should think about going into private-sector investigations too."

"Pay's better, for sure," I allowed.

Before he could reply, my seventeen-year-old daughter, Jannie, poked her head in and said, "Nana says your eggs are getting cold."

I put down my dry bag and went to the kitchen, where I found my youngest child, Ali, already finishing up his plate.

"Morning, sunshine," I said, giving him a hug. He ignored it, so I tickled him.

"C'mon, Dad!" He laughed, then groaned. "Why can't I go with you?"

"Because you're a kid and we don't know what we'll be facing."

"I can do it," he insisted.

Sampson said, "Ali, let your dad and me scope it out this year. If we think you're up to it, we'll bring you along on the next trip. Deal?"

Ali scrunched up his face and shrugged. "I guess. When do you leave?"

"First thing in the—"

My cell phone began to ring at the same time Sampson's chimed.

"No," John protested. "Don't answer that, Alex. We're supposed to be gone already!"

But when I saw the caller ID, I grimaced and knew I had to answer. "Commissioner Dennison,"

I said. "John Sampson and I were just heading out the door on vacation."

"Cancel it," said the commissioner of the Metro DC Police Department. "We've got a dead female, gunshot wound to the head, dumped in the garage under the International Spy Museum on L'Enfant Plaza. Her ID says she's—"

"Commissioner, with all due respect," I said, "we've been planning this trip for—"

"I don't care, Cross," he snapped. "Her ID says she's CIA. If you want to continue your contract with Metro, you'll get down there. And if Sampson wants to keep his job, he'll be with you."

I stared at the ceiling a second, looked at John, and shook my head.

"Okay, Commissioner. We're on our way."

JAMES
PATTERSON
RECOMMENDS

JAMES PATTERSON

THE FIRST LADY

BRENDAN DUBOIS

THE FIRST LADY

The US government is at the forefront of everyone's mind these days and I've become incredibly fascinated by the idea that one secret can bring it all down. What if that secret is a US President's affair that results in a nightmarish outcome?

Sally Grissom, leader of the Presidential Protection Division, is summoned to a private meeting with the President and his chief of staff to discuss the disappearance of the First Lady. What at first seemed an escape to a safe haven turns into a kidnapping when a ransom note arrives along with what could be the First Lady's finger.

It's a race against the clock to collect the evidence that all leads to one troubling question: Could the kidnappers be from inside the White House?

JAMES
PATTERSON

TEXAS
RANGER

★

& ANDREW BOURELLE

TEXAS RANGER

So many of my detectives are dark and gritty and deal with crimes in some of our grimmest cities. That's why I'm thrilled to bring you Detective Rory Yates, my most honorable detective yet.

As a Texas Ranger, he has a code that he lives and works by. But when he comes home for a much-needed break, he walks into a crime scene where the victim is none other than his ex-wife—and he's the prime suspect. Yates has to risk everything in order to clear his name, and he dives into the inferno of the most twisted mind I've ever created. Can his code bring him back out alive?

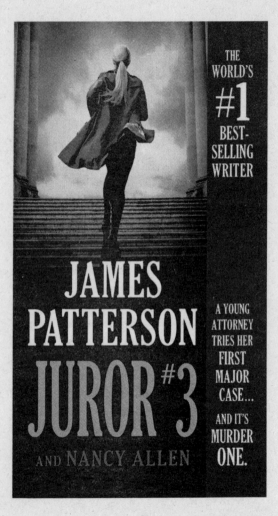

THE
WORLD'S
#1
BEST-
SELLING
WRITER

JAMES
PATTERSON
JUROR #3
AND NANCY ALLEN

A YOUNG
ATTORNEY
TRIES HER
FIRST
MAJOR
CASE...

AND IT'S
MURDER
ONE.

JUROR #3

In the deep south of Mississippi, Ruby Bozarth is a newcomer, both to Rosedale and to the bar. And now she's tapped as a defense counsel in a racially charged felony. The murder of a woman from an old family has Rosedale's upper crust howling for blood, and the prosecutor is counting on Ruby's inexperience to help him deliver a swift conviction.

Ruby is determined to build a defense that sticks for her college football star client. Looking for help in unexpected quarters, her case is rattled as news of a second murder breaks. As intertwining investigations unfold, no one can be trusted, especially the twelve men and women on the jury. They may be hiding the most incendiary secret of all.

JAMES PATTERSON

"No one gets this big without amazing natural storytelling talent— which is what James Patterson has, in spades." —LEE CHILD

THE CHEF

with **MAX DiLALLO**

THE CHEF

In the Carnival days leading up to Mardi Gras, Detective Caleb Rooney is accused of murdering a fellow member of the New Orleans PD. While fighting the charges against him, Rooney makes a pair of unthinkable discoveries: His beloved city is under threat of attack…and these would-be terrorists may be local.

Amid crowds of revelers, Rooney follows a fearsome trail of clues, racing from outlying districts into the city center. He has no idea what—or who—he'll face in defense of his hometown, only that innocent lives are at stake.

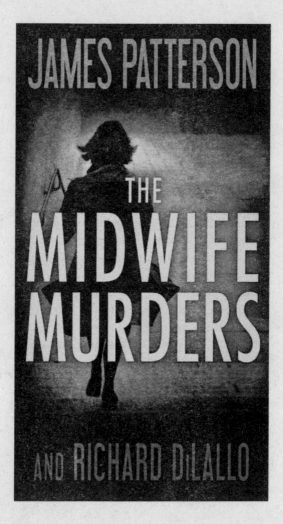

JAMES PATTERSON

THE
MIDWIFE
MURDERS

AND RICHARD DiLALLO

THE MIDWIFE MURDERS

To senior midwife Lucy Ryuan, pregnancy is not a condition, it's her life's work. But when two kidnappings and a vicious stabbing happen on her watch in a university hospital in Manhattan, her focus abruptly changes. Something has to be done, and Lucy is fearless enough to try.

Rumors begin to swirl, with blame falling on everyone from the Russian mafia to an underground adoption network. The feisty single mom teams up with a skeptical NYPD detective to solve the case, but the truth is far more twisted than Lucy could ever have imagined.

For a complete list of books by

JAMES PATTERSON

VISIT
JamesPatterson.com

Follow James Patterson on Facebook
@JamesPatterson

Follow James Patterson on Twitter
@JP_Books

Follow James Patterson on Instagram
@jamespattersonbooks